"All the things th[ ] **records aren't. It'**[ ] **before you opened your investigative agency.**

"Which makes me curious as to what you were doing before then," she added.

"I don't know what you're talking about."

"Why are you in hiding?" Valerie asked.

"I'm not in hiding. I run a business. I advertise. My number's in the phone book. You can check all that out—"

"Yes, I know. You told me. Except the man who recommended you seems to have disappeared. So...I'm not exactly sure anymore why you're here, Mr. Sellers."

"I'm here because I'm being paid to do a job—"

"And did that job involve trying to get me into bed?" she asked softly. "Or was that just some sort of...extra compensation you thought up all on your own?"

"No," Grey said seriously. "I don't have any hidden agenda where you're concerned...."

Dear Harlequin Intrigue Reader,

You wanted MORE MEN OF MYSTERY by Gayle Wilson—now you've got 'em! Gayle's stories about these sexy undercover agents have become one of Harlequin Intrigue's most popular ongoing series. We are as impressed by her outstanding talent as you, her readers, and are thrilled to feature her special brand of drama again in *Her Private Bodyguard* (#561). Look for two MORE titles in August and November 2000.

Also available this month, *Protecting His Own* (#562) by Molly Rice, an emotional story about the sanctity of family and a man's basic need to claim what's his.

There's no more stronger bond than that of blood. And Chance Quarrels is determined to see no harm come to the little daughter he never knew he had as Patricia Rosemoor continues her SONS OF SILVER SPRINGS miniseries with *The Lone Wolf's Child* (#563).

Finally, veteran Harlequin Intrigue author Carly Bishop takes you to a cloistered Montana community with a woman and an undercover cop posing as husband and wife. The threat from a killer is real, but so is their simmering passion. Which one is more dangerous…? Find out in *No Bride But His* (#564), a LOVERS UNDER COVER story.

Pick up all four for variety, for excitement—because you're ready for a thrill!

Sincerely,

Denise O'Sullivan
Associate Senior Editor
Harlequin Intrigue

Her Private Bodyguard
Gayle Wilson

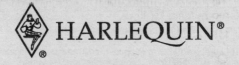

HARLEQUIN®

TORONTO • NEW YORK • LONDON
AMSTERDAM • PARIS • SYDNEY • HAMBURG
STOCKHOLM • ATHENS • TOKYO • MILAN • MADRID
PRAGUE • WARSAW • BUDAPEST • AUCKLAND

ISBN 0-373-22561-X

HER PRIVATE BODYGUARD

Copyright © 2000 by Mona Gay Thomas

This edition published by arrangement with Harlequin Books S.A.

® and TM are trademarks of the publisher. Trademarks indicated with ® are registered in the United States Patent and Trademark Office, the Canadian Trade Marks Office and in other countries.

Visit us at www.eHarlequin.com

Printed in U.S.A.

ABOUT THE AUTHOR

Gayle Wilson is the award-winning author of twenty novels written for Harlequin. She has lived in Alabama all her life except for the years she followed her army aviator husband—whom she met on a blind date—to a variety of military posts.

Before beginning her writing career, she taught English and world history to gifted high school students in a number of schools around the Birmingham area. Gayle and her husband have one son, who is also a teacher of gifted students. They are blessed with warm and loving Southern families and an ever-growing menagerie of cats and dogs.

You can write to Gayle at P.O. Box 3277, Hueytown, Alabama 35023.

Books by Gayle Wilson

FOR YOUR EYES ONLY
CIA
AGENT PROFILE

NAME: GREY SELLERS
DATE OF BIRTH: November 9, 1961
ASSIGNED TEAM: EXTERNAL SECURITY

SPECIAL SKILLS: Adapts to any situation or setting, expert marksman, rated in fixed- and rotary-wing aircraft, fluent in Russian.

AGENT EVALUATION: Strong sense of honor, loyalty and commitment to his former team. Despite a tough exterior, he hides a tender heart.

STATUS: Identity erased

CURRENT ADDRESS: Unknown…

FOR YOUR EYES ONLY

CAST OF CHARACTERS

Valerie Beaufort — Val had never wanted any part of the millions her father's company generated. Now she was stuck with the money and all that went along with it, including a private bodyguard. And someone who had murder on their mind.

Grey Sellers — The ex-CIA agent had left the agency and the External Security Team because of a mistake that had resulted in a good man's death. He never again wanted to be in a position where someone else's life depended on him. But now he was falling in love with the woman he had been charged with protecting.

Billy Clemens — Clemens would become the majority owner of Av-Tech Aeronautics if something happened to Valerie. With the millions involved, wasn't that a good enough motive for murder?

Porter Johnson — Porter had known Valerie all her life and had treated her like a daughter when she had lost her own father. Could he really be involved in what was going on?

Harper Springfield — Another of her father's partners, Harp had as much to gain by Valerie's death as any of the others.

Emory Hunter — Did Emory's soft Southern accent and courtly manner hide a murderer?

Autry Carmichael — The head of Av-Tech security formed his own theory of what was going on out at Valerie's ranch as soon as he discovered Grey Sellers was a man without a past.

Constance Beaufort — Connie, Valerie's stepmother, had been virtually cut out of her late husband's will. Could she be angry enough to kill?

For all the girls who post in my folder
(and for all you lurkers, too).
You are the best!
This one's for you!

Prologue

A hell of a way to acquire a few hundred million dollars, Valerie Beaufort thought, looking down on her father's flower-draped coffin. And she would have given all of it, of course, not to be standing here. They were his millions. Money she had never wanted. And didn't want any part of now.

"If there's anything we can do, Valerie, dear," Porter Johnson said, taking her hand and patting it gently, "you let us know. You know Betsy and I love you like our own daughters."

Porter's touch brought Val out of her heartsick reverie and made her realize that the brief graveside service was over. The people who had gathered around the final resting place of Charles Valentine Beaufort were already beginning to stream back to their cars, parked haphazardly along the edges of the vast cemetery.

She supposed she should have listened to whatever the minister had had to say about her father, but she didn't really need any eulogy to remind her of how he had lived his life. Or of how much she had loved him.

"There wasn't a better man in this world than Charlie Beaufort," Johnson said softly. "I never had a better friend."

Touched by the quiet sincerity in his voice, Valerie

leaned forward to press her lips against his cheek. His skin was as soft as old velvet, crepey with age. But then, Porter was even older than her father.

Actually, she remembered, he was the oldest of that small group of men who had founded Av-Tech Aeronautics. They had had no way of knowing then what an industry giant the tiny company they had started on a shoestring after the Korean war would become. Maybe if they had, things would have been different.

"So sorry about your daddy, honey," Emory Hunter said, as soon as Porter and his wife moved away. Emory patted her cheek, just as he had when she was a little girl. "Charlie was a real good man. Maybe the best I've ever known. That should be a consolation to you, just like the size of this crowd should be."

He indicated the hundreds of people scattered across the sweep of green lawn, centered by the tent they had set up over her father's grave. They hadn't lowered the casket yet. Maybe they didn't do that until everyone was gone. She wasn't really up on funeral etiquette, which was a good thing, she guessed.

"It *is* a consolation," she agreed, finding a smile for another of her father's partners, men she had literally known all her life. "And it helps to know he had friends like you."

"You call me in a few days, and we'll talk some about your old man. I know stories I bet he never told you. Probably didn't want you to know what a hell-raiser he really was," Emory said, laughing before his expression sobered. "It's good to talk about folks after they're gone. Healthy to remember the good times. It keeps them alive for us a little longer."

Hunter had never lost his Southern accent, despite the number of years he had lived in Colorado. Since he was now in his late sixties, Val didn't suppose he ever would.

"I will," she said, smiling at him. "I'll call, I promise. And thank you, Emory. Your friendship meant a lot to Dad."

He moved away, and Valerie turned to the next person waiting for her attention. Soon the faces and the condolences started to run together. She seemed to be repeating the same phrases over and over again, her mind a million miles away, just as it had been during the service.

All she wanted to do was to get this over and go home. Get out of these clothes and into a pair of jeans. Ride out the tension that had grown into an ache between her shoulders. Get the scent of hothouse flowers out of her nostrils and the sound of all these voices and their words of comfort out of her head.

That wasn't a lack of respect for her father. He would have been the first to agree that riding over the isolated landscape they both loved was a better idea than standing over his grave. Charlie Beaufort had loved the high desert and the mountains with a deep and abiding passion. Just as he had loved the ranch that sat in a small, sheltered valley in the middle of the tract of rugged land he'd bought more than forty years ago. He had built the main house and most of the outbuildings with his own hands.

During the past ten or fifteen years, however, when Av-Tech had really taken off, he hadn't had time—hadn't taken time, Val amended—to get away and visit it. When she was a little girl, they had gone out to the ranch almost every weekend. Piled in an old station wagon, her mother, father and Val would spend Friday evening driving out there, arriving long after midnight.

Some of her best memories of her father were associated with the ranch. Those were the memories she wanted to get in touch with. And those were the years she wanted to remember.

"Val, honey, if you've got a minute..." Harper Springfield whispered in her ear. ''While they're finishing up here...'' Hand firmly on her elbow, Harp, another of Av-Tech's founders, applied pressure to direct her away from the grave, where people were still waiting in line to speak to her and her stepmother.

Constance Beaufort's perfectly coifed blond hair and beautiful features were covered by a sheer black veil, her slender figure clothed in a black designer suit, black hose and black kid pumps. There wasn't a spot of color or a piece of jewelry, except for her gold wedding ring, of course, to spoil the image Connie was aiming for.

The grieving widow, Val thought as she turned away. Who had been grieving in earnest when she'd learned the terms of her late husband's will. Charlie Beaufort might have been foolish enough, Val thought regretfully, to marry a woman younger than his daughter. But thankfully, his lawyers had been smart enough to make him have her sign a prenuptial agreement.

There would be a generous settlement for Connie, plenty of money to live on, but she would get no shares of Av-Tech. And there, of course, was where Charlie Beaufort's real wealth lay.

Only when Val managed to pull her eyes away from her stepmother's artful performance did she realized where Harp was leading her. On a slight rise looking down on the grave site, the co-owners of her father's company were standing in a semicircle, waiting for Harp to bring her to them.

She had thought the firmness of Springfield's grip on her arm was an unnecessary and unwanted concern for her bad leg, but now it began to feel like some kind of strong-arm tactic. Although she would much prefer to believe the latter than the former, she couldn't imagine why her fa-ther's partners would think she needed to be coerced into meeting with them. Most of them had bounced her on their knees when she was a baby.

They were looking decidedly nervous, however, as she and Harp approached. Because she was now the majority owner of the company that had been their bread and butter for so many years? After all, they were of a different generation. They might have concerns about a woman directing an international company, especially one that specialized in cutting-edge missile delivery systems and the latest satellite technology.

The first thing she needed to do, Val decided, was let them know she had no intention of trying to run things. She didn't have the expertise, even if she had wanted to. And she didn't want to, of course. She had walked away from her father's money more than ten years ago. She wasn't going back to that life now. No matter what his will had said.

"We all thought we needed to talk about what happens next," Billy Clemens said as she and Harp walked up to the group.

Trust Billy to cut to the chase, Val thought. The most outspoken of the four men who had been her father's partners for more than forty years, Clemens was also Val's least favorite, although she could never quite pinpoint the reason. Billy was fond of saying that with him, what you saw was what you got. He was right. Val just didn't particularly like either.

Maybe her father hadn't, as well, Val thought, although he had never openly expressed any disparagement of Clemens. However, if her dad had arranged for his shares to be divided among his partners at his death instead of saddling her with them, Billy would now be the majority owner, and all the responsibility that went with the position would be his instead of hers.

"What happens next?" she repeated, although she certainly knew where this was heading.

"There's a lot of stuff going on with the company right now. A lot of contracts that have to be met, with some pretty substantial penalties involved if we don't meet them. I'm just wondering what you're planning to do about those."

"I'm planning to see those contracts are fulfilled," Val said. "And that the company doesn't have to pay any penalties."

"You're going to step into your father's shoes?" Harp Springfield asked bluntly.

"You all know as well as I do that no one can do that. Av-Tech was my father's life. If I try to step in, I'll botch it."

"You're the majority shareholder, Val," Porter Johnson reminded her. "Somebody's got to command the ship."

"Are you volunteering, Porter?" she asked softly.

There was little doubt what his answer would be. Johnson was suffering from prostate cancer. He wouldn't want the responsibility of the company. Of course, neither did she. As a matter of fact, Val doubted that any one of them, with the exception of Billy Clemens, would even consider taking over.

"You know better than that, Val," Porter said. "Your dad was the heart and the soul of this company. The last couple of years... Well, even Charlie wasn't able to see to everything."

She was grateful Porter hadn't made that sound any worse than he had. Her father's health had been failing for a long time, and she hated to admit she hadn't even been aware of how much. At least, not until his first stroke two years ago.

"That's why we're going to get someone in there who

can tell us what we need to do with the company," she said reassuringly.

"You aren't talking about selling?" Clemens asked. "You can't do that."

"Right now, all I'm talking about is hiring a management consultant," Val said. "Someone to look us over, examine the books, look at those contracts and make some suggestions. I think that's what my father should have done when he got sick. If he had been himself, he would have." There was a small pause, but no one challenged what she'd said, so she continued, thankful they were at least giving her the opportunity to tell them what she'd been thinking. "I've already asked our attorneys to locate someone with management expertise specific to our patents."

She was a little surprised at how easily those phrases came. *Our attorneys. Management expertise specific to our patents.* For someone who had spent years professing to have no interest in any of this, she talked a good game. Maybe she was more her father's daughter than she had realized.

"Your daddy didn't believe in consultants," Porter said.

"My daddy's dead, Porter. And up until the last couple of years he knew exactly what he was doing as far as Av-Tech was concerned. I don't. However, as the majority owner, I have a responsibility to the other shareholders— that's all of you, by the way—as well as a responsibility to the people who work for us. I'm going to get some help figuring out what's best for the company. I may not have taken an interest in all this before, but it's my responsibility now. I *am* Charlie Beaufort's daughter," she reminded them.

"And I'm *not* going to let the company he loved go down the tubes," she continued. "I want to get someone who knows what they are doing in place there as soon as possible. I hope you'll all be willing to cooperate with him." As her gaze circled their faces, she didn't see anyone who looked upset by that plan. Not even Billy Clemens.

"I think your dad would have been proud, honey," Emory said. "That makes a lot of sense to me. And frankly, it'll be a relief to know that what we started will be in good hands."

Now that Hunter had broken the ice, there was a polite murmur of what sounded like agreement. At least no one objected openly. It wouldn't have mattered if they had, of course. She had the shares to do whatever she wanted. Still, it was nice not to have a mutiny on her hands over her first decision.

"Now, if you'll excuse me, I have a long way to travel to get back home. I'd like to make it before nightfall," she said.

She didn't give them time to protest. She turned and retraced her steps down the rise. Her knee had begun to ache, and she was overly conscious of her limp. Of course, she always was when she knew someone was watching her.

As she passed by the tent, her stepmother was still holding court. Two of the men from the mortuary were beginning to take the flowers off the casket in preparation for lowering it into the ground. *Ashes to ashes,* she thought, turning her blurring eyes quickly away and examining the smoothly rolling green lawn with its dotting of trees and crosses instead.

And dust to dust. Goodbye, Daddy, her heart whispered.

Deliberately she wiped the scene from her mind, picturing him instead behind the wheel of that battered old station wagon, driving them out to the ranch for the weekend. Still young and happy, with all of life ahead of him, and her mother at his side. That was the way she wanted to remember him.

Behind her, she could hear the screech of the crank as it turned, lowering his casket into the ground, and her stepmother's voice, exclaiming to someone about the depths of her grief.

Four days later

"BODYGUARD?" Grey Sellers asked, his deep voice rich with disbelief. "What the hell makes them think somebody would need a bodyguard in *this* place?"

"That's what I'm telling you," Joe Wallace said, easing his bulk down into the chair across the desk. "Piece of cake. I'm gonna hire somebody to make these folks happy, so why shouldn't it be you? Take their money, pay some bills, enjoy the scenery."

The pay-some-bills part struck the right note, Grey acknowledged, and he wondered if Wallace could know that. There were more than a few unpaid bills piled on his desk right now. What *wasn't* piled there were cases.

Not that he was complaining about that, he admitted. At least, he hadn't been until the notices of nonpayment had started arriving. The ones that began with "Dear Valued Customer" and ended by threatening legal action.

"I'm not a bodyguard," Grey said, resisting temptation. The flat statement wasn't exactly a lie. He had the skills, and he'd had the training, all of it acquired at government expense. Grey had done a lot of things during the fifteen years he'd spent with the CIA. Not anything he could classify as pure bodyguarding, however. The closest he had come to that…

He blocked that memory, just as he always did. It was the thing that had driven him away from the agency and the team. Away from the only friends he had. Of course, after what he'd done, he doubted he could still consider many of them friends.

"So?" Joe asked, shrugging. "You don't have to know what you're doing 'cause she doesn't really need a bodyguard. This is a paperwork deal. Somebody snatches Valerie Beaufort, and this insurer might get hit for a loss, so they got to cover their butts. Only, you and I both know nothing's gonna happen. We've never had a CEO kidnapping out this way. Not that we got all that many CEOs to begin with," Wallace added with a grin. "They must have got us mixed up with California. I'm telling you, this is a piece of cake. And somebody's gonna get the job. Might as well be you. Easiest money you'll ever make."

"You know what they say about easy money," Grey said.

He was surprised to find he was thinking about it, however. He had to admit it was tempting. Hell, anybody looking for this Beaufort woman would probably get lost before they found that ranch. From what Joe had told him, it was at the back of beyond.

He took his booted feet off his desk and put the front legs of his chair down on the floor. Then he stood up and stretched the kinks out of his back and shoulders. Too many hours spent hunched over his desk this morning, trying to figure out how to keep his investigative agency afloat.

Investigative agency, he thought wryly. He supposed that did sound better than hole-in-the-wall-surveillance-of-straying-spouses-and-insurance-fraud-con-men service.

"Not really," Joe said. "Don't think I ever heard that one. So whatta they say about easy money?"

Grey walked over to where the air conditioner was sluggishly churning out air that didn't feel any cooler than that outside. He played with the controls a few seconds, and then turned around, letting the lukewarm current blow on his back. It would evaporate the moisture that was molding the soggy material of his shirt to his skin, and the chill that provided would at least give an impression of coolness.

"That it usually *isn't* easy."

"You need a new unit," Joe advised, ignoring the less than original observation about money.

"I need a lot of things," Grey said. *Starting with a stiff drink,* he thought. *A little hair of the dog.*

Since it was only ten o'clock on a typically noneventful weekday morning, however, he didn't announce that particular need to his prospective client. He didn't think it would be conducive to impressing Wallace with his dependability to say that he was hung over and just a little bit shaky as a result.

When he had opened his agency here over a year ago Grey had known things would be slow. At least for a while. He just hadn't known how slow. And since Joe Wallace was one of his few repeat customers, he didn't want to blow the guy's confidence. For some reason, Wallace seemed to think Grey knew what he was doing, and he couldn't afford to lose his business.

Wallace represented several major out-of-state insurers. And he had thrown Grey most of the surveillance cases he'd had during the past few months. The jobs Joe provided, investigating fraudulent insurance claims, along with a few calls from the locals asking Grey to spy on a straying husband or wife, had pretty much made up his caseload since he'd started.

It was boring stuff, no challenge involved, but he did it all with a dogged persistence, even on days like this. Even when he was hung over and aching for another drink. He did those jobs as well as he could because that was the way Griff Cabot had trained him. Nothing left to chance. Nothing ignored, no matter how insignificant it appeared.

He also did them because they provided him with food, a roof over his head and the occasional bottle of bourbon. Lately, it had been more than the occasional bottle, he admitted. Lying to himself wasn't something Grey Sellers did. He never had.

And at some time during the past year, Grey had decided he liked boring. If he didn't, he would learn to. After all, he had already had all the excitement he ever wanted. Enough to last him a couple of lifetimes, he thought bitterly, remembering again, without wanting to, the last mission he had undertaken for Griff Cabot and the CIA's very elite, very clandestine External Security Team.

"Take this job and get some of those things you need," Wallace suggested.

Grey's lips tightened as he tried to think why he shouldn't. Other than the fact that he didn't ever intend to be in that position again. The ghost that drove him to crave a drink way too early in the morning was too closely connected to protection. Or rather with a failure to provide it. A failure on his part.

"Easy money and somebody's gonna get it," Joe said, watching his face, maybe reading that need. "Might as well be you."

"What do I have to do?" Grey asked, knowing in his gut this was a mistake. And every time he hadn't listened to his gut—

"Look around. Make some security-type recommendations on the place. Do surveillance on the insured until they get something else set up. Do the paperwork." Joe nodded toward the packet of documents he had dropped on the cluttered desk.

Grey hadn't even looked at them. Paperwork was something he was familiar with. This couldn't be much different from the government red-tape-type crap he'd dealt with for years. Griff had taken care of most of that, but everyone on the team had occasionally had to do their debriefing on paper.

He again pushed those memories back where they belonged, and despite the pounding in his head, tried to wrap his concentration around the particulars of this case.

"And the policy isn't even on the Beaufort woman?" he asked, trying to remember the details Joe had mentioned before he had thrown in that pay-some-bills part and gotten his attention.

"The policy, as it's written," Joe said patiently, "covers the CEO of Av-Tech Aeronautics, which by virtue of her father's death last week, Valerie Beaufort now is. So someone at Beneficial Life finally figured out that the policy covers her. It's pretty standard. All the big companies have these things for their executive officers. The insurers agree to pay the ransom if a CEO is kidnapped. That kind of stuff."

"And there isn't any reason to believe she might really need protection."

Joe laughed. "The insurers are covering their butts. Just like I am. They'll make her set up some kind of state-of-the-art security system on that ranch. Until she does, they want somebody to guard this broad on a temporary basis," Joe said, shrugging. "That's the deal. Like I told you—piece of cake."

"Okay," Grey said, still reluctant, even as he heard the agreement come out of his mouth. And he was not completely sure why he was so resistant. More messages from his gut, he guessed.

"I got to provide them with a résumé. Your credentials. You got a sheet with the stuff on it, I can just fax it to them."

Leaving the air conditioner, Grey walked over to the battered black metal filing cabinet that stood in a corner of the tiny office. Pulling out the top drawer, the only one that had anything in it, he thumbed through the mostly empty folders until he found the one that contained the information he had put into the ads he'd placed when he had first set up the agency.

He handed one of the sheets to Joe and then sat back down behind his desk as Wallace read it. Joe looked at it a few seconds before his eyes came back up. The insurance agent took his pen out of his shirt pocket and put the paper down on Grey's desk, poised to write. "References?" he asked.

How about a supposedly dead ex-deputy director of the CIA, Grey thought, a little amused by the idea of putting Griff's name down. Cabot would vouch for him, all right, providing a postdated letter of reference if Grey wanted it, but he didn't intend to ask Griff or anybody else for any favors. Not to get a job he had reservations about taking in the first place. If these folks didn't like his credentials, they could get someone else.

"Ex-military," Grey said. "That's all on there."

"I mean somebody who could verify your qualifications."

"What you see is what you get," Grey said softly. "If they don't like it, they can get themselves another bodyguard to watch over their little heiress. You know, the one who doesn't really *need* a bodyguard at all."

Joe's gaze rose again, and he studied Grey's face a moment. He looked as if he wanted to ask other questions, but after a few seconds, maybe because of what was in Grey's eyes, Wallace put the pen back into his pocket and stood up. He folded the sheet Grey had given him and stuck it in the same pocket.

"There *ain't* nobody else," he said, smiling, his good humor restored. "Not out here. I know that, and you know it. Besides, they aren't gonna quibble over a résumé. This job won't last but a few days at the most. You give 'em somebody's name, and they probably wouldn't even take the time to check 'em out. So why bother, right? I'll vouch for you.''

Grey nodded, again wondering why he was doing this. His instincts were still telling him it was a bad idea.

When Joe reached the door, he hesitated before he opened it, looking back over his shoulder. ''Might be good if you stay out there twenty-four seven. You know, so if anything goes wrong, they can't come back on us and say, 'Well, that wouldn't have happened if…' You know,'' he said again, seeming to run down.

''You want me to stay out at the Beaufort place?''

''Might be best,'' Joe said. ''Until they get the security system in. Just as a precaution.''

''I got a business to run,'' Grey said, knowing how ridiculous that excuse was, even if Joe didn't.

''Yeah, well… Just a precaution, you know. And you got an answering machine and all.''

''I thought you said—'' Grey's protest was cut off by Joe's voice.

''Almost forgot. Here's the first payment,'' he said, walking back to lay a check on the desk. ''Retainer and the first week.''

Grey looked down at the nice round sum on the check. Fifteen hundred dollars would take care of most of those bills, at least the ones that had ''third notice'' attached.

''A thousand bucks a week plus expenses,'' Joe said. ''They'll want receipts for those. Bean counters,'' he said dismissingly.

Grey heard the door close before he looked up. Wallace was gone, and he was alone with a check on his desk and a job he didn't want but had, for some reason, apparently agreed to take.

''Son of a bitch,'' Grey said. ''Stupid son of a bitch.''

Angry with himself, he pulled open the bottom drawer

of his desk and poured a shot of whiskey into the small tumbler he kept there. He tilted his head and knocked it back, closing his eyes as the liquor burned all the way down to his empty stomach, producing a small, satisfying glow. He put the glass back into the drawer and recapped the bottle with fingers that trembled.

That telltale vibration bothered him. He had had the reputation of having the coolest head and the steadiest hands of anyone on the team. Steadiest hands of anyone except Hawk, of course, he acknowledged with a small, twisted smile.

At least he hadn't begun drinking it straight out of the bottle, he comforted himself caustically. That would probably come next. Probably right after his first encounter with Miss Valerie Beaufort and her millions.

Chapter One

Two things were clear immediately. The battered pickup parked in front of her house now hadn't been there when Val left a couple of hours ago. And she didn't recognize it as belonging to anyone she knew. Since she didn't get many visitors, especially ones she didn't know, both of those things made her wary. It was pretty hard to stray off any beaten path and end up out here. Her eyes studying the unfamiliar vehicle, she slowed her gelding to a walk, guiding Harvard slowly toward the ranch house.

The truck sported Colorado plates, along with half a dozen pings and dents. There was more dirt on its paint job than the normal surface dust a vehicle would acquire in making the trek out here. This one had been in need of a wash job for a while.

Her eyes traced over the porch, sweeping quickly over and then coming back to the shape that didn't belong there. Almost hidden in the late-afternoon shadows, a man was sitting in one of her mother's rockers, booted feet crossed at the ankles and propped on the wooden porch railing.

A black Stetson had been pulled down over his face as if he were asleep. Val would be willing to bet money that he wasn't.

The boots were well-worn, she noted, her eyes moving upward to assess the length of his legs—long, muscular and clad in faded jeans. And a broad chest covered by a chamois-colored shirt, the sleeves turned back, revealing tanned forearms that were crossed over the man's flat belly. Long-fingered hands lay totally relaxed on either side of his waist. As she watched, one rose, its thumb pushing the Stetson up off the man's eyes.

They were gray. Ocean-gray. Storm-gray. Rain-cloud gray. Valerie had time to come up with a couple of other totally inane analogies before he straightened in the rocker, putting his feet down on the porch and pushing the hat all the way back.

His hair was coal-black and just a little longer than she normally liked for a man. Val couldn't decide whether that was a stylistic decision on his part, or if he were just badly in need of a haircut. Her gaze came back to his face, but she found it hard to look at any feature other than those compelling eyes.

They were silver now, opaque in the shadowed light, and set in a frame of thick black lashes. Their color was the only softness in a face as harsh as the country that surrounded them. The features were lean and darkly weathered. It was obvious his nose had been broken at least once, maybe more, and it sat defiantly crooked above thin, hard lips.

"Ma'am," he said, touching his hat in the traditional gesture of respect. A respect missing from the silver eyes. They examined her face as thoroughly as she had examined his.

"Who are you?" she asked, her voice demanding, a little arrogant. That was a front, the tone developed long ago to hide her habitual nervousness at meeting strangers.

"My name's Grey Sellers, ma'am. Beneficial Life sent me."

There were a couple of slow heartbeats of silence.

"Sent you for what?" Val asked. She really couldn't

imagine. He certainly didn't look like any insurance salesman she'd ever seen.

"To be your bodyguard," he said.

For just a second there had been something behind those shuttered eyes. Amusement? Val wondered. The emotion had disappeared too quickly for her to be sure of its identification, replaced by the same bland politeness that was in his voice.

"My...*bodyguard?* Is this somebody's idea of a joke?"

"Not as far as I can tell. Their check was good."

This time his amusement was obvious. It underlay the deep voice and touched the edges of that hard mouth, tilting a corner.

"Let me get this straight," Val said. "Somebody *paid* you to come out here and be my bodyguard?"

The word was so ridiculous she almost couldn't bring herself to say it. It was one of those words that belonged only in the movies. Or on bad TV shows. The people she knew didn't have bodyguards. Not even the rich ones.

"Beneficial Life," he said.

"I don't have a policy with Beneficial whatever," she said. "Now, if you'll just get off my porch, Mr...?"

"Sellers," he supplied obediently, the upward quirk of his lips increasing minutely.

"Mr. Sellers," she echoed. "If you will just get off my porch *and* off my property, I'd be very grateful."

She had already begun to turn Harvard toward the barn when he spoke again. "They had a policy on your father, ma'am."

That stopped her. The wound of her father's death was too new for any information about him not to give her pause. When she turned back, Sellers was holding out a packet of papers.

Without reaching for them, she asked, her voice full of sarcasm, "And they sent *you* out here to pay it off?"

No one with half a grain of sense would trust this man with money, not as disreputable as he appeared, and they both knew it.

"No, ma'am," he said, still rather obviously amused. "If you're short of cash, I'm afraid it wasn't *that* kind of policy."

She took a breath, holding on to her temper. She realized that, surprisingly, she didn't feel any sense of threat. Even her initial wariness at finding a stranger on her porch had begun to fade, turning to skepticism instead.

"Then what kind of policy was it, Mr. Sellers?" she asked with studied patience, as if she were talking to someone who wasn't quite bright.

"You can look at the paperwork," he said, laying the packet on the railing. "But as I understand it, the policy assured the other owners that nothing untoward was going to happen to the CEO of Av-Tech Aeronautics."

"Nothing…*untoward*," she repeated. The word was as unexpected on his lips as his lean body had been on her porch.

"As I understand it."

"You're here to see that nothing *untoward* happens to me."

"Yes, ma'am," he said solemnly, but again there was a flash of something in the depths of those gray eyes.

"I don't think that there is a single *untoward* thing lurking around out here. Do you?" She raised her eyebrows and waited.

His gaze circled the neat yard and then rose to the mountains that loomed over the narrow valley where the ranch and the spring that fed it were located. It was that spring that made her small operation possible in all this barrenness.

"I deposited their check," he said, his eyes seeming to consider the line of fencing that faded off toward the barn.

She waited a moment to see if there would be some further enlightenment as to why he had thought she might be interested in that revelation. "And?" she asked finally.

"And frankly, I'd play hell giving that money back," he said, turning to face her again. The mobile corner of his mouth had inched upward a little farther, almost a smile. His eyes, however, were still carefully neutral. Still opaque.

"Well, I think that's probably going to have to be between you and them, Mr. Sellers. It seems to fall in the category of not my problem. I want you off my place in…two minutes?" she asked, looking toward the battered truck.

"I could do that, ma'am, providing my truck will start, of course. And sometimes that's doubtful. But I don't think they'd be any too pleased if I did. Beneficial Life, I mean."

"You know, I don't really give a damn whether they are pleased or not," Val said. "I want you *out.*" She didn't raise her voice, but the last word was sharp. And final.

"I wish I could oblige you, Ms. Beaufort. I really do. But I have a professional obligation, ma'am. I'm sure you, being the C-E-O of a big company and all, can understand that." He had said the initials slowly, emphasizing each, drawling them out mockingly. "I took their money, and now I'm obligated to do the job. Whether you or I like it very much," he added.

"You're planning on *protecting* me," she said, her anger building, "whether I want you to or not. Is that what you're trying to tell me, Mr. Sellers?"

"That's what I'm telling you, ma'am," he agreed solemnly.

"Don't you imagine that's going to be hard to do without my cooperation?" she asked, her voice falsely sweet.

"Well, it would certainly be easier *with* your cooperation, but I think I can probably manage the other," he said.

She drew a deep breath, feeling Harvard stir beneath her. He was probably responding to her tension. She was furious, but she wasn't sure at whom she was angrier. Beneficial Life? Av-Tech's attorneys for not telling her about this policy, *if* it even existed? Or with this smug son of a bitch sitting on her porch? She edged Harvard closer to the railing and reached out to retrieve the tri-folded packet of documents he'd laid there. When she had it in her hand, she backed the gelding.

"Get out," she said softly.

"They'll just send somebody else," Sellers said, his tone devoid now of the amusement that had lurked in it before. "They aren't going to leave you alone out here without some kind of security system in place. And I assume you don't have one."

She'd be a fool to tell him she didn't, of course, but she had never seen the need for security. When you lived at the back of beyond—in the devil's armpit, as her dad used to say—you didn't worry about the occasional burglary. Especially when there was nothing out here worth stealing in the first place.

"What would make you assume that?" she asked, controlling the gelding's impatience with the ease of long practice.

Grey Sellers held her eyes a moment before he unfolded his length out of the rocker and walked over to her front door. He opened it, and then he waited. Nothing happened, of course. There were no alarms. No automatic notification of the sheriff's office. Considering the roads that led to the ranch and the distance from the nearest town, by the time anyone from the Bradford County Sheriff's Department could get out here, anything that was happening would be long over with anyway.

Then Sellers walked over and pushed up the window behind the rocker he'd been sitting in. It wasn't locked. Val didn't worry too much about locking windows either, of course.

He turned to look at her, his hat shadowing his face. "Your alarm system doesn't seem to be working, Ms. Beaufort."

"That's because there isn't one. As you are well aware."

"So are they," he said. "The insurance company, I mean. Something happens to you, they pay Av-Tech through the nose. And they don't like paying. Can't say I blame them."

"What do you think is going to happen to me out here?"

"Nothing," he said. And then he added, his tone again amused, "At least, not as long as I'm around."

He came back to the railing, looking up at her from under the brim of that dusty black hat. Appropriate, she thought. This one certainly wasn't a member of the white hat brigade. Those shadowed eyes had seen too much.

And how the hell do I think I can tell that by looking into his eyes? she wondered in disgust. She seemed to have developed an eye fetish in the past few minutes.

Harvard snorted, tossing his head and working at the bit. Sellers put his hand on the horse's nose, running the heel down the length of it from between the gelding's eyes to the nostrils. He leaned forward and blew on them, an old horseman's trick.

"Easy, buster," he said. "Mind your manners." The words were low and caressing. The tone of someone who liked horses.

They'll just send somebody else, he had said. *They aren't going to leave you alone out here without some kind of security system in place.* And he was probably right.

She wasn't Val Beaufort, penny-ante horse breeder and trainer, anymore. She was the CEO of Av-Tech Aeronautics, and like it or not, there were certain restrictions that went with the position. Restrictions she couldn't do much about right now.

She would, she vowed. She wasn't going to live her life chained to that damn company as her father had. Chained to the headaches that went with it. *They'll just send somebody else.* They would. And she'd deal with that one when he arrived.

"Tell them I'll get someone out here to set up a security system at the earliest possible opportunity," she said.

"If you don't, they will."

"On my property? I think that's called trespassing."

"And *I* think the policy Av-Tech agreed to gives them the right to take adequate measures to safeguard their investment. Beneficial Life wouldn't have written it unless it did."

"I'll straighten this out as soon as possible, Mr. Sellers," she said, feeling that he was probably right and she was wrong. It wasn't a particularly pleasant feeling. "Thank you for making me aware of the policy. And now, if you would be so kind…"

She turned and looked pointedly at the truck again.

"They'll just send someone else," he warned the second time. "It'll take a few days to get a system in place. They won't leave you unprotected while that's going on."

"Then I guess I'll have another visitor tomorrow. In the meantime, it's a long way back to civilization. And it's almost dark, just in case you haven't noticed. The roads out here can be a little harrowing at night."

His eyes held on hers a long moment. Finally he touched his hat again and walked across the porch and down the shallow steps, boot heels loud on the wooden planks. He climbed into the pickup and closed the door. Val didn't move, almost anticipating what would happen next.

She wasn't disappointed. The motor ground a few times, but it never turned over. He had telegraphed that move with his comment about the unreliability of his truck. While he was waiting for her to get home, he had probably removed the wires from the spark plugs or something so the truck wouldn't start.

She could dismount and try it herself. Or she could ask him to pop the hood and let her look at the engine. If he had done much fancy tinkering with the motor, however, she'd just end up looking like a fool, which was something she worked hard at not doing. She knew far more about horses than she did about internal combustion engines.

For some reason, his interaction with Harvard flashed into her head. But just because he liked horses didn't mean he was harmless, of course. She took a breath, fighting frustration.

While he ground the motor a couple more times, she unfolded the papers she'd picked up off the railing. The heading at the top was Beneficial Life, and they looked official enough.

They'll just send somebody else. At least this one knew the back end from the front end of a horse, which was something in his favor. To her, anyway. And for some reason, Val wasn't afraid of him, despite what she thought she'd seen in his eyes.

The slamming of the truck's door brought her attention from the papers she held to the man who had presented them. He walked around the back of the pickup and stood looking up at her.

"I know what you're probably thinking," he said disarmingly. "I can give you Joe Wallace's number. You can call him and verify that he sent me out here, if that will make you feel any better. I'm not sure he'll be in the office this late, but—''

''There's a bunkhouse,'' Val said shortly. ''You can sleep out there tonight. I'll talk to Beneficial Life in the morning.''

''Fair enough,'' he said.

''And Mr. Sellers?''

''Ma'am?''

''I may not have a security system, but I *do* have a Smith & Wesson. And I know how to use it.''

''That's a real comfort to me, ma'am,'' he said.

The amusement was back in his voice, although his expression hadn't changed. There was no twitch at the corner of his mouth. Not a hint of laughter in the silver eyes. Just a rich layer of amusement in his voice before he turned and picked up a nylon gym bag from the bed of the truck.

Her eyes followed him until he had disappeared behind the barn. Then, realizing what she had been doing, she touched her heels to Harvard and headed him in almost the same direction.

GREY SELLERS WAS STILL fighting the urge to grin as he approached the bunkhouse she'd directed him to. It looked as well kept as everything else on the place. He wondered how much help she had. So far, he had seen no signs of human life other than Valerie Beaufort herself.

After he'd arrived this afternoon and discovered she wasn't home, he had wandered around a little. With an eye to security, he had told himself, justifying the snooping.

Although it had been a long time since he'd lived on a working ranch, he had immediately felt at home. It seemed to be the same kind of small-potatoes outfit he'd grown up on, minus the cows. Until a few minutes ago, however, it had looked as if he wasn't going to get a chance to savor this kind of life again.

Sitting on top of that big old roan, Valerie Beaufort might look fragile enough that a good wind would blow her away, but she had a mouth on her. And a very clear sense of what she wanted. Or what she didn't want, he supposed, in his case.

Grey wasn't sure what had changed her mind about letting him stay. Maybe just his winning ways, he thought, again fighting the urge to smile. His sparkling wit. Since he'd taken time to shave before he'd driven out here and had, in the process, gotten a really good look at himself in the mirror, he couldn't imagine it was his physical appearance. He looked rough. Like he'd been rode hard and put up wet. Which was pretty much how he felt.

The aspirin he'd taken before he'd left the office was wearing off. Driving out here over those narrow roads and looking into the afternoon sun the whole way hadn't helped the headache his hangover this morning had begun.

And he could use a drink, he acknowledged. He had deliberately left the bottle of bourbon in his desk drawer. He didn't drink while he worked. He never had. Griff wouldn't have put up with it, of course. Not from anybody on the team. Too many lives depended on them being able to do their jobs and do them well. Not that the booze had been a problem back then. That had all come about since—

He heard the squeak of the double doors at the front of the barn. They had made the same sound when he had opened them earlier this afternoon and taken a look inside. He glanced up and found that since the Dutch door at the back was standing wide open, he could see straight through the barn.

Valerie Beaufort was leading her gelding inside. He'd been right about the fragility, he thought, automatically assessing her figure, revealed clearly by the narrow-legged jeans and cotton shirt she was wearing. She was too thin for his taste. Small breasts and hips narrow as a child's.

She had pushed her hat back, revealing hair the color of leaves turning in the fall. No wonder she had a temper, he thought.

It took a second or two for his brain to register the other, although it should have been obvious from the first. Her stride was uneven. Noticeably so. An unexpected frisson of emotion uncoiled in the pit of Grey's stomach. And he wasn't even sure what it was he was feeling.

Head down, eyes on the ground, she hadn't noticed him watching her as she limped across the barn, the big horse docilely following. Despite the feeling that this made him some kind of voyeur, Grey couldn't seem to look away, and whatever he had felt in his gut when he'd noticed the limp stirred again.

She had been too damned prickly for him to be feeling sorry for her, he decided. But maybe this was why she was so standoffish, he thought, remembering that determined lift of her chin when she warned him she had a gun. Maybe it was this, instead of all that money, like he'd been thinking.

Just at that moment she glanced up, her gaze meeting his. Her eyes widened, and he was embarrassed to have been caught staring. He didn't allow his eyes to fall, however. He had a pretty good idea of how she'd interpret it if he looked away now.

Her lips tightened before she opened them to ask, "Did you need something else, Mr. Sellers?"

"No, ma'am."

Neither of them moved. Behind her, the gelding made some movement, but she ignored him. Her brown eyes, seeming too big for the small, oval face, held on Grey's challengingly.

"You can use any bed in the bunkhouse," she said finally. "Dinner's at nine. Later than you're used to, maybe, but I don't like eating while the sun's up."

"Are you inviting me to dinner, Ms. Beaufort?"

"Hospitality forbids that I let a guest go hungry, Mr. Sellers, even an uninvited one. Don't read anything else into the invitation, however. I figure having you come up to the house is easier than carrying a tray out there," she said, gesturing with her chin toward the bunkhouse behind him.

"Yes, ma'am," Grey said.

He realized that watching her limp across the barn had destroyed whatever perverse pleasure he had taken in baiting her. To do that now would make him feel petty, like taking cheap shots at someone who was not quite capable of defending herself.

Of course, she hadn't seemed to have a problem dealing with his sarcasm, so he knew that was all in his head— and he knew why. He didn't much like that reason being there, and he knew damn well she wouldn't. He suspected she wasn't the kind who would welcome pity, however dressed up it was and masquerading as something else.

"I don't want you to get the idea that it's an invitation to anything else, Mr. Sellers," she said, bringing his attention back with an unpleasant jolt. "I don't want to be your friend. I don't want any closer acquaintance with you. I didn't want to be your host, not even for one night, but it seems that choice has been taken out of my hands. So... Dinner. That's all."

"Grey," he suggested. "I don't get called Mr. Sellers often enough to feel real comfortable answering to it."

He smiled at her, the nice, safe, polite one he pulled out for little old ladies and loan officers and cops who were holding ticket books. Not the smart-assed one he'd been carefully pretending to hide while he sparred verbally with an attractive woman from across a porch railing.

Her lips tightened. "Nine o'clock, Mr. Sellers. No need

to dress up.'' She turned her back and began to unsaddle the horse.

From the quickness of her movements there was no doubt she knew exactly what she was doing, and that she had been doing it on a regular basis for a long time. Despite his previous acknowledgment that this was one proud, prickly woman, Grey set down the bag he was holding and walked into the barn. It was already dusk, the light from the dying sun fading quickly.

He was surprised at how much darker the barn's interior was than it had been outside. And surprised at how familiar were the smells. How evocative. He took a deep breath, inhaling a combined fragrance of hay, horse manure and oiled leather. Scents that would always mean home to him.

He walked toward the horse and his rider, watching as her small hands worked efficiently. As soon as she had loosened all the straps, Grey stepped forward, moving in front of her without warning. He lifted the saddle off and set it atop the rail of the nearest stall.

When he turned around, Valerie Beaufort's eyes were on his face. There was a bloom of heat in her cheeks, and her lips were set so tight they were nothing but a white line.

''Don't you *ever* do anything like that again,'' she ordered.

The madder she got, the quieter her voice. He had noticed that on the porch. Which must mean she was furious right now.

''I don't know what kind of men you're used to being around, Ms. Beaufort, but I was raised to be a gentleman. I would have done the same for any lady.''

''You're a lying son of a bitch,'' she said. ''You figured you'd just help the poor little cripple out, whether she needed it or not. Maybe get on my good side by showing what a gentleman you are. Or maybe you just wanted to feel better about yourself by doing your good deed for the day. I don't really give a damn why you did that, but if ever I want your help, I'll ask for it. If I don't ask, Mr. Sellers, then you leave me the hell alone.''

A matching anger grew as she spit words at him. Maybe it was the nagging headache he'd fought all day. The need for a drink that he hated like hell to admit. Or maybe it was pure guilt because she had come too close to the truth. Whatever the reason, his own rage suddenly boiled up past his normally well-developed self-control.

He grabbed her upper arms, locking his fingers around them hard enough to make her flinch. Her pupils dilated in shock. Ms. Rich-bitch Beaufort had probably never had a man touch her, he thought, in anger or any other way. With this kind of attitude, who the hell would want to? Despite the fact that his brain was already telling him he had made a huge mistake, he shook her. Not hard, just a single, sharp movement.

The bones of her upper arms were thin under his hands. As childlike as the rest of her appeared to be. Vulnerable. And realizing that should have destroyed his anger. It should have made him ashamed of the fact that he was manhandling someone so much smaller than he was.

Someone who was also…crippled. It was the word she had used. He didn't like having it in his head. The fact that it *was* there, just as she had accused, seemed to fuel his anger.

"I don't know what's wrong with you, lady," he said, his voice low and deliberately menacing, his hands still gripping her arms. "I came out here because I was hired to do a job. And because I need the money. Believe me, I don't want to be your friend, either. And if you think offering to feed me gives you the right to be rude, you need to rethink your policy on hospitality. I would have taken that saddle off for any woman. That's how I was raised. You can be damn sure, however, that being nice to you is a mistake I won't make again.''

He released her so abruptly she staggered. He fought the urge to grab her elbow and steady her until she regained her balance. Instead, he pushed between her and the flank of the roan and strode angrily across the barn and then outside to where he'd left his bag. He scooped it up without looking back and walked into the bunkhouse, slamming the door closed behind him.

The noise didn't help his headache appreciably. Neither did the blood that was pounding through his temples. It had been a long time since he had really lost his temper. A long time since anyone or anything had driven him out of the fog of apathy that had surrounded him since he'd quit the External Security Team. He couldn't even begin to explain why he had lost it now.

But it made him ashamed. And exposed. As if he had opened himself up and revealed to this woman that all the gears and cogs that were supposed to be turning smoothly inside his head had gotten a little out of whack. Or maybe, considering what he'd just done, a lot out of whack.

He threw the bag on top of the bunk nearest the door and watched the dust lift in a small cloud around it. She'd probably file a complaint. He hoped it was with Beneficial Life rather than with Joe Wallace. After all, he could con Wallace with some tale about why this hadn't worked out.

And he'd have to pay back the money somehow. He didn't have a clue how he was going to manage that. He sat down on the edge of another bunk and put his aching head into his hands.

Way to go, hotshot, he thought, everything he had said to her running through his head. The way to win friends and influence people.

I don't want to be your friend, Valerie Beaufort had said. He sure as hell couldn't blame her for that.

Chapter Two

Valerie stuck her fork into the pork chop on her plate, making another neat row of holes. When Grey Sellers hadn't shown up for dinner, she had sat down at the table a few minutes after nine, feeling righteous. And indignant. And then nauseated.

I rode too far in the afternoon heat, she told herself.

You acted like a jackass, her conscience jeered, because a man had the nerve to take the saddle off a horse for you.

Which he did for all the wrong reasons.

Feminist bull. Since when is it a crime for a man to help a woman?

When he does it for the wrong reasons.

You're a mind reader? You know for sure why he was moved to do that terrible thing to you?

Tired of the internal conflict and especially of trying to answer that last question, Val pushed back her chair, picked up her plate and carried it over to the garbage can. She opened the can with the foot pedal and dumped the battle-scarred pork chop, the roll and green beans in. Then she set her plate in the sink and turned to look at the serving bowls on the kitchen table. *It's a shame to waste all that food,* she thought.

Especially when there's a hungry man out in the bunkhouse who would probably be more than willing to take care of it for you. A man you invited to dinner under the guise of hospitality and then attacked because he reciprocated with what was possibly nothing more than an act of kindness of his own.

Some act of kindness. He grabbed my shoulders hard enough to bruise, she reminded herself, determined to hold on to her anger because she hadn't found a way to let go of it without admitting she'd been partially at fault in the situation.

She advanced on the table and began to pick up dishes and carry them over to the counter. She didn't open the garbage can again until she had everything transferred, but even then she couldn't bring herself to throw the food away.

Instead, she took another plate out of the cabinet, almost slamming it down on the counter, and piled two pork chops, three rolls and the rest of the green beans onto it. She set the plate on a tray, along with the bowl of fruit salad and a fork, a spoon and a knife. Then she took a clean napkin out of the drawer and spread it over the top.

She stood looking down at the covered food for a few seconds before she reached across the sink and turned on the lights out in the yard. She picked up the tray before she could change her mind and carried it through the door, pushing the screen open with her hip.

When she rounded the corner of the barn, she could see a dim light coming from the bunkhouse. The patch of ground where she was standing was still in darkness, however, out of range of the lights from either building. *Safe,* she thought, grateful for the concealing shadows. Safe from what? the voice of her own logic, which she was beginning to despise, taunted.

Still reluctant to face the man she had yelled at this

afternoon, she had to make herself walk over to the door and knock, balancing the tray on her hip. There was no sound from inside the bunkhouse, and no answer to her rather tentative tap. After a couple of minutes she knocked again, more forcefully this time, and then she turned the knob, pushing the door inward.

"Mr. Sellers?" she called.

There was still no response, so she pushed the door wider and stepped inside. The bunkhouse appeared to be empty. Maybe he was out doing another security check, she mocked mentally. She had been aware that he was making a check of all the windows and doors while she had been cooking dinner. She had already locked them as soon as she had come inside, of course, so he hadn't had any reason to complain about her security measures.

She set the tray down on the table in front of the pot-bellied stove and turned to leave. For a moment her eyes surveyed the building her father had built. Pretty primitive by any standard. There were six bunks, three on each side; the table she had put the tray on and its four chairs; the stove; and bookshelves that held a variety of puzzles, games and books.

All of it was covered by a fine layer of silt that the desert wind had brought in. She hadn't cleaned out here in a long time because no one had lived in the bunkhouse in years, which was exactly the way she wanted it.

Her father had accused her of being a recluse. Maybe she was. But the confrontation with Grey Sellers this afternoon made her know she didn't regret the life she had chosen. She didn't need that kind of upheaval again, especially not now.

That kind of upheaval. She repeated the phrase, wondering why she had used it in relation to Sellers. There was nothing in *this* situation that was anything like the other.

Her eyes rose, sheer instinct maybe, and found him watching her from the doorway that led to the bunkhouse's communal bathroom. His black hair was wet, glistening with blue highlights under the glare of the bare, swaying electric bulb. Obviously he had just gotten out of the shower, which was why he hadn't answered her knock or her call.

He was wearing the same jeans he'd worn this afternoon, but he was barefoot. And he was in the process of rebuttoning the chamois-colored shirt. As he did, those gray eyes, which had taken her breath this afternoon, rested inquiringly on her face.

His long fingers continued to work the buttons through their holes, one after the other, not seeming to hurry over the task. The open edges of the shirt revealed a flat brown stomach, centered by an arrow of dark hair. Her eyes had time to trace down it, all the way to where it disappeared into the waistline of his low-riding jeans, before he got to that last button, pulling the shirt together and destroying her view.

"I brought your dinner," she said, forcing her gaze back up.

For some reason, her mouth had gone dry, so that the words were hard to articulate. She hoped he wasn't aware of the effect that glimpse of his body had on her normally guarded emotions.

He glanced at the tray of food she had set down on the table, and then back at her. "Thank you, ma'am," he said.

"And I wanted to apologize for...flying off the handle at you this afternoon," she said, forcing the words out and hearing their clipped coldness.

It was a grudging apology at best, but her people skills

were rusty. And this man seemed to have the ability to throw her off balance, just by looking at her. Just by that subtle movement at the corner of his mouth, which was happening again.

As if he knew something amusing, but didn't intend to share. As if he were laughing inside. Laughing at her? she wondered. Paranoia, she chided, pulling her eyes away from his lips.

"I don't like people assuming I can't do whatever I set out to do," she continued doggedly, determined to get this out of the way, to offer some explanation as to why she had reacted as she had this afternoon, without getting too close to the painful truth that she hated being treated as if she were handicapped.

"I didn't assume anything about what you can or can't do, Ms. Beaufort," he said, his voice without inflection. "I told you. I was raised to be a gentleman. Old-fashioned, I guess. At least nowadays. But since you were obviously offended, I apologize. For…everything," he finished softly. "I assure you, nothing like that will ever happen again."

His eyes held on her face, saying more than his words. Those were probably meant to make up for the fact that he had put his hands on her. Except he hadn't even mentioned that. There had been no apology for manhandling her.

Of course, she acknowledged, he wasn't the only one who was not explaining everything. Usually she just ignored people who made a point of noticing her disability. With him, she had made a big deal of it. And if she were honest, she would have to admit that she knew why.

This was the first man she had been attracted to in years—more years than she wanted to remember. The first one to affect her with this subtle sexual tension since she had broken her engagement to Barton Carruthers.

Nothing like that will ever happen again, he had promised. The "that" carefully unqualified or defined. And she was equally unwilling to pursue a discussion of that physical contact. Grey Sellers would be gone in the morning. She would see to that, even if she had to drive him into town herself and then send someone out here to tow his truck off her property.

When she had, she'd talk to Wallace or to the insurance company, and all of this nonsense would be over. Maybe she had overreacted this afternoon—she wouldn't deny that—but there was no need to continue to do so. Grey Sellers had chosen to ignore the fact that he'd touched her, and she would, too.

"And thanks for bringing the tray out," he said, his voice low. "I figured the invitation to dinner had been rescinded."

Rescinded. As strange a choice of words for the man he seemed to be as *untoward* had been. But the soft sincerity in his voice made her conscious again that she didn't feel threatened by him. She hadn't, not even when he'd shaken her. His action had been only a reflex, a reaction to her anger and her accusation.

"Good night," she said, deliberately breaking the connection that was growing between them. She didn't want to know any more about Grey Sellers than she already did. She didn't want to think about him any more than she already had.

She limped across the room, conscious that her footsteps echoed unevenly on the old boards. Conscious that his eyes were on her, even if she couldn't see them. *Let him watch. Let him get a good look,* she thought, suddenly angry and unsure why.

After tomorrow, she told herself again, things would go back to normal. At least, as normal as they could be until she had gotten rid of the albatross that was Av-Tech.

And the sooner she did that, the better, she decided, shutting the door of the bunkhouse firmly behind her. All the way back into the house, however, it seemed she could feel the force of those silver eyes, still watching her.

"IT'S OKAY," Valerie crooned to the stallion, keeping her voice low and soothing. "Easy now. Easy, boy. Everything's okay now, you big old bad boy."

This on top of everything else, she thought, feeling the tension, which she had spent most of the nearly sleepless night trying to destroy, seep back into her neck and shoulders.

Being tense wasn't a real good thing, of course, when you were dealing with a spooked horse. And despite her continued attempts at reassurance, the black was still upset, head up and ears forward.

One reason she had chosen Kronus as her first stallion was because of his disposition. For a stud horse, he was remarkably well behaved. She had watched him work, and his previous owner had vouched for him. And since she had owned the stallion, he had never given her any cause to question that reputation.

Until today. As soon as she'd come out of the house this morning, shortly after dawn, she had heard him banging in his stall. He had even splintered one of the rails, which meant she didn't want to leave him in the tiny holding pen until she could make repairs.

Probably better to put him into the corral, she had thought. The other horses were all in the pasture that surrounded the spring, so there would be nothing to bother him out there. Nothing beyond whatever it was that had made him so edgy already.

He'd be in a less confined space and less apt to do himself damage. She took her eyes off the black long enough to glance back into the stall she had just led him out of. It was inside the simple enclosure that she had built herself when she decided she needed to buy her own stud. Granted, the building was very small, but it had seemed plenty secure, and it was far enough from the barn that he didn't cause problems with the other horses.

She could see nothing in the stall to provoke this kind of display. However, a lot of things could spook a horse, from an unexpected or unfamiliar noise to a piece of plastic blowing along the ground.

Maybe Kronus sensed there was a stranger on the property. As she led the jittery stallion by the bunkhouse, her eyes focused briefly on the door, still closed against the growing light. She realized that she had been aware of that door the whole time she'd been in the yard.

Anticipating when her uninvited guest might open it? she wondered, leading the stud toward the corral. If so, it was an anticipation she didn't want to feel. Despite her resolve, however, she remembered the impact of Grey Sellers' eyes. And that small tug of amusement at the corner of his mouth.

She had been momentarily distracted by that memory, but her attention was abruptly brought back to Kronus, where it should have been all along. He had been nervous throughout the short journey. Now he threw up his head, jerking against the lead, and jigging to the side.

She shortened the nylon rope by changing the position of her hand, intent on controlling his head. She was by his shoulder, right where she needed to be. Even so, she could sense the gathering of muscle in those powerful hindquarters, his front hooves even seeming to lift a fraction from the ground.

Val knew that he just wanted to be gone, just to get away from whatever was frightening him. That flight instinct was highly developed in horses, and that's exactly what Kronus wanted to do. Just get the hell out of here.

Although she was talking to him the whole time, she could feel his tension building. And she still couldn't understand why. There was nothing—

He jerked his head up, pulling strongly against the lead she held, the whites of his eyes showing. She stayed with him, fighting to keep control. They were so near the safety of the paddock. If she could just get him through that gate and inside.

She reached for the gate with her free hand, and Kronus crow hopped, trying to pull away. He dragged her a few inches away from the fence before she was able to get his head back down.

She could feel her bad knee beginning to tremble, however, as it always did under strain. She ignored it, gritting her teeth against the pain, and grimly hung on as he jumped to the side again.

It would be dangerous for the horse to let him get loose, as crazy as he was acting. Although her land was fenced around the perimeter, there were too many ways he could do damage to himself if he got away out there.

Where it wasn't covered with the dust he'd kicked up, Kronus' ebony hide gleamed, his eyes still showing white. He reared again, and she held on for dear life, grateful for the leather gloves that kept her hands from being burned by the nylon rope.

When he came down, she was forced to back up a little to get out of his way. Her bad knee buckled, throwing her to the side. As she tried to regain her balance, the stallion lurched into her. The move was not deliberate, but it was effective. Still off balance, and hanging on to the lead for dear life, she fell, banging the side of her head on one of the rails of the corral before she hit the ground.

Even with the impact of her skull against the wooden post, she didn't lose consciousness. The air around her thinned and darkened, however, and as she fought to stay conscious, she realized that she was still clinging to the lead. Instinct, maybe, but probably a foolish one, given the horse's panic.

She couldn't seem to will her muscles to release it and let Kronus go. Her only thought was that he could be seriously injured out on that rock-strewn terrain.

Of course, she could be even more seriously injured lying almost under his feet. She edged to her right, hunching her shoulder, as the horse reared again, almost jerking the lead out of her hand. Just then, a flash of long, blue-jean-clad legs appeared in her peripheral vision.

"Let it go," Grey Sellers commanded, as the horse reared again, totally panicked now.

Knowing she had no choice, she released the rope. Grey had already wrapped his arm around her body and now he lifted, pulling her up and back, just as the horse came down, hooves striking the ground, too close to where Val had been only a heartbeat before.

Then the stallion whirled and took off toward the open and away from the two humans who were still on the ground. It took a second or two for Val to realize the potential for danger in what had happened. Another couple to become aware that she was practically sitting in Grey Sellers' lap, her back against the solid muscle of his chest, his arm still around her, just beneath her breasts.

He was holding her so tightly it was hard to breathe. Or maybe that was simply delayed reaction to the events of the past few seconds. And that's all it had taken for everything to get out of control.

Weak and disoriented, she leaned her head against his shoulder, fighting a wave of nausea. She looked up at the turquoise sky, breathing through her mouth.

"All right?" Grey asked, his voice at her ear, his lips so close that the warmth of his breath touched her cheek.

She nodded, turning her head a little so she could look at him. As she did, the abrasiveness of his early-morning beard brushed her temple. After a moment, he turned to look in the direction in which the stallion was rapidly disappearing, thundering over the dry ground.

Val knew he could run for several miles without encountering any fencing. As for the other obstacles he might tangle with on that high desert range, that was in the hands of fate. She said a quick prayer for the horse's safety, watching him grow smaller and smaller as he raced toward the backdrop of the mountains.

When the stallion was no more than a dark speck, Grey turned to her, his voice touched with the same humor she had heard in it yesterday. "Is he always like that? 'Cause if he is, lady, you've got a hell of a lot of nerve."

"He's never done anything like that before," Val said truthfully.

"Any idea what set him off?" Sellers asked, echoing her own questions.

She shook her head, trying to think what could have happened in the stall to make him so edgy. And there had been nothing at all on the way to the corral that had called for that reaction. She had no explanation for the horse's uncharacteristic antics.

"All I know is, he's going to get hurt out there," she said, struggling against Grey's hold. His arm was still wrapped around her rib cage, her small breasts resting on top of it.

He loosened it at her first movement, and she began to push awkwardly off his lap, embarrassed by the intimate position of their bodies. *Emergency,* she told herself, determined not to overreact as she had yesterday.

He would think she was some kind of neurotic. Afraid of men. Afraid of having any contact with them.

She got to her feet, but when she put weight on her leg, a shard of agony lanced through her damaged knee. The vertigo closed in again. When the world swam back into focus, seconds later, thankfully she wasn't back on the ground. She was still standing, but she was leaning against Grey. His arm was around her again, supporting her competently and impersonally.

"I hit my head," she explained, looking up into his eyes.

In the morning light they were like smoke, less opaque than last night. Suddenly he took her chin in his hand and turned her head. She was too surprised to resist, despite the flutter inside that his touch set off.

She quickly realized Grey wasn't looking at her face, however. He was examining her temple, the one that had struck the wooden railing when Kronus had knocked her down. She watched his eyes widen slightly before they came back to meet hers.

"Looks like you're going to need a few stitches," he said.

She put her fingers over the injury, finding it unerringly, although she hadn't been conscious of pain. She winced as she touched the gash.

Vertigo threatened once more, and, determined not to faint in his arms like some stupid Victorian, Val bit the inside of her cheek hard enough to compete with the burn at her temple and the ache in her knee. Although it hurt like hell, the sharpness of the bite had the desired effect, clearing her head.

"It's nothing," she said, more worried about her stud than about herself.

"Might leave a scar if you don't get it sewed up."

When she laughed, his eyes widened again. Did he really think she cared about a scar? Of course, he couldn't know how many of those she already had. And she sure wasn't concerned enough about this little cut to drive into civilization to get it stitched up. She had more important things to attend to. Like seeing to her most recent investment, whose black hide was at this moment very vulnerable, as he ran like a mad thing over some pretty rough territory.

"I have to catch him," she said, pulling away from Grey's hold. Thankfully, there was no vertigo when she moved this time.

Limping heavily, each step sheer torture, she made it as far as the fence, a matter of two feet, before she realized that catching the black was going to be an impossibility. She could barely walk, much less do what she needed to do to find him and bring him back.

"By the time you get mounted," Grey said, "he'll have disappeared. And you aren't going to track him on that ground."

It was possible she could still ride, she decided, assessing the pain in her knee with the ease of long practice, but he was right about the other. Even if that rocky ground lent itself to tracking, she couldn't manage the dismounting and remounting that process would almost certainly require.

"I can't just let him go."

"You can until we get that tended to," Grey said.

"But he's my animal. My responsibility," she protested.

"And *you're* mine, Ms. Beaufort," he said quietly. "Or have you forgotten?"

She had. She'd forgotten that this man had been sent out here to be her bodyguard. *Bodyguard,* she thought again, ridiculing the concept. And she never responded well to being told she couldn't do something. At least, not since her accident.

"This is different," she argued, her eyes drawn back to the fading trail of dust.

"Nothing in my instructions said there were things I'm not supposed to protect you from. I think that covers concussions and possible bleeding inside the skull. And I told you," he said, "I've already spent their retainer. I'll go get the car."

She grabbed for his arm, jarring her leg again, and got sleeve instead. "I can't just leave him out there."

"I don't think you've got much choice," Grey said.

She didn't, she admitted. At least, not as far as getting on a horse and hunting Kronus down was concerned. However, there was nothing to say that Grey couldn't do that for her.

Of course, he wasn't getting paid to look after her stud. That was not why Beneficial Life had given him that retainer he kept talking about. But what did she have to lose by asking him? she thought. Except maybe her pride. And she would gladly trade that to have Kronus safe and sound.

"*You* could go after him," she suggested softly.

"I could. *If* I didn't have you to look after."

"You don't need to look after me. I'm not in any danger. He's the one who could get hurt. And," she added, thinking this might sway him, "he's a very valuable piece of horseflesh."

That was the absolute truth. The stud represented every

bit of the profit she had made last year. That wasn't the primary reason she wanted Grey to go after him, of course. She just didn't want the horse to be seriously injured. Maybe he'd calm down after he'd run himself out, and then—

"My responsibility is doing the job I was paid to do," Grey said.

"Meaning you'd want to be *paid* to go after the horse?" she asked. "I think that can be arranged. Will you take a check? I'm afraid I don't have much cash on hand. Of course, I may not have enough for you in my bank account. Just how much is it going to cost me, Mr. Sellers, to get you to go after my horse?"

There was a silence before he said, "It must be hell to be that cynical."

"Not cynical," she denied. "Just experienced. Money seems to have an almost mystical influence on people."

"Not on me, Ms. Beaufort. Sorry to disappoint you. And the sooner we get that place on your head treated, the sooner I can get back out here and try to track your horse."

"By then it may be too late."

"Take it or leave it," he said, stooping to pick up the black Stetson from the ground and beating it against his leg to knock the dust off.

"I should have known a horse wouldn't mean much to someone like you," she said angrily. She wasn't even sure what she meant by that, but it felt good to make the accusation.

She began to limp away from him, heading toward the pasture and using the fence for support. Her leg seemed to get tighter and more painful with each step.

"I think you can probably afford another horse, Ms. Beaufort. Your life is another proposition. You only get one shot at that."

The edge of sarcasm in that first sentence was obvious, just like his comment about being sorry her father's policy wasn't the kind that paid out cash. Both remarks said "rich bitch" so loudly he didn't have to. It was a tone Val had heard most of her life, at least until she had moved out here, and, furious, she turned to face him.

"Kronus represents every bit of profit I made last year, Mr. Sellers," she said. "Just for your information. But this isn't about money. Not everything is, you know."

She regretted saying that as soon as the words came out of her mouth. Like yesterday she didn't seem to be able to control her tongue when she was around him. Somewhere deep inside she knew why. That knowledge wasn't something she wanted to deal with right now, however.

"I want to look at his stall, so maybe you better join me," she said instead, injecting sarcasm to keep her voice from betraying her. "If whatever spooked Kronus is still in there, you'll be right there, ready to *protect* me from it."

THEY DIDN'T FIND ANYTHING in the stall to explain the horse's actions. Grey wasn't really surprised. If something like a snake had spooked the stallion, it would have been long gone. And somehow he didn't think that would have caused exactly the reaction he'd just seen. Maybe the horse would have been upset, but he wouldn't have been out-and-out loco once he was away from the danger.

His eyes were examining the broken board when he became aware that Valerie Beaufort was sitting on the ground of the stallion pen, her back against its rough boards, eyes closed. As he watched, she put her head down on her bent knee.

She didn't move, even when he walked over to stand in

front of her, although she must have heard his footsteps. "You okay?" he asked.

Her head came up, eyes open, wide and very dark. Pupils dilated? Or did they just look that way because her face was so pale? Shock? Or concussion? he wondered. The gash at her temple was still bleeding sluggishly. The hair around it was matted with blood and even the shoulder of her shirt was stained.

"A little dizzy," she said, putting her forehead back on her knee. The other leg, the one that she favored when she walked, was stretched straight out in front of her.

"Come on," he said, holding out his hand.

She lifted her head enough to look at it and then up at him, but she didn't reach for his outstretched fingers. She shook her head once, and then rested her forehead on top of her knee again.

"We need to have somebody take a look at that cut," he said. "You may have a concussion."

"I'm just dizzy."

"All the more reason—"

"I told you I'm not driving into town for this scratch," she said, overriding his attempt to make exactly that suggestion.

He watched her a moment more, weighing his options. He knew a fair amount of first aid. Even if she did have a concussion, all a hospital would do would be to keep her overnight and observe her. He could do that here, of course.

However, observing Valerie Beaufort all night wasn't something he was eager to do. Whenever he looked at her, something happened in his gut that he didn't understand.

Maybe it was her vulnerability. That little-girl-lost look. Or maybe she had been right before, although he didn't like the idea any better than he knew she would. Maybe it *was* the fact that she limped. All he knew was that the thought of her being injured or in danger had become far more personal than any assignment should be.

"You can walk. Or I can carry you," he said harshly. "It's strictly up to you."

Her eyes came up again at that. Widened first with shock that he would talk that way to her, then becoming defiant. He meant what he said, however, and something in his face or in his voice must have told her that. Her mouth tightened, but finally, after a long moment of studying his eyes, she put out her hand.

As his fingers closed around it, there was again that unwanted frisson of emotion in the bottom of his stomach. Maybe because her life was his responsibility, and because it had been in danger this morning. Or maybe, he acknowledged bitterly, it was because he knew he wasn't good enough anymore to handle that kind of responsibility.

Chapter Three

"Taken to banging your head into brick walls now, have you?" Halley Burgess asked Val with a grin.

His big fingers were gentle, however, as he swabbed the clotted blood off the gash on her temple. Even if they hadn't been, Val doubted she would have felt it much, considering the size and volume of her headache.

It had grown with each rut Grey had driven over to get her here. After his ultimatum, she hadn't bothered to argue with him anymore. She had handed over the keys to her Jeep and given him the directions to Halley's clinic on the outskirts of Rainsville.

Halley had been her doctor since she had moved out to the ranch ten years ago, although she could count on the fingers of one hand the number of times she'd visited him. In spite of her thinness and her limp, she was as healthy as the proverbial horse. Except, as the doctor had just suggested, when she had been banging her head against something that was equally hard.

"Actually, it was a fence post," she said.

She was sitting on the end of his examination table, thankful Halley hadn't made her lie down. She felt less like an invalid—and a whole lot less like a fool—sitting up.

"How'd you manage to do that?" he asked.

"The stud horse I bought from Kirby Gills went loco this morning. He knocked me down, and when I fell, I hit my head on the fence."

"Went loco?" Halley echoed.

"Just…went crazy. Totally spooked. I still don't have any idea what set him off."

Halley didn't say anything in response. Apparently he had cleared away enough of the dried blood to finally get a look at the wound under it. At least he had stopped dabbing and talking. After a moment he moved back, dropping the bloodstained gauze pad he'd been using onto the tray beside him.

She turned her head carefully, looking up at him. "So what's the verdict? Am I going to live?"

"I expect so, but your friend was right. Needs a few stitches to pull that together, as fragile as the skin is there. Maybe take four or five. Then you'll be right as rain."

"No concussion?" she asked.

"I didn't say that. Eyes look good, though," Halley said, assessing them. "Head hurt?"

Val hesitated. She had a lot of experience living with her various aches and pains, and she hated to complain about any of them. An evaluation of her head injury was part of what she had come here to get, however, so it seemed stupid not to give Halley all the information that would allow him to make one.

Of course, she hadn't exactly come voluntarily. And she suspected that Grey would ask about the possibility of a concussion, which was why she had mentioned it to Halley in the first place. And with a bang on the head there *was* always the chance of internal bleeding—which she didn't want to risk.

"It feels like somebody's working inside my skull with a jackhammer," she said truthfully.

"I can give you something for that. Make you a little

drowsy, but that's okay, since you aren't driving. That guy that brought you in a new hand?'' he asked.

He lifted his eyes from hers and raised his eyebrows, an obvious signal to his nurse, who was standing on the other side of the examination table. Halley was probably indicating that he was ready for the local he would use to deaden the area around the cut before he sewed it up. One prick as opposed to several.

''Or is he something else?'' the doctor asked, his eyes coming back to her as the nurse moved to the other side of the room.

''Something else,'' she agreed.

''Boyfriend?''

''Oh, please,'' she said dismissingly, her tone mocking.

''Not a ranch hand, and not a beau. You keeping secrets from old Doc Burgess, Valerie?''

''Maybe I should. The truth sounds pretty far-fetched,'' she warned. ''Actually, it sounds downright ridiculous. And I don't particularly want to become a laughingstock.''

The nurse handed Halley something, keeping it behind Val's back and out of sight, as if Val wouldn't know what was going on. She couldn't help smiling at that not-so-subtle subterfuge.

''I could use a good joke,'' Halley said as he prepared the needle.

Val grimaced at the sting. She wasn't sure if Halley's comment about needing to hear a good joke was a reaction to her amusement at the nurse's tactics or to her saying she didn't want to become a laughingstock. And it didn't really matter. She supposed she would have to tell him the truth in any case.

''He's my bodyguard,'' she said.

Halley's hands hesitated, hovering a couple of inches over her temple. ''Did you say…bodyguard?''

She started to nod, but he had already put his fingers on

her chin, turning her head slightly to position it. He slid the needle in once more, on the other side of the gash this time. The local anesthetic must have already started to work, because the sting wasn't nearly so bad.

"I told you it was ridiculous," she said. "Something to do with an insurance policy the company took out on Dad. It seems that when I inherited his part of Av-Tech, I also inherited that policy. Its terms require that I have a security system on the ranch. Since I don't, they sent him out to guard me until I can get one put in."

"Well, he looks tough enough to handle most any kind of security," Halley said. "Bodyguard, huh?"

She heard his chuckle as he took the suture needle the nurse handed him. It would take a minute or two for the local to take effect, so she suspected that she was going to have to give Halley the whole story while they waited.

"If he's supposed to be guarding you, how come he let that horse beat you up?" he asked.

"He's the one who dragged me out from under him." Then she hesitated, knowing what she was about to say was the truth, even if she wasn't overly eager to confess it. "I guess if he hadn't been there, I could have really been hurt."

"Is that when you reinjured your knee?" Halley asked.

She had been grateful when the doctor had made no comment on her limping progress into the examination room. Her leg had stiffened up royally on the ride over here, so that climbing out of the Jeep had been a test of will. Grey had offered his hand, and again she had been forced to accept, leaning on his arm as they slowly made their way inside the office.

The feel of his fingers lingered in her head. They had been rough, a little callused. A working man's hands. And under her forearm they had felt every bit as strong and steady as they looked.

"I think I did that when I went down," she said. "Maybe it twisted under me. With all that was going on, I honestly don't remember."

"I'll take a look at that, too."

"Thanks, Halley, but believe me, I know everything there is to know about taking care of my leg," she said.

She could hear the tinge of bitterness in her tone, and she couldn't imagine why it was there. She had torn up her leg—literally—in a riding accident when she was thirteen.

Her pre-adolescent bones hadn't had much of a chance when a horse every bit as big as Kronus had crushed her leg under him. Worse than the broken bones, however, there had been nerve and ligament damage. Even the orthopedic specialists her father had called in had shaken their heads at the mess.

She had had several operations since the initial reconstructive surgery, but whatever improvements they had wrought had been minimal. Despite her father's periodic nagging, she had stopped going in for reevaluation.

After twenty years, her leg was something she lived with. She knew she was very lucky to have as much mobility as she did. It didn't affect her ability to ride, and she usually didn't think about the other restrictions it imposed. *Usually.*

"Well, *I* suspect caring for it should include staying off your feet for a few days," Halley said. "Your bodyguard know enough about horses to tend your stock?"

"I haven't asked him."

"We'll get you fitted with a pair of crutches, and then find out. If he can't handle it, we'll see what we can do about getting somebody out there to help you out for a while. After all, I hear you aren't exactly strapped for cash right now. Might as well use all that money to get help when you need it."

Val didn't bother to argue, but it wasn't a matter of being able to get help, of course. For her, it had always been more a matter of being able to admit she needed it. It appeared that it still was.

AFTER HALLEY FINISHED the stitching, he insisted that she let him adjust a pair of crutches—one he kept on hand, he said, for patients who needed them temporarily. Val had a pair at the ranch, although she hadn't resorted to them in years. The last time was when she had slipped and wrenched her knee trying to cross the spring-fed stream that ran through her property.

She thought the pair she'd used then was still in the top of the barn, but she wasn't sure. And it would probably be easier just to accept the loan of these than to argue with Halley.

"What do you know about this guy?" Halley asked, looking up at her from where he was squatting at her feet to adjust the second crutch. "This bodyguard of yours."

"Not much," she admitted. "The insurance company hired him. He's temporary until I can get someone out there to put in a security system. Or until I can unload my part of the company," she added under her breath, even though that was an idle threat. The company was her responsibility now. And responsibility was one of the things her father had drummed into her.

Halley's head came up. "You're going to sell your shares in Av-Tech?" he questioned, his tone clearly expressing disbelief.

"I can't really sell them, not the way the partnership is set up, but what I know about running a company like that would fit under my thumbnail," Val said.

"Okay, take a few steps," Halley suggested, still stooping at her feet, his mind seeming to be back on his own area of expertise. "See how they work."

Obligingly, she swung across the room and then back, grateful for the change of subject. She didn't have any problems manipulating the crutches. Maybe it was like riding a bike.

"You can always hire somebody to run the company for you," Halley said, watching her movements critically.

"We're looking for a management consultant right now."

"What about the others? Your dad's partners?"

"They're all as old as or even older than he is. Than he *was*," she amended, realizing what she had said.

Her dad's death was still too new to feel real. On the ranch she had been able to pretend everything was still the same. Her father and his new wife in Boulder, living their lives as she lived hers. And instead... After a moment she strengthened her voice and went on with her answer to Halley's question.

"I don't know that any of the others are interested in managing it. Or really capable of it. I think I owe it to Dad and to them to see that management of the company ends up in the hands of someone who *will* be competent to run it. And Av-Tech employs a lot of people."

"Still do mostly defense work? Government contracts?"

"More satellite delivery systems than anything else."

"We've stopped hitting 'em with bombs and started beaming sitcoms down on their heads," he said, grinning at her. "Not sure which is worse."

She laughed. "Me, either."

Halley seemed to know about as much about Av-Tech as she did, which wasn't much. Distancing herself from her father's company and its success had been a deliberate choice, one she had made a long time ago. Almost ten years now, she thought, a little surprised by the realization of just how long it had been since she had walked away from that privileged lifestyle.

"I've pulled the Jeep around to the front door."

At the sound of that deep voice, Val turned too quickly and was forced to take a small hop to maintain her balance. Grey Sellers was standing beside Halley's nurse, just inside the door to the examination room.

Only in a tiny, rural clinic like this would that happen, Val supposed, and she didn't like that it had. His presence in this room, which only seconds before had seemed very private, and very safe, was disconcerting.

Halley put his fist on the floor and pushed up, groaning theatrically as he got to his feet. "Halley Burgess," he said, holding out his hand to Grey.

"Grey Sellers."

"I understand you're Val's bodyguard," the doctor said, his voice revealing his amusement at the whole idea.

The gray eyes flicked to hers before they refocused on the doctor. Grey had probably guessed Halley's amusement was simply a reflection of her own. Maybe he even thought Val had been making fun of their situation. Or of him.

"For the time being," Grey said, looking back at the doctor. There was no answering humor in his tone.

"Val told me," Halley said. "Know anything about horses?"

"Enough," Grey said, his eyes again meeting hers.

She found herself wishing Halley had been a little more discreet. Of course, he had no way of knowing about the underlying tension between her and her "bodyguard," but she didn't think the doctor's attitude was helping the situation.

"We're trying to decide if Val needs to get someone from town to stay out there and take care of her animals while she's stove up. I thought maybe you could do it. Since you're already living there.''

''I can do that,'' Grey said.

''*And* take care of Val? I want her off that leg for a few days. You have my permission to hog-tie her if you have to.''

There was a small, awkward silence. During it, Grey's eyes didn't revisit her face.

''I think I can probably manage both,'' he said finally.

Val wondered if she were the only one who had been aware of how long it had taken him to agree. She hadn't been pleased with Halley's suggestion, and she could imagine Grey wouldn't have been, either. There had been animosity between them from the beginning, and now Halley was proposing that Grey play nursemaid.

''I don't think that will be necessary,'' she said, looking at Grey. Again her words seemed clipped, even to her own ears. ''There are usually plenty of people looking for work around here. We'll check the bulletin board at Hank's before we head back.''

''I just didn't figure Mr. Sellers' employers would be too eager to have a stranger living out on your place right now. You can't be too careful nowadays. Or am I wrong?'' Halley asked him.

''I'm sure we can manage on our own for a day or two,'' Grey said, without really addressing Halley's question.

You can't be too careful nowadays. For some reason those words echoed in Val's head. After all, Grey Sellers was a stranger, too. Here they were making arrangements for him to take care of her in a very different way from what he'd been hired to do, and as yet she knew almost nothing about him.

Yes, he had brought papers, and yes, they had looked official, but what did she *really* know about this man? She had intended to call both Beneficial Life and Joe Wallace this morning and check him out. Of course, that was before Kronus had disrupted her plans.

Now it seemed more important than ever that she do that. She had gotten stuck with Grey last night because his truck supposedly wouldn't start. But if he hadn't been there this morning, things might have been much worse than they were, she admitted.

That didn't mean, however, that she should stick her head in the sand about the dangers inherent in letting a stranger move in at her place. Taking at face value what Grey Sellers had told her about the policy and about his employment by Beneficial Life wasn't the smartest thing she could do, even if his actions this morning had temporarily lulled her suspicions.

"I'm sure you can," Halley said in answer to Grey's quiet claim. He even sounded as if he believed it. "You call me, Val, if the prescription doesn't help with the headache or if you have any of those other symptoms I mentioned. And stay off that leg. There's nothing that needs doing bad enough out at your place that it can't wait a day or two."

"My horses are used to getting fed very regularly."

"So, let him do it. I doubt there's much bodyguarding to be done, other than having to save you from the occasional rampaging stallion," Halley said, grinning again. "What do *you* think caused the horse to act up like that, Mr. Sellers?"

Halley's question seemed offhand. Maybe he was just making conversation. Val found she was interested in hearing what Grey had to say, however, which made her wonder why she hadn't asked him before.

Because I was too busy getting my tail over my shoulder about the rich-bitch crack. To be fair, he hadn't called her that, she reminded herself. She had read that into his tone.

"If he hadn't been in his stall when it started, I would think maybe he'd gotten into something," Grey said.

"Gotten into something? Like locoweed, you mean?" the doctor asked.

"Maybe," Grey said, shrugging a little.

"Except he was in his stall," Val said.

"Maybe your oats fermented in this heat," Halley teased.

"Or maybe he's just a stallion that got spooked," Grey said. "It doesn't take much."

"Well, I'm sure the two of you will figure it out," Halley said. "Take care of our Val, Mr. Sellers. She's pretty beat up. Keep her off her feet and out of harm's way, you hear me?"

"That's exactly what I'm getting paid to do," Grey said. This time he did allow his gaze to focus on her face, and in those cold gray eyes was a challenge.

"DIDN'T HE MENTION something about picking up a prescription?" Grey asked as he climbed back into the Jeep.

At Val's insistence he had stopped to check out the bulletin board at Hank's. She had stayed in the car, but even from where she was sitting, she could see that there were only a few notices on the board. And according to Grey, there wasn't a single one posted by anyone looking for work.

She had the prescription Halley had given her in her shirt pocket, but she didn't intend to get it filled. She would take a couple of aspirin when she got home. She had given up taking anything stronger a long time ago. Getting off pain medication wasn't a battle she intended to ever have to fight again.

"I have the same thing at home," she lied.

Grey nodded and put the Jeep into gear, backing out of the parking space. They drove a while in silence. After a few minutes, Val closed her eyes against the pain of her headache, wondering if she had made another pigheaded mistake in not getting something for it. After all, taking medication for a temporary injury was very different from courting dependence, which she had done after she'd crushed her leg.

"You all right?" Grey asked.

"I'm fine," she said tightly, opening her eyes again.

She was aware that he had taken his eyes off the road to glance at her, but she didn't turn to face him. Instead, she looked out the window, watching the familiar landscape fly by.

Grey was driving faster than she usually did, as if he had driven these narrow, twisting roads all his life. He drove as he had done everything since he'd shown up at her place yesterday—with a seemingly effortless competence and a great deal of self-confidence.

Ex-cop, she wondered? Military? There was something about him, some indefinable air that suggested that. And since they were going to be cooped up in this car together for a couple of hours, she realized this would be the perfect opportunity to ask some of the questions about his background that she probably should have asked last night. Then, when they got home, she could begin to verify whatever he told her. And at least those questions would steer the conversation away from any further discussion of her, her health, or her feelings.

"So how did you get to be a bodyguard?" she asked, keeping her eyes on the scenery whipping by beyond the glass of the passenger-side window.

He didn't answer immediately. The silence went on long enough that, despite her determination, she turned to look at him. All she could see was his profile. His eyes were on the road ahead, his lips thinned and set.

Apparently Grey didn't like talking about himself any

more than she did, she thought. What was good for the goose, however, was certainly good for the gander. At least in this case.

"I have an investigative agency in DeFarge," he said.

She waited, but there didn't seem to be anything else he wanted to add. "An investigative agency?" she questioned. "Investigating what? I mean, what exactly do you do?"

"Surveillance mostly. Some antifraud work for out-of-state insurers who have questions about claims made against them here."

Which was probably how Beneficial Life had come up with his name. He was fairly local, as local as one got out here, and he did other kinds of work for them. That all made sense.

"You don't normally do bodyguard assignments?" she probed.

If possible, the line of his mouth flattened even more. "Not normally," he agreed.

"Does your background qualify you for that kind of work?"

The resulting silence seemed tense. Maybe he didn't like her questioning his expertise. Or maybe he just didn't like her.

She had a right to question his experience, however, although she had no reason to believe he wasn't competent. She certainly couldn't doubt his courage. He had effectively demonstrated that this morning.

"I mean…do you have some kind of law enforcement experience?" she asked, talking to fill the uncomfortable stillness. "FBI? Secret Service?" The last suggestion seemed almost mocking, and she hadn't intended it to be. "There must be *some* reason Beneficial Life called on you, Mr. Sellers. Besides proximity, I mean."

She turned her head, looking full at him now, determined to wait him out. After a moment his eyes flicked over to hers. They didn't hold, their attention required by the road. They had rested on hers long enough, however, for her to read the anger in them.

"Maybe competence," he suggested softly, his gaze straight ahead. "If you have a complaint, Ms. Beaufort, you should take it up with Beneficial Life. They're the folks who hired me. But you're right, of course. They did have some reason to do that besides proximity. Why don't you ask them what it was?"

"Oh, believe me, Mr. Sellers, I intend to," she said. She turned her head again, pretending to study the passing scenery.

THE BLACK WAS STANDING head down in the corral when they pulled in to the yard. Grey remembered what he'd thought as he looked into the mirror yesterday morning. The bit about being rode hard and put away wet. The stallion appeared to be in pretty much the same condition he had been in about then.

"Thank God," Valerie Beaufort breathed when she saw him.

Grey knew that the first thing she would want to do would be to check the stud over for any serious injury. Grey couldn't blame her for that. If this were his animal, he would want to do the same thing. He wanted to do it anyway, and he didn't have any financial or emotional stake in the stallion.

Valerie had her door open before he could get the Jeep stopped. He had pulled up as close to the front steps of the ranch house as he could, thinking that would give her less distance to have to traverse on the crutches. He had used them a time or two, and as he remembered it, there was nothing pleasant about the experience, especially during the first couple of days as your hands and your arms were making the painful adjustment.

Valerie was out of her seat belt and then out of the car before he had gotten his own door open. She started around the front of the Jeep, using her left hand on the top of its hood for support. It was obvious she was headed toward the corral. Grey opened the back door and retrieved the crutches from the back seat, carrying them with him around the opposite side of the vehicle to meet her at the front.

"Here," he said, holding them out to her.

He figured that he wasn't going to do much good trying to talk her into going into the house without letting her at least check the black out. She pulled her eyes away from the horse, looking up at him as if she had forgotten he was there, just as she had obviously forgotten about the crutches. Her eyes fell to them and then rose again to his.

"Thanks," she said abstractedly.

She took the crutches and, leaning back against the Jeep, fitted them under her arms. As soon as she had, she straightened and began to move again toward the paddock. She stopped when she reached the fence, looking over the rail at the exhausted animal.

"Hey, old boy," she called softly.

The horse didn't look up, not even when she whistled, a low, melodic two-note call. The stallion's ears didn't even twitch. By that time Grey was standing at the fence beside her. She looked up at him, brown eyes full of anxiety.

"He's worn himself out," Grey suggested. "That doesn't necessarily mean there's anything wrong with him."

She nodded, obviously wanting to believe him, and then she began to move again, making her way behind him and around to the still-open gate. Grey followed, aware of the subtle play of well-toned muscle in her thighs and buttocks and back as she swung the crutches, moving between them efficiently, like someone who had had a lot of experience.

Again he felt that twinge of emotion. He supposed it was only natural to wonder what had happened to Valerie Beaufort to cause her limp. He resisted sticking his nose in other people's business, but he admitted that in this case he was curious. Of course, *asking* her that question wasn't something he ever intended to do. If she wanted him to ignore the fact that she limped, then he damn well would pretend he'd never even noticed.

Val reached the horse and, removing her left hand from the grip, she balanced on her crutches, running her palm over his back. The horse didn't respond, except for a periodic twitching of his skin. Valerie took the crutches out from under her arms and held both of them in her right hand, a little away from her side. Then she slowly bent the knee of her good leg, lowering her body until she could put the crutches down on the ground.

She reached out for the lead, and the stallion sidestepped uneasily. Val froze. Then slowly she reached out again, ignoring the dangling rope and beginning to check the stallion's near foreleg, running her hands down it, examining it carefully for heat or swelling or abrasions.

Grey wasn't real sure he would want to be stooping right under that horse, given the behavior they had witnessed this morning. However, the animal seemed too spent to move, much less offer any threat.

As he watched, Valerie tried to pick up Kronus' hind leg to examine his hoof. The horse shifted his weight in response, and, unbalanced, Val fell back, ending up on her bottom in the soft dust of the corral. Even from where he was standing, he had heard the involuntary gasp. The ground wasn't hard enough or the distance she had fallen great enough to cause any degree of pain, so he knew she must have jarred the injured leg.

He controlled his inclination to go into the corral with her. He wanted to help her up, help her check out the horse, just…help her, he acknowledged. Her words yesterday had been pretty explicit, however. *If I want your help, I'll ask for it. If I don't ask, Mr. Sellers, then you leave me the hell alone.*

So, he decided, he would do exactly what she'd asked and leave her the hell alone. Surprisingly, however, given her attitude toward him last night and this morning, he was finding that far more difficult than it should have been.

She pushed up off the ground, putting her palms flat in the dirt and balancing again on one leg. The one she favored was stretched out almost straight in front of her, parallel to the ground. Again she reached for the black's leg.

This time he shied away from her hand, moving a few feet away. Far enough to be out of Val's reach, Grey realized. Watching intently, he had unconsciously put his hands on the top rail, wrapping his fingers over it. Holding it too tightly, he realized, feeling the bite of the rough wood. He forced himself to loosen his hold.

It would take him about thirty seconds to ascertain if the horse were injured. And he knew he was as capable of doing that as she was. *If I don't ask, Mr. Sellers, then you leave me the hell alone.* And she wasn't asking, he reminded himself.

Instead, she stood up, bringing the crutches up with her. Still balancing on one leg, she fitted them under her arms. Then she swung over to where the stallion was standing, head down and black hide twitching.

Crooning coaxingly, her voice soft and very relaxed, she reversed the procedure she had just employed to stand up. She lowered herself by bending the one sound leg, laid the crutches down beside her, and reached for the stallion's lead.

Again he sidestepped, running a few feet before he stopped again. It had been obvious from that movement, however, that he was favoring his left foreleg.

Again Valerie picked her crutches up off the ground and stood. By this time, Grey's stomach was knotted with an unwanted tension. He wasn't sure whether what he was feeling was anger or fear or frustration on her behalf. Or a combination of all.

Or maybe, he conceded, it was a grudging admiration. Stubborn Valerie Beaufort might be. And as proud as the devil. But she had guts. He would give her that. He knew a lot about people with guts. And even more about those without.

Once more Valerie approached the horse. His head was up a little now, and he was watching her. As she came near him, crutches creaking, he would move, always keeping about the same distance between them. Never allowing her to get close enough to look at, much less touch that injured leg.

"Damn it," she said finally, after she had followed him around the corral for several fruitless minutes. She had kept up a steady stream of sweet talk, her voice soft and infinitely patient, as she tried to get close to the horse. Her tone in the sudden expletive was totally different, her frustration clearly expressed in its volume and force.

She stopped in the middle of the enclosure, seeming to realize she was fighting a losing battle. Grey was still holding on to the top railing, his hands occasionally releasing and then tightening as his own frustration had built.

She turned toward him. Grey allowed his eyes to meet hers, trying to keep all the mingled emotions he had experienced during the past few minutes from being reflected in them. She looked away, briefly focusing on the stallion.

Finally, after a few seconds, she turned, hopping on one foot, so she was facing Grey.

"Do you think you could check out that leg?" she asked. "And then maybe put him in a stall in the barn. I'll feel better about him being in there, I think."

He could tell what it had cost her to ask him for that favor. It was in her eyes, and even in the set of her narrow shoulders. In the taut line of her mouth.

If I don't ask, Mr. Sellers, then you leave me the hell alone. He supposed he should be feeling some satisfaction right now, considering the tongue-lashing he'd been given for trying to help her. Maybe he should be celebrating that she'd been forced to do the very thing she had bragged she wouldn't do. She had asked for his help.

It was painfully obvious, however, that she hadn't wanted to. And just as obvious that she felt as defeated by her inability to see to the stallion as he could possibly have wanted her to feel yesterday while she was reading him the riot act.

If this was a victory, he didn't feel much like celebrating. There was no sense of triumph in witnessing this woman brought down to a level of helplessness he knew instinctively she would hate. One *he* would have hated. So instead of wanting to celebrate this defeat, he wanted to pick her up and carry her into the house and put her to bed.

The phrase reverberated in his head. The usual term when Grey Sellers was thinking about any woman in connection with a bed would have been "take her to." And that had a very different connotation from what he was feeling right now, he admitted.

Almost despite himself, he wondered what she would be like in bed. Would that pride and stubbornness and redhead's temper be reflected there? And if so...

If so, he told himself disgustedly, he wasn't the man

who was going to find out about it. He had come here to do a job. And he didn't need the kind of complications a woman like this would be in his life.

Actually, he didn't need complications of any kind. That's why he had chosen to be where he had been when Joe Wallace had approached him about this assignment. Where he would be still if, like a fool and acting against all his instincts, he hadn't agreed to take this job.

"Mr. Sellers?" she questioned.

"I'll be glad to check your stud," he said.

He unwrapped his hands from the rail, finding that they ached from the pressure he'd exerted to hold them there. Then he walked toward the open gate. He was aware that she wasn't watching him. Her eyes had gone back to the stallion.

Only her concern for the animal had prompted this request. If she had been the one needing help, hell would have frozen over before she asked him for it. Grey knew that, and for the first time since this battle of wills had started, his lips tilted.

You've got guts, lady. I will give you that, he thought. And Grey Sellers' small smile was admiring. After all, he had been taught in a hard school just how important that particular quality was. And how very rare.

Chapter Four

"S-e-l-l-e-r-s," Val spelled slowly into the phone. "First name Grey, like the color. I'm not sure if that's with an *a* or an *e,* but it's unusual enough that there can't be more than one. Wait a minute, Autry," she said, remembering belatedly that she might have Grey's name in print.

She stretched over the table beside the chair she had collapsed into as soon as she'd undressed. The packet of documents Grey had brought out to the ranch with him was lying there, almost out of reach.

Her fingers barely captured the edge of the papers, and she pulled them over to her, being careful not to move her injured leg. She had it propped across a couple of bed pillows stacked on the chair's matching ottoman. If she stayed perfectly still, the pain was bearable. Turning or twisting the knee was another proposition entirely, as was putting any weight on it.

"I've got something from Beneficial Life right here…" she said into the phone as she opened the packet and hurriedly thumbed through its pages. She couldn't find any mention of Grey Sellers anywhere in them. They seemed to reflect only the terms of the policy. "Nope, sorry. His name's not here."

"You think that means this guy's lying about Beneficial sending him?" Autry Carmichael asked.

A few years younger than the founders of Av-Tech, Carmichael was the company's head of security. He had served under her father in Korea. Too young and broke after the war to have any money to invest in the fledgling aviation company—or at least that's what Autry always said if anyone asked—he hadn't become a partner. To Valerie, and to her father as well, Carmichael had always been as much a part of Av-Tech as any of the others.

"No, they sent him, all right," she clarified. "I verified that with the company by phone. However, they don't even have a résumé on him. Apparently he was hired by the independent agent who handles their claims in this part of the state. It seems they just took the agent's word for Sellers' competence."

"Sounds pretty slipshod to me," Autry said.

Val smiled. Autry didn't like slipshod. And he sure didn't run a slipshod operation at Av-Tech. Her dad had always said Carmichael was the best hire he'd ever made. That was one reason she had called him this morning. That and the fact that Autry was a trusted friend and, like her father's partners, almost as close to Val as if he were family.

"This is supposed to be only temporary," Val explained. "I have to get a security system installed. It's a requirement of some policy the company took out on Dad. As soon as the security is in place, I understand he'll be gone. Oh, and I could use a recommendation about who to call to have that system put in."

"Want me to handle it?" Autry asked. "Send somebody from the company out there?"

"Maybe they wouldn't like it if we did this in-house. Maybe that would void the terms of the policy or something. I don't even know why we have this policy in the first place. I've got a call in about that, too. But until I have all this straightened out, is there somebody respected in the security field that you could recommend for me to get to come out here? I don't really need a bodyguard. Or want one," she added.

"Sure. I can even make the call and set it up. Get them to send somebody out to look around and give you some recommendations. Develop a plan for your place. It'll probably take a few days after they do that part to get the techs out there to install the stuff," he said apologetically.

"So about how long are we talking?" Val asked.

"I'd say…less than a week from the time I call them. Maybe a little more. That sound okay?"

A week, Val thought in dismay, remembering the tension in the car when she had started asking Grey questions. It had been thick and very uncomfortable, and there had to be a reason for his reluctance to answer.

She also remembered, however, the gentleness with which Grey's big hands had examined Kronus, moving over the horse with a practiced expertise. She had been enormously relieved when he'd determined that the limp they'd observed was nothing more serious than a rock embedded in the frog of his front hoof.

Grey had then run his hands over every inch of the animal, talking to him the whole time. After the examination was over, Kronus had seemed relieved to be led back to the safety of the barn. Maybe as relieved as she was to see him there.

Then, after helping her into the house, and without being asked, Grey had set out for the pasture to check on the rest of her animals, which was where he was right now. Even after her conversation with Beneficial Life, however, she still didn't really know the first thing about her bodyguard. For all she knew, Grey Sellers could be an ax murderer. Her lips twitched, fighting a smile. If he were, she thought, he had shown a remarkable restraint thus far in dealing with her.

"A week's okay, I guess," she said. "But ask them to get on it as soon as they can, please."

"I've got a little pull with these guys. We've given them some business in the past. They're the ones who came in and updated the system at your dad and stepmom's new place, so they should be okay with Beneficial. I didn't realize at the time that Charlie wanted that update to meet the terms of this policy, but that must have been it, don't you think?"

"Probably," Val agreed, unwillingly picturing her step-mother standing by her father's grave. She and Connie would never be close, of course, but she knew she should call her. Just to check on how she was doing. Her father would have wanted her to. And she had promised to call Emory Hunter, she remembered.

"So, you still want me to run a background check on this guy? I mean, if he's only going to be there a week and as long as you know that Beneficial Life *did* send him…"

Autry sounded as if he didn't think they needed to do that. *You can't be too careful nowadays,* Halley had said. And you really couldn't be, Val thought.

"Just do the same kind of check you'd do if you were going to hire him, Autry. Nothing fancy. Can you do that for me?"

"Sure. Be easier if I had his social security number. You don't happen to have that, do you?" Autry asked, his tone indicating that he knew it was a long shot.

"Just his name. I don't think this agent sent anything else on to Beneficial Life. I've been trying to contact the independent, but he's out of his office, and I hate to ask the secretary this kind of stuff."

"You could ask the guy himself," Autry suggested.

"He's not the most forthcoming individual I've ever met."

"Secretive?"

"Closemouthed," she said, choosing her words carefully.

"That's not a bad trait in an investigator. I'd be more worried if he were some big-mouth blowhard."

"Well, that's not the case," Val said, smiling a little at the contrast. "Just do the best you can to check him out and then let me know what you find. I've got this guy living out here, and since we're pretty isolated..."

She let the sentence trail. Despite her common sense and Halley's warning, despite what she had just said to Autry about their situation, she realized she wasn't afraid of Grey or at all nervous about his being on the ranch.

She hadn't been from the first. There was an air of danger about him. Even a little mystery. But her personal radar, pretty well honed, had not detected any sense of threat. Not even when he had grabbed her shoulders and shaken her, something she normally would never have tolerated from anyone.

"Want me to come out there and look after things for you, sweetie?"

Valerie laughed, but even as she did, she knew that if she told Autry she'd hurt her leg, he probably would come. Like her father's partners, he had always been a little overprotective.

"And what would Av-Tech do without you in the meantime?" she hedged. "I'm fine. Honestly. I just think in situations like this, it's smart to know who you've employed. Even if it's an indirect employment."

"I'll do some nosing around and let you know what I find out. I'm not the CIA, remember."

They laughed together, and then a small silence developed across the line. Finally Autry spoke into it.

"I wanted to tell you again how sorry I am about your dad. He was a good friend. And a real good man."

"Thanks, Autry. That means a lot to me, especially coming from you. He loved you a lot, you know."

Another small silence before Carmichael said gruffly, "You take care now, baby."

Autry was obviously glad to have gotten the condolences out of the way. Not that Valerie doubted they were heartfelt. Men of his generation—her father's generation—didn't find talking about their feelings easy. Maybe men of her generation didn't either, she thought, picturing Grey's set lips when she had started asking questions.

"I will," she assured him.

"I'll call you as soon as I know something worth telling you, good or bad."

"Thanks," Val said. "I owe you, Autry."

She put down the phone and looked up to find Grey standing in the doorway, watching her. *This is getting to be a habit,* she thought, suddenly conscious of how short the worn cotton nightshirt she had put on was.

Her knee had swollen enough that the jeans were binding. And the house had seemed hot when they had first arrived, so she had gotten undressed and put on something cool and comfortable, without even considering the possibility of having a man barge in on her. Her state of undress wasn't something she'd ever before had to be conscious of out here.

"I didn't think you needed to get up and open the door," Grey said, probably reading her dismay. "So I didn't knock."

"How did it go?" she asked, fighting to control her embarrassment by pretending to ignore it.

She could feel the heated blood moving into her throat, however. That was one of the problems with having the kind of skin she had been cursed with. It was just too damned revealing. Just like the nightshirt she was wearing.

Of course, Grey was also pretending, she realized. Carefully pretending not to notice the exposed leg, with its network of old scars, stretched out on the ottoman before her.

"They're all right. Whatever affected the stallion," he said, his voice amused, "it hasn't spread. You've got some fine animals, Ms. Beaufort."

"Thank you," Val said, feeling a sense of pride in the compliment, despite her discomfort.

"Looks like prime breeding stock."

"That's what I do. And training to saddle, mostly for the youth market. Small-scale, but it pays the bills."

He nodded, his eyes mocking. Only then did she realize how ridiculous that sounded coming from her, someone who had just inherited a company worth several hundred million dollars.

However, her quarter horses had paid her bills for years. And she was finally building a reputation in the small world she had chosen to inhabit. After struggling for so long to keep her head above water financially, it was hard to think about herself as a rich woman. She didn't feel rich, but Grey Sellers knew that she was, of course.

The silence stretched. It seemed they might have used up their store of polite conversation. The next few days were going to be pretty strained around here if they could find nothing to talk about but her horses. Of course, after Grey knew the routine and where everything was, she probably wouldn't see him much during the course of the next week.

Her eyes fell to the packet of papers lying on her lap, and she felt a surge of guilt. He couldn't know what she had been doing, she reassured herself. This was only the Beneficial Life policy, which he surely expected her to read.

"What would you like for lunch?" he asked.

The question caught her off guard, and her eyes came

back to his face. She hadn't even thought about food, more concerned about Kronus and her mares. More concerned about getting her phone calls made while Grey was occupied. More concerned about the pain in her knee and in her head than her hunger.

Before she had gone outside this morning, she had had her usual bowl of oatmeal. However, there were no supplies in the bunkhouse, she remembered. Leaving food out there was too much of an invitation to rats and other, even less desirable invaders. And the building hadn't had any human inhabitants in a long time. It was after two o'clock now, and Grey must be starving.

"I'm not much of a cook," he continued, "but I can manage to put together at least enough for our mutual survival, I think. Sandwiches? Soup? Frozen dinner?"

All of which Val had in her kitchen, either in the pantry or in the chest-style freezer on the back porch. And none of which sounded particularly appealing. She wasn't sure she wanted anything to eat, but it was obvious he did.

So much for her intentions to be hospitable. She couldn't let him stay here and not feed him, not as far from civilization as they were. Automatically, she reached for the crutches she had laid on the floor by her chair.

"You're supposed to stay off your feet," Grey said. "Just point me in the general direction of the food and give me some clue as to what you might like."

"The kitchen's back there," Val said, shifting in the chair enough to indicate the hall behind her. When she did, she was aware that the nightshirt rode up on her bare thighs. She tugged it down again as she turned back to face him.

"I think you'll find everything you listed in your culinary repertoire is in there," she said, feeling the blood rush under her skin and talking mainly to cover her unease. "There's a freezer on the back porch, which has a pretty good supply of frozen dinners. I'm not much for cooking from scratch.''

"Is anybody?" he asked. "At least not anymore. So…what sounds good to you?''

She hesitated, thinking that if he were really going to fix lunch, she ought to try to eat something, if only to be polite. Despite the agreement Grey and Halley had come to this morning about his playing nursemaid, none of this was in his job description. The fact that he was offering to fix her something to eat was simply an act of kindness.

Or was it an act of pity? some perverse part of her wondered. After all, Grey had watched her get knocked humiliatingly on her butt again and again out in the corral this morning. Maybe he just felt sorry for her. She had learned a long time ago, another lesson learned the hard way, that her limp affected some men like that. They wanted to take care of her. And normally, she neither needed nor wanted to be taken care of.

Or maybe Grey just wanted to get her back on her feet as quickly as possible so he could go back to doing what he'd been hired to do. Which hadn't been waiting on her hand and foot. And, she realized suddenly, if he were going to undertake these extra duties, which would allow her time to heal, she should offer to supplement whatever Beneficial Life was paying him.

"Your choices aren't really all that wide," he said, questioning her delay in answering. "I told you. I can only manage simple things. Soup, sandwich, frozen dinner.'' Again he enumerated the items he'd offered her before.

"I guess I need to increase your salary if you're going to become chief cook and bottle washer around here.''

She had tried to inject a trace of humor into the end of that suggestion, but she could tell it hadn't come off. Not according to his eyes. They held on her face, long after her words had faded, and their gray was the slate of the high desert sky just before snow.

"Everything's about money to you, isn't it, Ms. Beaufort?"

Val took a deep breath, both angered and embarrassed. "Actually, hardly anything is about money to me, Mr. Sellers. I know you don't believe that, but... I just don't like imposing on people," she finished.

"You just don't like accepting help," he said. His inflection mimicked hers exactly. "No matter the circumstances."

She couldn't deny it. She hated asking for help. Hated having to admit there were things she couldn't do. And she knew that was all connected to her disability. She acknowledged that, at least to herself. It wasn't something she had ever discussed with anyone else, however. Not even with her father. She didn't want to discuss it now.

"No, I guess I don't," she said finally. "I don't think many people in...my circumstances would."

Again he nodded, his eyes less cold. "There's a time for standing on your own two feet. And I certainly applaud your desire to do that," he said, his tone as quietly intense as hers had been. "But there's also a time for asking for help. Or at least for accepting it gracefully when it's needed."

"I know," she said.

She couldn't have managed the horses on crutches. Especially not Kronus. The stallion had already proven that to her. She needed help, and Grey had offered it—freely and apparently without any expectation of being compensated. And she... She had screwed up big time by offering him money. Again she had come off sounding like some rich bitch.

"Soup," she said, forcing her eyes back up to meet his. She hadn't even been aware they had fallen. Maybe that had happened when his lecture had struck too close to home for comfort.

"Any preference?" he asked.

It seemed he had said all he intended to about her insulting offer to pay him, and she was infinitely grateful.

"Anything that's on the shelf," she said. "Living alone, I only buy what I like."

"Fair enough."

He took a step or two farther into the room, and then he stopped, almost beside her chair. His eyes examined her knee for a few seconds. "That's an impressive collection of railroad tracks you've got there," he said.

Her heart was beating too fast, but again she forced herself to look up into his eyes. A long way up. If this was some kind of test, then damn it, she wasn't going to fail again.

"They ought to be impressive," she said, relieved that the breathlessness she felt wasn't reflected in her voice. "I spent years acquiring them."

"We'll compare scars some day," he said.

Then he moved away, walking past her chair and into the hall that led to the kitchen. She took another breath, closing her eyes in relief. When she opened them, her gaze found the ugly, reddened reminders of the numerous surgeries she'd had. *We'll compare scars some day.* Since none of his were any more visible than hers were when she was dressed, she wondered if that implied anything like what her brain was suggesting.

The length of *his* bare legs exposed to view—long, muscled and roughened with dark hair. She knew from the way they moved under the material of his faded jeans that they would be as strong and as dark and as masculinely beautiful as his hands.

She thought about the flat brown stomach she had glimpsed as he had unhurriedly pulled the edges of his shirt together last night, his fingers moving methodically down the line of buttons. There had been no visible scars on the tanned skin.

Thinking about his body, she realized a different heat was moving through hers now. Not caused by embarrassment. This was something she hadn't felt in years. Something she had never expected to feel again. Had never really wanted to feel again.

And with good reason. *Very* good reason, she reminded herself. Her eyes dropped again to her knee, exposed and vulnerable, with its obscene network of scars. The skin beneath them was too white, untouched by the sun. Untouched.

This was a lesson she had learned long ago. A painful one that she didn't need any further instruction to remember. Men were interested in her for only one reason. And nothing had changed about that during the past ten years. If anything, with her father's death, it would only have gotten worse. A whole lot worse, she acknowledged.

So there was no need to start fantasizing about Grey Sellers' body. No need to even think about what he had meant by the phrase he had so casually dropped into this conversation. They were never going to "compare scars." She wasn't ever again going to make the mistake of letting a man get under her skin. Or under her guard.

She wasn't the same woman she had been ten years ago. There was nothing needy or vulnerable about her now. Again her eyes fell to her knee, as she deliberately replayed Bart Carruthers' words in her head. Her former fiancé had taught her a very painful lesson, perhaps, but it had been a valuable one, which she would never forget. Not as long as she lived.

A HELL OF A LITTLE SERMON you gave out there, old buddy, Grey Sellers told himself sarcastically as he opened the pantry door and surveyed its contents. *Yes, sirree, you just go right ahead and tell everybody else how they should live their lives. Especially since you've done such a damn fine job with yours.*

He couldn't believe he had spouted all that crap about knowing when you need help and being able to accept it. Who the hell did he think he was kidding? He wrote the book on *not* being able to admit to needing help.

And in his case, a lot of people had tried. Griff, for one. And Hawk. He had dismissed their efforts as if they didn't mean anything. Even worse, he had done it as if the people themselves didn't mean anything to him. And nothing could have been further from the truth.

He blocked the remembrance of his behavior, blindly selecting a can of soup. He started opening and closing cabinet doors, searching for a microwavable bowl to put it into. He noticed that his hand was trembling as it closed over the handles. He told himself it was because he'd had nothing to eat today, not even a cup of coffee, much less his usual five or six.

His head was beginning to throb almost as painfully it had yesterday afternoon, and he wasn't sure which of those deprivations—food or caffeine—was responsible for today's headache. Maybe both of them.

When he opened the next cabinet door, he hesitated. Almost without his volition, his hand held it open long after he had ascertained that its shelves didn't hold bowls. On the middle one sat a full bottle of whiskey, the seal intact.

And given the kind of day this had been, it looked damned tempting. Almost as tempting as the long, shapely length of Val Beaufort's legs, which had been revealed by that abbreviated nightshirt she was wearing.

Of course, her legs hadn't been the only thing the thin cotton hadn't hidden. She wasn't wearing a bra, and the nipples of her breasts had pushed tantalizingly against the fabric.

When he had opened the front door, it had been almost impossible to pull his eyes away from them. As soon as she'd hung up the phone, however, she had glanced up and had seen him standing there. He'd had to use every bit of self-control he possessed to force his gaze to focus on her face.

Self-control, he thought. *Self-control. You remember that, old buddy. That's where you don't indulge in everything you have the urge to indulge in.*

He closed the cabinet door and his eyes at the same time, holding the latter tightly shut. The woman in the other room was his employer. His responsibility. And none of the things he was thinking right now had anything at all to do with the requirements of his job.

He opened his eyes slowly, and then deliberately turned his back on the cabinet he'd just closed. There was a thick earthenware bowl in the drain tray. Relieved that he wouldn't have to do any more searching, he walked over and carried it and the soup to the can opener.

Just because he had screwed up on one job didn't mean he was no longer capable of seeing something through to the end, he told himself doggedly. He had been telling himself the same thing for a couple of years now. Maybe, he thought, just maybe, it was starting to sink in.

Once he had taken Ms. Beaufort's lunch in to her, he would come back in here and fix himself a sandwich. And make a pot of coffee, he promised his headache. He placed the soup, which was tomato, into the microwave and pressed buttons until it started to whir. As he waited, his eyes drifted again to the doors of the last cabinet he'd opened.

Easy way out, he thought. *And you're the one who's all of a sudden gone on the lecture circuit, telling people how to live. You're the one who's got a job to do here, and the quicker you put all this into perspective, the better off you'll be.*

He turned his head again back to the microwave and, watching the bowl turn slowly around and around, he didn't bother to acknowledge exactly what "all this" meant. He knew, however, that it was tied up with what he had felt this morning as he'd watched Val Beaufort struggle with that stallion without the least trace of fear. And with what he'd felt this afternoon, watching her hobble around, trying to catch up to the brute that had put her on those crutches, trying to hold him long enough to take care of him. And even what he had felt looking down on that scarred and swollen knee, he acknowledged.

But it had a lot more to do with what he had felt when he'd become aware of the small, taut peaks of her breasts, erotically revealed by that knit T-shirt every time she took a breath. "All this" had a whole lot more to do with those than with anything else.

Valerie Beaufort wasn't someone whom he should have even been thinking about in that way. She wasn't in any way, shape or form the kind of woman he should be interested in or could afford to be interested in. Especially not like that.

The fact that he *was* thinking about her in that way was almost as troubling to him as the sight of that unopened bottle of whiskey. And almost as tempting.

Chapter Five

"Did I manage to screw up the soup?" Grey asked.

Val looked up at the sound of his voice, and then down at the almost untouched bowl of soup he'd brought her earlier.

"There's nothing wrong with the soup," she said. "I'm just not hungry. Maybe the heat. Or the excitement this morning."

"Or maybe it's my cooking," he said as he took the tray off her lap. "I have to admit, this doesn't look too appetizing."

As the soup had cooled, an orange-red skim had settled over the top. It hadn't looked that way when he'd brought it, and it had tasted fine. Valerie just hadn't been able to make herself eat.

"Honestly..." she began.

"How about a sandwich?" His offer came almost on top of her words of protest, but she shook her head in response.

"Really, I'm just not hungry."

His eyes assessed hers a moment. "Did you take your pills?" he asked. "You want me to round them up and bring them to you?"

As soon as she'd gotten settled in the chair, Val had taken two extra-strength, over-the-counter tablets of pain medication. The bottle was still on the table beside her. Unconsciously, her eyes considered it, trying to estimate how long it had been since she'd downed those two. Despite the fact that they hadn't made much of a dent in the pain, she knew that not enough time had passed to repeat the dosage.

"I'm fine," she said. "Just a little...bushed."

His eyes were still considering her face. Since the mirror in the bathroom where she had gotten undressed was well lit, she knew exactly what she looked like. The line of Frankenstein-like stitches Halley had put in on her temple was relatively neat, but by no stretch of the imagination could it be called attractive. She hadn't put on makeup before she'd gone out this morning, and she certainly hadn't bothered with that when she'd gotten home.

She *had* tried to get the dried blood out of her hair, dabbing at it with a wet cloth, but she knew she would have to shampoo to get it all. And considering the ache in her head and her leg, that was way down on her list of priorities.

Under the steady appraisal of Grey's eyes, however, she found herself wishing she had made more of an effort to clean herself up. And she then wondered why she felt that way, especially in light of her recent mental diatribe against men.

Finally Grey nodded, his lips pursing a little, and then, without saying anything else, he carried the tray out of the room. Val put her aching head back, resting it on the top of the chair, and closed her eyes, listening to his footsteps fade away.

And then listening to them return. They stopped beside her. She opened her eyes, not bothering to lift her head from the chair. This time he wasn't looking at her. He had picked up the over-the-counter pain medication and was examining its label instead.

"Is this what you took?" he asked.

Is that any of your business? she thought, but she didn't deny it was, her eyes holding on his face.

"I thought you had a prescription."

"I did," she said. *About fifteen years ago.*

"Then why take these?"

This time it was her lips that tightened. The medication hadn't done her headache or the pain in her knee much good, so the question was certainly valid. She just wasn't sure she was required by their relationship to share the equally valid answer.

Why not? she thought. The battle she had fought and won wasn't anything she was ashamed of, and she wasn't out to impress Grey Sellers. Or was she? If so, she had to wonder why.

"Because I spent too many of my teenage years addicted to painkillers and walking around in an overmedicated daze," she said bluntly. "Once I weaned myself off them, I swore that would never happen again. So…" She nodded toward the bottle he held in his hand.

His eyes, looking down into hers, changed subtly. His control was so practiced, however, that she couldn't read much from them or from his expression.

"Any other questions?" she asked softly, expecting embarrassment if nothing else. Most people were thrown by the open admission of addiction, especially in connection with someone like her. She hardly fit the stereotype.

"You need me to help you to the bathroom?" Grey asked.

His tone was so matter-of-fact, so totally unrelated to what she had just confessed, that it took her a moment to comprehend what he had said. And when she did, she almost laughed.

Her disclosure hadn't elicited anything like the discomfort she'd been expecting. Only a rather prosaic offer for assistance with a necessary body function. Which told her two things. Grey Sellers wasn't easily shocked, and he was prepared to take his nursing duties seriously.

"Thank you, but no," she said, struggling not to smile. He certainly knew how to destroy the drama of the moment. Or maybe that should be the melodrama, she acknowledged.

"Just let me know," he said. "Oh, and I made some coffee. I missed my normal potful this morning. You want a cup?"

She thought about it. Maybe the caffeine would help the stuff she had taken to kick in. But it might also keep her awake. And she figured there were going to be enough aches and pains and troubling images running through her head tonight to accomplish that without any additives helping out.

She shook her head, and he nodded again.

"I'll be in the kitchen. Give a yell if you need anything."

"I know what Halley told you this morning, but... I mean, it's not that I'm not grateful for what you're trying to do, but you don't have to wait on me. I'm not helpless."

His lips moved, the small, upward tilt of one corner that she had noticed as he had sat on her front porch challenging everything she said. Mocking her. And she realized just now that she hadn't seen this particular movement since then.

"Believe me, Ms. Beaufort," he said, "I don't think you're helpless. Anybody who locks horns with that black on a daily basis is tough enough to tangle with a pair of crutches. And you used them as if you've had some previous experience with those."

She didn't say anything in response. That had sounded like a compliment. And the last part was true, of course.

"I knew when I took this job that there wasn't much

bodyguarding to be done,'' he continued. ''Beneficial Life is paying me to be here, however. As long as I am, I might as well make myself useful.''

''And have you had experience at…'' She paused, trying to think of a delicate way to ask if he'd ever done any nursing.

''At being useful?'' he filled in when she hesitated.

And then he laughed, a pattern of small creases forming attractively at the corners of his eyes and in his lean cheeks. It was the first time she had seen him laugh, and as with that intriguing twitch at the corner of his mouth, she was fascinated by what laughter did to the hard planes and angles of his face.

''I'm always up for a new experience,'' he said.

Just as when he had mentioned comparing scars, the image those words created in her mind had nothing much to do with the context of the conversation. *Always up for a new experience.* He hadn't meant anything sexual by the comment, and she knew it, so she couldn't imagine why something sexual had been the first thing she thought of. She didn't really have that kind of mind.

''I guess that's good,'' she said, ''since things are a little different than when you accepted this job.''

''It'll work out,'' he said. ''As long as we…''

''Don't get into one another's hair?'' she suggested.

''I was about to say as long as we're honest with each other. But I will try to stay out of your hair, since you mentioned it. If you need me, give a yell. Unless you do, I'll assume you can handle whatever comes up.''

Again Val's mind took the words out of context, and for a moment she didn't seem able to formulate an acceptable answer. Finally she took a page out of his book and simply nodded.

He didn't move for a few seconds, looking into her eyes. She had the strangest feeling that he was considering bending down and putting his lips over hers. Her intuition was so strong her own lips parted in anticipation. Instead, he turned and, boot heels echoing on the floor, walked back toward the hallway.

She was conscious of the strongest sense of disappointment. Almost of desertion. Both of which were ridiculous. She should have asked Halley about the possible side effects of concussion. Apparently she had hit her head a lot harder than she'd realized. Hard enough to make her forget she wasn't interested in men? Hard enough to make her start fantasizing about a stranger, a man about whom she literally knew nothing? She took a deep breath and closed her mouth.

A couple of days and things would be back to normal, she told herself. She'd be back on her feet and wouldn't feel so vulnerable. Or so needy. There was no reason for her to feel either of those things. After all, she had everything she *needed*. She had been perfectly content living alone on this ranch for the past ten years. And nothing had happened to change that. Absolutely nothing, she told herself firmly.

THE HOURS OF THE NEXT three days passed grindingly slowly. There wasn't much Valerie could do except sit and worry. About her horses. About Av-Tech. And especially about what happened in her head whenever Grey Sellers brought her a meal or a report about what was going on outside.

Kronus had shown no more tendency to spook, thank goodness. And according to Grey, everything else on the ranch was running smoothly. He and the guy from the security firm had spent a couple of hours walking around the place and then a couple more on the porch, heads together over a sketch pad.

Apparently they'd been in complete agreement about

what was needed. When the salesman had brought in the plan they'd devised, she hadn't bothered to argue with anything they wanted to do. Carmichael had assured her these people were the best in the business, and Grey was Beneficial Life's official representative here, so she figured she should leave the details of what was needed to satisfy the terms of the policy up to them.

Before her father's death, she would have panicked at the projected cost; now she had simply instructed the security firm's rep to have the bill sent to Av-Tech. After all, if it weren't for the fact that this policy went along with the shares she'd inherited, she wouldn't be having this system put in. The company could pay for it in lieu of any salary she was due—however brief her tenure—as chief executive officer.

She had been expecting a call from Autry concerning his background check. She had also thought he would be interested to know how the security consultation had gone. He hadn't called back by the evening of the third day, however. By then, she had ditched the crutches and was hobbling around with increasing ease, her hand on the wall or a convenient piece of furniture whenever she needed extra support.

Tonight she had even managed a shower, as opposed to a bath. Despite the stitches, she had risked a shampoo, finally getting the last of the dried blood out of her hair. As a result, she was feeling a lot more like herself.

Under the invigorating spray of hot water, she had decided this was the last day she was going to be housebound. She might not be able to work, but at least she could be out in the fresh air and sunshine, watching Grey do all the things she normally would be doing. Which was, she admitted as she carefully rubbed strands of wet hair between the two sides of her towel, something she was looking forward to with too much anticipation.

During the three days he had cared for her and her animals, she had become more and more attracted to Grey Sellers. He helped her only when it was necessary and without making her feel like an invalid. He kept her informed about her horses and everything else that was happening on the ranch. And gradually, the tension that had been between them had evaporated.

At least on her part it had turned into a different kind of tension, she acknowledged. The kind that grew between a man and a woman who were forced by circumstances into some kind of intimacy. As the two of them had been.

When she made that admission, her hands stilled over their task. She leaned closer to the fogged bathroom mirror, for the first time in a very long while studying the features of the woman reflected there. Discounting the stitches and the bruising at her temple, it wasn't a bad face. Even with them, no one would run away in horror.

It was a little thin. And her eyes seemed too big for that thinness. Mouth too wide. The dusting of freckles across the bridge of her nose was more noticeable because it was summer and because she sometimes went out without remembering sunscreen.

Not a bad face, she thought again, but certainly not one that would ever stop traffic. Or entice a man's notice, she reminded herself. Not without the Beaufort millions behind it.

Those had always been enticing enough that she had never been without a steady boyfriend while she was growing up. Not even after the accident. She had limped to proms and parties, never suspecting the reason she didn't have to go unescorted was because her name was Valerie Beaufort instead of Valerie Smith.

She could thank Bart Carruthers for that wake-up call. She supposed she really should be grateful to her former fiancé. And if calling off their wedding at the last minute hadn't been so damned painful, she might be. Actually, telling her dad *why* she was calling it off had been worse than anything else. Even worse than the initial pain of overhearing Bart's remark. Worse than sending back all those gifts.

For some reason, maybe because he was the one who had been so successful, her father had considered the entire fiasco to be his fault. It wasn't, of course. It wasn't anyone's fault, Val had finally concluded. It was just the way the world worked.

She jumped at the unexpected knock on the bathroom door, shocked out of her foray into the past.

"Yes?" she called, lowering the towel.

"I'm going out to the bunkhouse for the night," Grey said, his voice muffled by the old-fashioned solid-core door between them. "Just checking to see if you need anything before I do."

He had been washing their dinner dishes when she'd decided to take her shower. Although he had asked this same question every night since she'd been hurt, she hadn't really expected him to knock on a closed bathroom door and ask it tonight.

"I'm fine. Thanks," she added.

She had an urge to open the door between them and look at him before he disappeared into the darkness. Maybe because she knew she would be changing the status quo of their relationship tomorrow. If she were up and out, then she wouldn't need him any longer to bring her meals, which meant...

Which meant she'd probably see less of him than she had been. She watched her lips tighten in the mirror, and then deliberately she forced them to relax.

"I almost forgot," he said. "You had a phone call. Someone named Autry."

Almost without her direction, her hands put the wet

towel down on the lavatory. She limped across the couple of feet that separated her from the door. Her hand closed over the knob, and she hesitated a second before she opened it. When she did, his eyes came up to her face, surprise clearly revealed within them.

And then they fell to the low neckline of the sheer white nightgown she was wearing. It was a lot more feminine than her usual nightshirts, and she couldn't explain why she had chosen it. No more than she could explain why she had opened this door.

"Did he say he'd call back?" she asked.

His gaze rose slowly to her face, the same unremarkable face that had stared out at her from the clouded glass only seconds ago— thin, freckled and surrounded by damply curling strands of reddish-brown hair. Except he wasn't looking at her as if he saw that very ordinary collection of features she had just seen. There was something else in the gray eyes.

Something…heated, she realized in wonder. Something she had only caught a glimpse of once before, and then it had been quickly hidden. She knew him well enough by now to understand that she would never have been allowed to be aware of what he was feeling if he hadn't intended her to. Whatever was in his eyes was so powerful, however, that it sent a jolt of molten sensation all the way down into the pit of her stomach.

"I think *you're* supposed to call *him,*" Grey said.

She nodded, throat tight, mouth suddenly dry.

"Boyfriend?" he asked.

Despite the current of sexual awareness that had just flared between them, she laughed. And watched that subtle play of movement at the corner of his lips again. His eyes were dark, almost smoky. And still heated.

"One of my father's friends. My father's age."

He nodded, but his eyes didn't release hers. "I guess

I've just been anticipating that...someone would eventually show up out here to check on you.''

"Boyfriend-type someone?"

He nodded again. His gaze had touched on her lips as they moved to form those words before it rose again to her eyes.

"I don't have one of those. Living out here..." she began, and then realized she didn't owe him any explanations as to why she was unattached.

"Plays hell with your social life," he suggested.

"Pretty much."

He put his thumb and forefinger on her chin, turning her head. She didn't resist. After the first shattering sensation of his fingers moving against her skin, she had realized he was just looking at the line of stitches Halley had set.

"Didn't get that wet, did you?" he asked.

"No more than I could help. I just couldn't bear having blood in my hair anymore. And besides..."

She hesitated, almost hating to announce her recovery. Hating to destroy the rapport that had developed between them during the past couple of days. She couldn't deny, not even to herself, that her initial suspicions of him had faded. It was hard to be antagonistic to a man who was feeding you. Looking after your horses. A man who might even have saved your life.

Which was only what he was getting paid to do, she told herself. Protecting her from danger was exactly why he was here in the first place, she reiterated, fighting whatever was happening inside her chest. Inside her stomach. And especially fighting the sweet ache that was moving into her lower body as she stood looking up into those gray eyes.

To him, what he had done that day hadn't meant anything else. Just part of his job. And she needed to get the idea that it *had* been anything else—anything personal—out of her head.

"I'm well enough to be up and around," she made herself say. "I need to be moving my knee a little, recovering function."

His eyes were on hers again. "Are you sure?"

"I'm sure," she said softly. "I've had lots of experience." And then she added, "At this, I mean."

His mouth moved again, one corner slanting upward. He was obviously amused by that disclaimer. *Why wouldn't he be?* she thought. Annoyed at that totally inane and unnecessary addition, her eyes fell in embarrassment. She had no idea why she had said it. There *was* no reason, except an attempt to be provocative. Which, considering the way she looked right now, she couldn't possibly believe she was.

"But not at...other things?" he asked, his fingers still touching her chin.

Whether under their direction or her own, she was again looking up into his eyes. She didn't answer, because seeing what was in them, she couldn't seem to formulate words. Not any kind.

And then his head began to move, tilting to one side to align his lips over hers. Which had already parted in anticipation, just as they had that first night when he'd stood so long beside her chair.

She had thought then he was going to kiss her, and she had been wrong. Now she held her breath, unwilling to do anything that might break the spell that had been broken before. This time he didn't walk away. His head continued to lower toward hers, which he raised with the gentle pressure of his fingers.

When there could be absolutely no doubt about his intent, her eyelids fell, shutting out reality. Transferring what was happening into that realm of fantasy she had been inhabiting for the past three days. The place where she had imagined his lips moving over hers. His arms closing around her to ease her against the same hard chest she had leaned into the day he had pulled her out of Kronus' path.

He released her chin, and his lips, dry and warm and incredibly pleasant, settled lightly over hers. She was aware on some level when his hands closed over her upper arms, almost exactly as they had the day he'd arrived.

Tonight, however, the intent of his fingers was so different. There was no anger in the way they held her. No anger in the way his tongue pushed inside her parted lips. No anger in the way hers met his, moving together in a slow tangle of heat and desire.

She did desire him. She had known—and had denied—that desire almost from the first time she had seen him. Now she couldn't deny it. And she no longer wanted to.

He deepened the kiss, his hands releasing her arms to slide around her back, pulling her close. Her breasts brushed against the muscles of his chest and then were flattened against them. And the ache that had been between her legs seemed to ignite, sending heat spiraling upward, into nerve endings, veins and muscles. Burning them. Branding them.

The feeling was infinitely sweet, awakening a longing she had hidden so long and so deeply that the sudden need it produced was sharp, verging on painful. Automatically, trying to assuage that pain, she moved nearer to him, pushing her lower body into his, seeking some kind of appeasement for the demand clamoring through her senses.

The thin cloth of her nightgown offered no barrier between them and no shield against his body. In response to her movement, Grey bent his knees and then straightened them, pushing the heat of his erection upward into the most sensitive part of her anatomy.

Her gasp of response was too revealing, she supposed,

but right now she didn't care. All she cared about was getting closer to him. Feeling his strength pressed all along the length of her body. Feeling him.

At the involuntary sound she had made, however, his mouth released hers. He turned his head a little, his lips resting on her cheek instead. She could feel his heart racing against her breasts, and that excited her, too.

"I didn't mean to hurt you," he whispered. "I don't ever want to hurt you."

"You didn't," she breathed, turning her head enough that her mouth was again under his.

Daringly, she ran her tongue around his lips, and he pulled her tighter, bending her back and pushing his tongue once more into her mouth. Ravaging it with an expertise she hadn't expected. One of his hands slipped down to spread over her hips, and he lifted her so she was again in contact with his arousal.

And she wanted to be. She had been conscious of every move this man had made during the past three days. Conscious of the way his hard muscles shifted under his clothing. Conscious of his hands. Of his eyes. Of the way the corner of his mouth expressed whatever he was thinking. *Conscious.*

And yet so unknowing. Aching for his touch without acknowledging that ache, that need. Now that she had, she knew there was no going back. For the first time in ten years, she had allowed herself to admit she wanted this. She wanted this man's hands on her body and his mouth over hers.

And of all the men she had met in those long, empty years, the one she wanted was one she knew nothing about. A stranger, who was as protective of his own privacy as she was of hers.

And with this surrender, she had opened herself up again to a world of pain that could hurt like no other. Certainly beyond any of the physical agonies she had ever suffered. She didn't understand why she had done this. All she knew was that it was far too late to question that she had. And right now, with his arms around her, his body so close that, except for a couple of layers of too-thin fabric, they were one, she had no regrets.

The kiss went on and on, their mouths and their tongues finding ways to lengthen it. Finding ways to explore each other. His left hand joined the right one, which was still cupped under the softness of her bottom, and he bent his knees again, lifting her into him, grinding his pelvis against hers.

His breathing was ragged, and she liked that she had the power to make it that uneven. She could feel the hot moisture seeping out of her body, increasing in response to the slow movement of his hips. To his tongue. To his hands.

Suddenly he straightened, pulling the front of his body out of contact with hers. His hands found her back, soothing upward, and then he gripped her shoulders again, holding her in place as he took a step backward. She opened her eyes, feeling that same sense of desertion she had felt the first night. A sense of incompleteness. Of loss.

He was looking down into her face, lips closed, almost flattened, even that mobile corner unmoving. And she wanted it to. She wanted to see that faint display of amusement. Of mockery. Even if it were mocking that this was happening between two people who had begun as antagonists. She wondered if he were as amazed by this feeling as she was. She needed him to be.

"Grey," she said softly, knowing nothing else to say. Nothing beyond his name. All her brain could devise.

"That got a little out of hand," he said softly.

Her mind examined the sentence. There was nothing wrong with the words. They were certainly an accurate portrayal of what had occurred, at least on her part. Her emotions had certainly gotten out of hand. They—he—had broken the strict control she had exercised over them for almost a decade.

She nodded, still holding his eyes, trying to read what he was thinking. And feeling.

"I didn't mean for that to happen," he said softly.

She nodded again, the pleasurable excitement beginning to fade. She didn't know exactly why. There was nothing wrong with what he had said. She hadn't meant for this to happen either.

"I think maybe I better go," he said.

The words hung in the air between them, like the breath of steam and the scent of shampoo that still pervaded the small room. Was he waiting for an invitation to spend the night? Here in the house? An invitation to spend the night in her bed?

As the thought formed in her head, however, she knew that this was wrong. Wrong for them. For her. It was too soon. Too sudden. Too…dangerous. She didn't know this man. She didn't know anything about him, except that his touch could reduce her to a person she hadn't been in years. Could reduce her to being a woman again. Vulnerable. Needy. Wanting.

And that was a leap she wasn't sure she was ready to make. She could admit to that doubt, just as long as his tongue wasn't moving against hers. Just as long as his hard erection wasn't pressed into her body, imprinting hers with its heat and power.

Too soon. Too sudden. "Maybe that would be best," she agreed, her voice as soft as his.

"You okay?" he asked, examining her face.

She nodded, feeling the burn of tears at the back of her eyes despite her assurance. She fought them, determined not to allow her eyes to fill. She held them on his face by sheer force of will and with the same stubborn determination that had always allowed her to get through any experience, no matter how difficult—or how painful—it was.

"I'm fine," she whispered.

Apparently there was enough of what she was feeling revealed in her face or her voice to make him suspicious. One of his hands rose to brush a strand of damp hair off the temple that bore the evidence of Kronus' rampage. Then he bent his head and put his lips gently against the line of stitches.

"You sure?" he asked, his breath warm against her skin.

"I'm sure," she said. "Don't worry about me."

After a few seconds, he nodded, his mouth brushing tantalizingly over the new scar. She closed her eyes, the tenderness of that movement producing a need almost as sharp as when he had first touched her, had first put his lips over hers.

"Lock up," he ordered. "I'll see you in the morning."

His hands released her arms, and he turned away. He didn't look back as he disappeared into the hallway. She took a step into the safety of the bathroom and leaned weakly against the lavatory, propping her left hand on the rim. Then she opened her eyes and turned her head to look again at her reflection.

There was something very different about the woman who stared back at her now. Something in the eyes, perhaps. Dark and very wide. Almost dazed. A little misty with unshed tears.

Or maybe it was in the shape of her mouth, swollen with a man's hard kisses. Or in the reddened cheeks, burnished by the abrasiveness of a man's whiskered cheeks.

Different. Vulnerable. Needy. And already hungry again for what had just happened. *Too soon. Too sudden.* And way too dangerous.

THE KITCHEN WAS DARK because he had cut off the lights when he had finished the dishes and readied the coffeemaker to self-start in the morning. He had intended to go out through the front door, but when he'd left the bathroom, he had ended up back here instead. He knew why, of course. It seemed to be a night for indulging. After all, he had already given in to temptation and tasted one very forbidden pleasure.

For almost four days he had been fighting the urge to kiss Valerie Beaufort. Days he'd spent admiring her courage, not only in dealing with the stallion but in admitting why she hadn't stopped in town to pick up that prescription. Watching her cope uncomplainingly with pain and injury and with being forced to accept his help, and doing it pretty graciously, considering that she damn sure didn't want it.

Tonight, seeing her in that so-sheer-he-could-take-pictures-through-it nightgown, he had lost the battle. Which meant he had lost this one as well, he acknowledged, opening the cabinet door and wrapping his fingers around the neck of the whiskey bottle. He stood there a couple of long heartbeats, thinking about all the good reasons he shouldn't do this.

He was on an assignment, even if it was bogus as hell. He was getting paid to do a job, and he *never* drank on the job. Cardinal rule. People could get killed.

But people had been killed, he remembered bitterly, and he hadn't been drunk then. Just mistaken. Wrong. Incompetent.

And so having a drink is going to make you more competent, old buddy? his mind jeered.

Having a drink is going to let me sleep, he argued, *despite what just happened.* Despite the ache in his groin. Despite the fact that it had been too long since he'd been with a woman he cared two hoots about. Way too long since he had wanted to be.

And he wanted to be with this one. He had given up trying to figure out why. She wasn't all that good-looking. Certainly not so beautiful that she should be irresistible. And she didn't like him worth a damn.

He took a breath, his fingers unwrapping from around the neck of the bottle. She hadn't exactly kissed him like she didn't like him, he admitted. She had kissed him just like he had kissed her. Like she wanted him to make love to her, maybe even as much as he wanted to make love to her.

Loneliness? he wondered. Who could know? He just knew that she had responded as passionately to that kiss as he could have wanted. And that didn't make this battle any easier. Frankly, it just made it harder.

His fingers closed around the bottle again, lifting it off the shelf, and taking it with him as he crossed the kitchen to the back door. He hesitated, his free hand on the knob. If he intended to drink himself to sleep he needed a glass, he supposed. It had always been a matter of pride—about all the pride he had left, he admitted—that he hadn't yet resorted to drinking straight out of the bottle.

For a moment, Valerie Beaufort's face was in his mind's eye, as clear as it had been when he had been looking down at her, pulling her slender hips up into contact with his like he had the right. Like she wasn't Ms. Valerie Beaufort, CEO and majority shareholder of one of the biggest companies in the state. Hell, in the nation. Like he was somebody she would want rubbing his body against hers.

She did, his alter ego reminded.

Only because she doesn't know…

He stopped that thought before the images that went with the words could form. And then, almost angrily, he turned the knob, knowing that drinking straight out of the bottle tonight wasn't going to be a problem. At least, not one that was going to be nearly so hard to deal with as the problem he was leaving behind him in this dark and silent house.

Chapter Six

When the phone rang, the sound was jarring in the night-time stillness. A little shocking, even, because it was so unexpected. A lot of people had called the week her father died, and several the first of this week, but those calls had gradually tapered off. Valerie didn't think the phone had rung at all in the past two days. Not since she'd given the security firm's representative directions out to the ranch.

And this call, whoever it was from, was an intrusion she didn't want to deal with right now. She had other things to think about. All she had been doing since Grey left. She had been sitting in the same chair she had occupied during the past few days, thinking about what had happened. About what it meant.

When the phone pealed again, she reached for it reluctantly. *Anyone except Connie,* she prayed in the split second after her hello.

"Can you talk?"

Autry. She had even forgotten that Grey had said he'd called. Or at least she had put it out of her mind, concentrating instead on other things Grey had said. Far more important things.

Until she heard his voice, the possibility that this might be her father's old friend hadn't even crossed her mind. And then his question, "Can you talk?" caught her off guard. It was so cloak-and-daggerish, which was, however, right down Autry's alley.

"Of course I can talk," she said, almost amused.

"Where's your bodyguard?"

"In the bunkhouse."

By then, her numbed mind was beginning to operate well enough to understand what this call was about. She had asked Autry to check up on Grey. However, the feeling that she should find out more about the man who was living on her ranch had certainly dissipated during the three days since she had done that, and after tonight…

"You sure he can't hear you?" Autry demanded.

"I'm positive. Why are you being so mysterious, Autry?"

"You wanted me to check on Sellers."

After tonight, that request felt like some kind of betrayal. A lack of trust. *Except I don't exactly have a spotless record about knowing who to trust,* she thought, the admission bitter.

Besides, she *had* asked Autry to get the information for her, and apparently he had already gone to the trouble to do it. Maybe a lot of trouble, considering the time that had passed since she'd asked him. She should at least hear him out.

The clandestine way Autry was going about this conversation made it sound as if he had discovered something unsavory in Grey's past. If he had, she wasn't sure she wanted to hear it now. *Of course you do,* her logic insisted. *You were burned before by trusting the wrong man. Grow up.*

"So what did you find out?" she asked, forcing herself to say the words, holding her breath as she waited for his response.

"Not a damn thing," Carmichael said. Something in his

tone made that statement less reassuring than it should have been.

"That's good," Val said. Then, when the silence on the other end of the line continued, she added, "Isn't it?"

"I mean literally nothing. This guy's got no past, Val. Not a real one, anyway."

"Everybody has a past," Val said.

"That's right," Autry said. "And when somebody doesn't, it sets off alarms. Makes guys like me real suspicious."

"I don't think I'm following you."

"Everything we do in our lives leaves a record. Birth, death, schools, military, jobs. You do it, and it's in a computer somewhere. Payroll, income taxes, social security. There's some kind of record."

"And you didn't find any of those records for Grey Sellers?"

Despite Val's acknowledgment that she didn't want to hear this, Autry had her hooked. Not with the fact that there was nothing bad about Sellers, but by the fact there was nothing at all. Even she understood how unlikely that would be. *Unlikely, hell,* she thought. It was impossible.

"Not a trace. No address before he moved out here. No records of verifiable employment. No previous records at all."

"What does that mean? Verifiable employment?"

"It means nothing that left any marks. He may be able to name names of companies where he supposedly worked. Maybe even get somebody to say, 'Yeah, we employed him for such and such a period,' but the fact is nobody paid payroll taxes for him. No W2's. No 401K's. No nothing."

"I think he was in the military," Val said, although she couldn't remember why she had come to believe that.

"Not according to government records."

"This doesn't make sense."

"Unless somebody cleaned his files."

"Cleaned his files?"

"Deleted all records pertaining to someone named Grey Sellers."

"Maybe that's not his real name," Val suggested.

"Maybe not, but that's the one thing we *do* have. A birth certificate. Issued thirty-eight years ago, right here in Colorado, as a matter of fact. And the individual on that birth certificate has a social security number."

"But nothing else?" she asked, incredulous.

"Nothing that stands up to examination. At least not until early last year when he showed up out here."

"So…what exactly does this mean? If somebody destroyed all records in his past."

Again the silence stretched. "I'm not sure," Autry admitted finally. She heard the breath he released. "But this isn't an amateur job, Val," he warned. "It's not something that can be done easily, at least not when it's done this completely. Somebody with a lot of know-how cleaned up after our boy, which is why it took me so long to get a handle on it."

"Because…there were criminal activities in his past?"

A sense of dread stirred in her stomach. She didn't want to hear this. She had already been trying to come to terms with the difficult realization that she might have begun to fall in love again.

The *last* thing she had ever intended to do—and with a man she barely knew. Now Autry was telling her that getting close to Grey Sellers wasn't only emotionally dangerous. It might be physically dangerous, as well.

"Not necessarily criminal," Carmichael said, and some of the tension eased in Val's chest. "I have to admit this looks like a hide. After forty years in this business, you get a feel."

"A hide?"

"Witness Protection, maybe. Something like that. But probably official, in any case. I'm still working on it, honey, but I thought you should know what I'd found out, especially since he's staying out there."

"Who goes into Witness Protection? I mean, isn't that for criminals who have testified against other criminals?"

"Or witnesses to crimes. Undercover cops whose identities have been blown. All kinds of people, actually. Anybody who needs protection and who is valuable enough to the government that they're willing to provide it."

There was another silence as she thought about what he'd told her. "If Grey Sellers needed protection himself, would he be running a protection agency?" Val asked.

Something wasn't right here. It didn't *feel* right. None of this, not the suggestion that Grey was in hiding or that he was guilty of some wrongdoing, fit with the man she had lived with so closely these past few days.

She didn't doubt that what Autry was telling her was true. He had been in this business too long to make a mistake about something like this. Besides, she had known from the first there was some mystery about Grey. But as Autry had said, even if he were in protection, that didn't mean he had done anything wrong.

She remembered wondering if Grey had been in law enforcement, so maybe he was someone who had had his cover blown and had been forced to "reinvent" himself. Not necessarily one of the bad guys.

"Running a protection agency might be the perfect cover," Autry said. "After all, who would suspect someone who is *in* protection himself would be in the business?"

"Ex-cop?" she asked. That would be the kind of scenario she preferred, of course, which was why she had suggested it.

"It's possible," Autry said, his tone skeptical.

"But you don't believe it?"

"I don't have enough information to know what I believe."

"So what do we do now?" Val asked.

"I keep looking. And *you* be careful. I don't like people who pretend to be one thing when they're something else. This guy's a phony, no matter what else he is."

To Autry, and to Val's father, being a phony was the worst thing anyone could be. Her ex-fiancé had certainly been one. Val believed her stepmother was, too, which was one of the things that had kept a distance between them. And Grey...

She took a breath before she spoke again. "Thanks, Autry. I'll be careful, I promise you. And as soon as the security system is in, he'll be gone."

"Have you gotten in touch with that independent agent? The guy who sent him out there?"

"Not yet," Val said.

She didn't admit that she hadn't tried again after that first morning. Joe Wallace might very well have been back in his office and highly accessible for the past three days, and Val wouldn't have known because she hadn't called him.

"Keep trying. Feel him out. See if you think they're in on this together."

"In on what, Autry? What do you think they could possibly be after out here?" she asked, her voice sharp with exasperation because she could think of no explanation for what was going on. And she hated being in the dark. "I don't have anything of value except a few horses. If somebody wanted to steal them, they could just load them up out in the pasture one night and drive them away. They wouldn't go to the trouble of sending out a fake bodyguard."

"I don't *know* what they're after, honey. I don't know enough to even venture a guess. Maybe nothing. Maybe I'm all wet, and this guy's background has nothing to do with you at all. But you need to remember that you're a very rich woman now. That means all kinds of vultures will be coming out of the woodwork, with all kinds of schemes and scams, hoping to find you're vulnerable. Hoping to take a bite out of what you've got."

"I know," she said softly.

Hoping to find you're vulnerable… Those words had hit painfully close to home. She *had* been vulnerable. And she hadn't even known it. Not until Grey Sellers—or whoever the hell he was—had tilted her face and put his lips over hers.

Nothing had changed, she thought bitterly, except that the buffer of being Charlie Beaufort's daughter and one step removed from his money was gone. Now they were *her* millions, and she had been pretty damned naive to think she could escape the merciless fortune hunting she had moved out here to avoid.

She had taken herself out of the public eye, out of society and, she had hoped, out of that particular danger ten years ago. Her dad's death had put her right back in, whether she wanted it or not. Was Grey Sellers simply the first to realize she was fair game? The first to mount an attack?

"If…" Autry began, and then his voice faded. Again she heard the breath he drew before he spoke again. "If something happened to you, Val, what would become of your shares?"

If something happened to you… That wasn't anything she had ever thought about before. Or had reason to. She was only thirty-three years old, for God's sake. But Autry was right; she *was* a very rich woman now. So that was a legitimate question, especially coming from someone with his background.

"My shares would be divided among the other partners," she said, "in proportion to what they already own. It's a pretty standard partnership agreement. Or at least that's what the lawyers said."

"I just wondered," Autry said hesitantly, "since you inherited your dad's shares..."

Although she had known she was named as her father's heir in his will, all she had expected to inherit was the ranch. She had begged him years ago, just after her broken engagement, to arrange for his shares to be divided between the other partners at his death. She had no interest in either the technology that was at the heart of Av-Tech or in the wealth the company had brought him. As far as her own life had been concerned, that had truly been the root of all evil.

Then, when the will was read, she had discovered that her dad had done the one thing she had asked him not to do. He had left his share of the company to her, along with the unwanted responsibilities that went along with it. Like this one.

"I *could* leave them to an heir. Any of the partners can—to their children or their wives. But if any of them... If any of us dies without an heir, then our shares revert to the partnership and would be divided among the others."

"In your will—" Autry began.

"I don't have a will, Autry," Val broke in. "I never needed one before, since I didn't own anything but my horses."

"You do now," he said.

He was right, of course. And despite the partnership agreement, she wasn't sure how long it would take for her shares to be transferred to the other partners if something happened to her. They were all elderly, some of them in ill health, so they needed their assets, even those in the company, to be liquid. If something happened to her, it might be easier for them to get access to her shares if she put that same stipulation that was in the partnership agreement in a will. It was what she had wanted her father to do.

"I'll call the lawyers in the morning," she said. "I'll get them on it as soon as I can, I promise. I don't know why they didn't press me to make a will. I needed to check with them anyway on how their search for someone to manage the company is coming along. Maybe prod them a little."

"That's all well and good, honey, but it wasn't really why I was asking. You were trying to figure out what somebody might have to gain by sending a man out there who isn't…exactly what he seems to be."

"What are you trying to say?" she asked.

"If this guy tries to put a move on you…" Autry began.

A coldness moved into her lower body, exactly where the sweet heat of desire had stirred only a couple of hours ago. Val's mind flashed back to that humid bathroom. To Grey's lips descending to meet hers. To the feel of his hands cupping under her bottom to pull her into contact with his body.

"Or whatever the current terminology is," Autry continued awkwardly. "You know what I mean. I just want you to be aware that if he does something like that, it might not be…exactly what it appears to be."

"You mean the man might be after my money rather than after me? What a shocking idea," Val said. She thought she had controlled her tone remarkably well, considering. Apparently Autry wasn't fooled by her attempt at sarcasm.

"I'm sorry, honey. I know…" Again he hesitated. Since Carmichael was one of the few people aware of why she had called off her wedding ten years ago, she knew he was choosing his words with care. "Look, I'm just trying to do what I think Charlie would want me to. As a friend. His *and* yours. That was just a friendly warning. A word to the wise. I know you're too smart to be taken in by some scumbag after your money."

"Once burned," she said, "twice shy. Isn't that the way it's supposed to work?"

"Val…" Autry said.

"It's okay, Autry. That's all behind me. I never think about it anymore. Or about him. And I promise you I *am* a lot wiser than I was back then."

"Then this guy hasn't tried anything?"

"He's tried some cooking," Val said, deliberately lightening her voice, forbidding the old bitterness, or the new, to show. "And caring for the horses. He hasn't tried getting me into bed, if that's what you're worried about."

"More than forty years in security makes you suspicious," Autry said, his voice indicating his relief. "Pretty ridiculous to suggest that just because there's some mystery about his past, that he would do *that*, I guess."

"Considering…" Val said the word under her breath.

"What was that, sweetie?"

"Nothing. Look, I'll call the lawyers in the morning and get everything taken care of. I don't know why I hadn't thought about a will before. Too much going on, I guess. And I never wanted those shares. I tried to tell Dad that. I thought, after Bart, that he understood."

Autry laughed. "Once Charlie made up his mind, it was pretty hard to tell him anything. Glad you took after your mother in that respect."

It was surprising to realize Autry didn't know she hadn't. She was just like her father. When she made up her mind to something… Except, of course, in the case of Grey Sellers. She didn't want to even think about how gullible she had been in the case of Grey Sellers. *Once burned, twice shy.*

"I'll call you after I talk to the lawyers," she said again.

"You sleep tight, honey," Autry said. "And don't you worry. Everything's under control."

Yeah, right, Val thought as she replaced the receiver. *Everything except me.*

GREY CAME AWAKE with a start, his mouth open and dry, his heart pounding as if it were trying to drive its way out of his chest. He was breathing as if he'd been running.

In the nightmare he had been. Not that it ever did any good. *Dream,* he thought, forcing himself awake. *Just the dream.*

He was sitting straight up in bed, the sheet knotted in both fists. He closed his eyes, willing his breathing to deepen. To even. Willing his racing heart to slow.

There was nothing he could do now to stop what had happened. He was two years too late. All the adrenaline in the world, rushing through his bloodstream until it tore him from an alcohol-induced sleep, couldn't get him there in time. Nothing could change what had happened.

His breathing began to ease. He closed his mouth, licking dry lips. He knew where he was now. On a ranch. Valerie Beaufort's ranch in Colorado. Not there. Not there.

You can't go back, Griff had told him. But then, Griff probably didn't know about nightmares. Because you always go back in nightmares.

He opened his eyes, aware of the hot ache behind them, and was surprised at how dark it was in the bunkhouse. There had been a moon earlier tonight, riding high against the clouds, and the smell of rain had been in the air. He had stood in the open doorway, breathing it in. Trying to get the scent of her out of his nostrils. Trying to get the thought of her out of his head.

His eyes searched the room, looking for the bottle he had held as he had stood there in the moonlight, drinking straight from its mouth and trying to forget what he had done. He had been way out of line to touch Val Beaufort. Apparently there was nothing left now of self-discipline. Nothing of self-control. Nothing at all left of the man Griff Cabot had trained.

Lost again in those regrets, he only gradually became aware of the sound, probably because it had been simply a background to the horror of the dream. But it had been going on since he'd been awake, he realized. Maybe what had pulled him out of sleep.

It was a distant banging, which came at fairly regular intervals. Unlatched shutter blowing in the wind? Barn door? And with that thought came the knowledge of what this noise must be. The black was trying to kick his way out of his stall again.

Grey threw off the sheet and stood up. Too quickly, he realized, feeling the room spin sickeningly off its axis. He sat down on the edge of the bunk and put his head in his hands, breathing through his mouth. After a moment, he opened his eyes.

His jeans were lying on the floor in front of him, right where he had dropped them when he'd stumbled into bed. He bent forward carefully to pick them up, trying not to set off the vertigo. Obviously he hadn't been asleep long enough for the effects of the alcohol to wear off.

Still sitting on the edge of the bunk, he thrust his legs into his pants and, one hand on the bunk, pushed himself slowly into a standing position, relieved to find the room wasn't circling anymore. He pulled his pants up without fastening them.

Then he slipped his bare feet into his boots, refusing to search for his socks in the darkness. His shirt was nowhere in sight. Of course, he could have turned on the light, but just the thought of that bare, dangling bulb made his head hurt. He walked across the wooden floor, fastening the buttons on his jeans as he did. When he opened the door, he was grateful for the wind whipping in through it. Maybe it would clear his head.

It had started to rain, big drops thudding into the loose, dry soil of the yard and pinging like hail against the tin roof of the bunkhouse. The air was electric with the approaching storm, which was what had set off the stallion, of course. No mystery about his antics tonight.

Grey put his hand on the railing beside the three low steps, using it to steady himself, just as he had used the mattress. The world was still slightly distorted by the whiskey he'd consumed, although the feel of the air on his face was helping. As he headed toward the barn, a thread of lightning split the sky, followed seconds later by the distant rumble of thunder. And in the background was the steady thud that had awakened him.

Wind-driven dirt swirled before him. He glanced at the ranch house, which was still dark, its doors and windows securely closed against the coming storm. If the noise the horse was making was enough to drag him from sleep, however, Val should be able to hear it.

He couldn't decide whether he wanted her to or not. He didn't exactly need another encounter with Valerie Beaufort. He hadn't been able to maintain the necessary distance between them when he was stone-cold sober.

He opened the double doors at the front of the barn, and the banging was immediately louder. He waited a few seconds, allowing his eyes to adjust to the darkness of the interior, before he began to walk toward the black's stall.

As he approached, he realized that the noise wasn't coming from there. The top half of the back door of the barn, that Dutch door through which he had first watched

Val without her being aware that he was, had come unlatched.

The wind was catching it and slamming it again and
again against the side of the barn. A few seconds after it
hit, the door would start to drift closed again, drawn back
by unbalanced hinges, only to be caught and slammed
backward by the next gust.

Grey hurried down the aisle between the double rows
of stalls toward the rectangle of lesser darkness made by
the open half of the door. As he passed the black, he
glanced over at the animal. The stallion was moving restlessly, reacting to the impending storm and the noise of
the door. Considering that both of those were going on,
however, Kronus seemed remarkably calm.

Grey grabbed the door the next time it swung inward.
The wind fought to rip it out of his hands, but he pulled
it closed and secured the hasp. He stood a moment in the
resulting quietness, just listening. The rain had increased
to a downpour, pounding noisily onto the roof of the barn.

All the familiar scents of his childhood seemed stronger
in the darkness. The smell of the thirsty earth, drinking in
the moisture. The scent of hay, its normal dryness enriched
to odor by the humidity. Horse smells, compounded of old,
well-oiled leathers and the rich fecundity of the animals
themselves.

He walked over near the black's stall, more as a precaution than because of any real concern. If the banging
door hadn't spooked the stallion, it was unlikely that the
steady sound of the rain would. Or anything else, he
thought.

"You're really a good boy, aren't you?" Grey whispered soothingly. He didn't reach out to touch the black.
He was a stranger and he didn't want to do anything to
set him off. "That's nothing but some wind and rain out
there. Nothing worth getting rattled over, is it."

"Is he all right?"

He turned at the question and found Valerie standing in a narrow opening between the big double doors of the barn. The white of her nightgown was stark against the surrounding darkness, but he couldn't see her face.

"He's fine. The top half of the back door came unlatched. That's what was banging."

She said nothing in response to his explanation. Maybe she was looking toward the door to verify it was properly fastened now. He couldn't tell, because he could see only a ghostly white silhouette. Then, unexpectedly, there was another flash of lightning, the summer kind that lingered, flickering, for a few seconds, illuminating the figure in the doorway.

Valerie was holding something over her head, probably a poncho, judging by the shape. Almost like an X ray, the lightning revealed the outline of her lower body through the thin fabric of her nightgown. And then it was gone, the barn and the sky behind it plunged into darkness again.

The grumbling thunder that followed the lightning was no louder than the sudden rush of blood through Grey's ears. He couldn't hear the rain anymore. It felt as if a vacuum had formed around him. A cone of silence. Blocking sound. Blocking everything but the thought of Valerie Beaufort standing in that door, her gown plastered by the rain to her bare skin. More revealing than if she'd been nude. And far more tantalizing.

"I wonder how that happened," she said, her voice puzzled.

"The wind," Grey said, his mind not occupied by the problem of the errant door. It was filled with other images. With the remembrance of all those sensations from earlier tonight. When her body had been pressed tightly against his. When she had responded to the touch of his lips as if she had just been waiting through the days he'd spent here for him to kiss her.

She moved, stepping into the barn and pulling the doors closed against the driving rain. The darkness seemed complete, but somehow, in spite of it, Grey was aware that she was walking toward him. Or at least coming down the center aisle, maybe headed toward the back door, which meant that she would pass very close to where he was standing. Close enough that if he wanted to, he could reach out and touch her.

Touch her. The words echoed in his brain, and he fought the power of them. Drunk, he told himself. That's where the thought that touching her would be a good idea had come from—from the effects of the alcohol.

This wasn't anything that should be happening between the two of them. She was his employer. And more important, his responsibility, which made her off-limits. Way off-limits. He had almost lost control before. And right now…

Right now, it would be a whole hell of a lot better if he wasn't in such close proximity to the woman he was supposed to be protecting. Of course, *not* being in proximity wasn't exactly the way bodyguarding was supposed to work, he acknowledged.

His eyes must have adjusted to the lack of light, because suddenly he could see her. She materialized out of the darkness, close enough that he could smell her, the faint hint of shampoo evoking the unwanted memories of what had happened in the bathroom.

"He really is all right," she said softly as if she hadn't believed him. "I swear when I heard that noise…" She lowered the poncho, being careful that the plastic didn't rustle.

"I know," Grey said, trying not to breathe. Not to think.

Not about her, at least. "I thought the same thing, but not even the noise the door was making spooked him."

"Do you think somebody might have...done something to set him off?" she asked. "That morning, I mean."

"Like what?"

"I don't know. Hurt him. Given him something. Halley mentioned locoweed."

"Fed him something, you mean?"

He didn't really believe that's what had happened. Stud horses were unstable by nature, and despite what he'd said to the doctor that day, he had pretty much attributed the horse's wildness to that.

"Or drugged him," Val said softly.

She had been thinking about this for a while, Grey realized. The thought that someone might have tampered with her horse hadn't just occurred to her. He wondered why she hadn't mentioned it to him before.

"With what?" Grey asked.

That wasn't something he knew much about, but he supposed there were substances that could make a horse go crazy, just like there were drugs that could make people seem psychotic.

"I don't know. I thought about calling my vet and asking if he knew of anything that might have that effect."

"You really think he might have been deliberately spooked?"

She hesitated before she answered. When she did, it didn't seem to have any bearing on what they'd been talking about.

"Autry Carmichael called back. After you left the house."

"The Autry who *isn't* a boyfriend?"

"Actually, he's head of security at Av-Tech."

"And he suggested someone might have done something to the black?"

"Not really. We didn't talk about that. Not specifically."

He waited, but she didn't seem inclined to go on. After a moment, she laid the poncho carefully on the floor and walked over to the stall. The black reached his head out toward her, and she ran her hand soothingly down his nose.

She was near enough now that the same sweet fragrance of soap and shampoo that had been in the bathroom tonight surrounded Grey. Near enough that he wondered if she could smell the whiskey on his breath. Even if she could, he supposed it was too late to start worrying about what she might think about it. He should have thought about that a couple of hours ago.

"You waiting for me to ask what you *did* talk about?" he said.

She turned her head, looking directly at him for the first time. She was so near he could have put his fingers under her chin again. Near enough that not more than one step separated them. Near enough that if he took that step—

"We talked about you," she said.

He wished he thought that might mean something good, but the tone was all wrong. "What about me?" he asked.

If Carmichael had been checking up on him, Grey knew he wouldn't find much. That had been one of the provisions of his "retirement." The CIA didn't want anyone to be able to connect him with the company or, more specifically, with the External Security Team, which had still been in existence at that time.

"Not much," she said.

"Maybe that's because there isn't much to find."

"That's exactly what Autry said," she said. "That's what made him suspicious—that there's not much there to find. Would you like to explain why?"

"I afraid I don't understand."

Really bad dialogue, Grey thought, even as he said the

words. And not very original. With all his training, he ought to have been able to do better than that clunker.

"I think you do. I think you understand very well. All the things that should be in your records aren't. It's as if you didn't exist before you opened your investigative agency. Which makes me curious as to what you were doing before then."

"Carmichael just didn't know where to look." Grey stalled, trying to think how much he could tell her. Or how little.

"He knows what he's doing," she said, "but the records have all been wiped clean. Professionally," she added for emphasis.

"Carmichael told you that?"

"Don't play games," she said sharply. "Whatever this is all about, you aren't the least bit surprised that there are no records on you. You may be surprised that Autry could determine that, but those are two totally separate issues."

"I don't know what you're talking about," Grey said.

He had realized there really wasn't much he could tell her. Not without breaking the terms of his agreement with the agency. Not that he gave a rat's ass about that, other than the fact that at one time he would never have considered breaking his word.

And once he would never have considered taking a drink while he was on assignment, he reminded himself. Or considered getting involved with a woman he was responsible for protecting. One by one the standards he had once lived by seemed to be slipping from his grasp. And he didn't even know how it had happened.

All he knew was that it seemed to have something to do with the way he had begun to feel about Valerie Beaufort, maybe as early as the morning she'd chased the black on crutches, trying, despite her own injury, to take care of her horse.

"Why are you in hiding?" she asked.

"I'm not in hiding," he said, injecting a thread of amusement into the denial. Acting as if the thought of that were ridiculous. "I run a business. I advertise. My number's in the phone book. You can check all that out with Joe Wallace."

"Or with Beneficial Life. I know. You told me. Except Beneficial Life has nothing on you either, other than Wallace's recommendation. And Wallace seems to have disappeared. So...I'm not exactly sure anymore why you're here, Mr. Sellers."

"I'm here because I'm being paid to do a job—" he began.

"And did that job involve trying to get me into bed?" she asked softly. "Or was that just some sort of...extra compensation you thought up all on your own?"

It took a second for him to understand what she had just asked. Maybe the booze. Maybe the fact that he'd been worrying more about how good this Carmichael might be. It had never crossed his mind that Val might think what had happened between them had anything to do with what her friend had discovered.

"No," he said softly. That was God's truth, of course. The job Joe Wallace had given him had nothing to do with what was between the two of them.

"Was it just because I'm so physically attractive? I'm just so damned irresistible that you just couldn't help yourself?" Her voice was mocking.

There was no right answer. And it was obvious she had already made up her mind.

"There's nothing..." he began, and then knew she wasn't in the mood for explanations. Actually, he wasn't sure he could give her one. The fact that he was so attracted to her had been surprising as hell to him, as well.

"I don't have any hidden agenda where you're concerned," he said instead.

She laughed, the sound softly bitter. "*Everything* with you seems to be hidden. I'm just trying to figure out why. And why you're out here."

"I was hired to protect you," he said.

"Against what?"

"Against...whatever."

"Fortune hunters?" she asked, her voice still amused.

"Not unless they intend to do you harm," he said.

"I think we could probably safely assume they do. Maybe not physical harm. But then, who knows? Money makes people do all kinds of strange things. Does it have that effect on you, Mr. Sellers? Does it make you do all kinds of strange things—like try to take a woman you barely know to bed?"

He didn't answer. Nothing he could say would make any difference to what she was feeling. She had put what Carmichael had told her together with his kiss and drawn her own conclusions.

"I want you off my property in the morning," she said.

The words were clipped, her tone cleared now of any inflection except anger. She began to move away, and he grabbed her wrist. She turned back to face him, her eyes meeting his, and she didn't try to pull free. In the dimness he could see no fear in her face, despite the fact that she was out here alone with a man she obviously didn't trust.

"You didn't hire me," he said. "I don't think you can fire me."

"You hide and watch," she said softly, her voice very cold.

"Beneficial Life—"

"Probably won't be too pleased when I tell them that you've been drinking on the job."

It stopped him, just as she'd intended. "I think they'd

like it even less if I left you alone out here and unprotected," he countered after a moment.

"Don't you think it's interesting that nothing dangerous happened to me until you showed up? I'll bet they would."

"You think *I* did something to the black?" he asked, finally understanding what she had been suggesting earlier.

"I think it's strange that it happened the morning after you show up out here to *protect* me. And to a horse I'd never had a problem with before."

"You think I'm trying to harm you?"

"Not really. If I did, I'd be a fool to have come out here tonight, wouldn't I?" she said. "And I'm not a fool, Mr. Sellers, whatever else I may be."

"What could I possibly have to gain by spooking the black?"

"The opportunity for a little heroism in the face of danger. The chance to insist on nursemaiding me, which put us in close proximity for several days. And as a result, you hoped I'd fall right into your arms. Was that the drill? And for an encore to tonight's performance in the bathroom, a banging door and a meeting in the barn. You knew I'd come when I heard that noise. Were you planning a little midnight roll in the hay? You even seem to have dressed for the part," she accused, her eyes leaving his to consider his bare chest. "I think I saw this one when it first came out. I don't need the rerun."

"What happened tonight—" he began.

"Did you have to get drunk to face the seduction scene? Too bad you couldn't have talked Wallace into taking the bodyguard role. Maybe his stomach is stronger than yours."

"What the hell's the matter with you?" he asked softly.

Despite the bitterness, so blatant it dripped like venom from every word, he hadn't really known what she was talking about until now. Until that last accusation.

"Been there," she said. "Done this. I want you off my property before I wake up in the morning," she said again.

"I'm not after your money," he said. "Neither is Joe Wallace. Beneficial Life hired me, strictly on his say-so. Which isn't all that unusual in my business. There's nothing else going on here."

"And making love to me was all your idea? No ulterior motives in that, of course."

"Some," he said.

There was a small silence.

"Are we finally getting somewhere near the truth, Mr. Sellers? They say confession is good for the soul."

It probably was, but his confessing skills were as rusty as all the others. However this turned out, he owed her the truth about this, at least. Judging by the pain underlying the mockery in her voice, this was a truth she needed to know.

"I'm attracted to you," he said. "That isn't a crime. And that attraction has nothing to do with your money."

She laughed again, and he felt anger surge into his body in a way he hadn't felt in a long time. Maybe because for a long time there hadn't been anything he cared enough about to get angry over. And he didn't quite know why he was so furious now.

"You don't believe that?" he asked.

"Not since I was old enough to know better. I know who—and what—I am. I have no delusions."

"And what are you?"

"I'm a *very* ordinary woman. Ordinary face. Ordinary body. Not someone likely to provoke some kind of instant attraction. Not from someone…like you. You wouldn't look at me twice if you passed me on the street. You know that. And I know it."

The hell of it was, Grey admitted, she was right. He probably wouldn't have. He had tried to explain his attraction to himself. Maybe it was her courage. Her stubbornness. The fact that she didn't give up. Maybe even the vulnerability he had sensed under her very genuine toughness.

"Believe me, I wasn't looking for this to happen," he said.

"I just kind of swept you off your feet," she said mockingly.

He lifted his other hand and cupped the back of her head, pulling her toward him. She didn't resist, but he didn't really give her time. Or warning. He put his mouth over hers, thinking as he did that at least it would shut her up.

He wasn't sure what he was trying to prove by kissing her again. Maybe that she was wrong about him. Or maybe he was simply reacting to the pain that had been mixed up in all that mockery and bitterness.

Her mouth didn't open to his as it had before, however. Without struggling, she merely endured the movement of his lips over hers for a long time. Finally he lifted his head, looking down into her eyes, feeling in the center of his chest the coldness they were projecting.

"Don't be here when I wake up tomorrow," she ordered. "I want you to be nothing but a bad dream, the kind of nightmare that disappears with daylight."

She twisted her wrist, trying to pull it out of his grasp. He was reluctant to let her go with everything unresolved, but he didn't know what else he could say or do to convince her she was wrong. After a second or two, he released her. There were some battles you could win, and some that shouldn't even be fought. This was probably one of the latter.

Because he had had no business falling in love with Valerie Beaufort. It couldn't go anywhere. So what did it matter what she thought about him?

She stood there a moment, her eyes still on his, before she finally turned away, disappearing into the same storm-touched darkness from which she had come.

Don't be here when I wake up tomorrow, she had said. He wouldn't be.

Chapter Seven

Grey had acknowledged that Wallace would still be asleep, even as he had punched the agent's home number into the cellular phone. And he suspected Joe wouldn't be any too happy to be getting this particular call, not at any time of the day, but especially before dawn. He had been right in both suppositions.

After this fiasco, however, he wouldn't be getting any more business from Joe Wallace anyway. All it would take would be one conversation between the insurance agent and Val Beaufort, and that would pretty much be a done deal.

"Because she kicked me out," Grey said in response to Joe's bewildered question. He had delivered the news that Wallace needed to round up a replacement without offering any explanation as to why, but he should have known the agent wouldn't let it go at that. "I'll hang around until you get somebody else out here, but you better make it quick."

"Who am I going to get at…" There was a pause while Wallace checked the time. "At five frigging o'clock in the morning? What the hell do you think—"

"The security system should be installed in a day or two." Grey interrupted the stream of profanities. "Until then get the security guard from the grocery store. Hire a rent-a-cop. Or come baby-sit Ms. Beaufort yourself. I don't give a damn how you manage it. Just get somebody out here and do it now.''

"What'd you do to make her kick you off the place?''

"I pissed the lady off. It wasn't all that hard. Ms. Beaufort's got a few hang-ups.''

Grey regretted the words as soon as he said them. They felt like a betrayal, although technically, he supposed they were true. Of course, Grey recognized that he had a few hang-ups as well. He just wasn't announcing his to Joe Wallace.

"Hang-ups like what?'' Joe asked, sounding more interested.

"Like thinking somebody's after her money,'' Grey said.

That was enough of an explanation. All he was prepared to give, in any case. He knew Wallace would eventually get an earful from Val about the rest.

"Considering how much of it there is,'' Joe said finally, "she probably ain't wrong about that.''

"Get somebody,'' Grey ordered again.

"You're still out there, aren't you? Hell, you haven't gone off and left her alone, have you?'' Joe said, sounding disturbed.

"I'm on a ridge looking down on the ranch. She told me to get off her property, and I did. I'll hang around a while, but give it another couple of hours, when the sun gets good and high, and it's going to be mighty uncomfortable up here.''

"I can't just manufacture somebody to take your place. You gotta give me a little time.''

"That's exactly what I'm giving you,'' Grey said. "A *little* time. You want her protected, you get your ass in gear and find somebody before my nose gets sunburned.''

He punched the button on the cell phone, cutting off

Wallace's protests. He knew he was putting the agent in a bad position, but he couldn't help it. Joe had said there was nothing to this assignment. If he really believed that, he shouldn't have any trouble finding someone to take over.

And what if Joe's wrong? he thought. After all, Valerie Beaufort *was* an extremely rich woman. But just because she was rich, he told himself, didn't mean she was in danger. The possibility of somebody kidnapping her for ransom was, as Wallace had suggested, highly unlikely. And Grey didn't know any reason why anyone would want to hurt her.

All Wallace needed was a warm body to fulfill the terms of the Beneficial Life policy and to cover his ass. Surely he could find somebody who could fill that bill. And until he did...

Grey lifted his binoculars and focused them on the ranch below. In the lemon-pale light of the rising sun, everything looked as peaceful as a picture postcard. The lights hadn't come on in the house, so he assumed Val was still asleep.

He leaned back against the rock behind him, laying the binoculars in his lap. He had stopped at this spot on the day he'd first driven out here, figuring from the map that this ridge would look down on the Beaufort place. Climbing down here then had been a lot easier than doing it in the dark a few minutes ago.

The narrow ledge where he was sitting was not only a good vantage point for looking down on the valley below. He had found it was a pretty good place for thinking as well. For clearing his head. He wished the aspirin he'd fished out of the glove compartment of the truck would kick in, but despite what he'd told Joe, thanks to the overhang above him, he was out of the sun. Out of sight. And out of excuses.

He had blown it. He'd had a chance to get enough

money to pay his bills and to keep his agency afloat. And he'd blown it because he couldn't keep his hands off the woman. A woman he had been hired to protect. He closed his eyes against the throb in his head, thinking about the past few days. Thinking about her. Thinking about all the ways he'd screwed up.

And the whole time, in the back of his head, like a toothache, was what Val had said about the stallion. Could somebody have deliberately set him off? And if so, for what purpose? If anyone wanted to hurt Val, that seemed a roundabout way to go about it. But still…

Without giving himself time to think of all the reasons he shouldn't, he picked up the cellular phone again and punched in another number. It was one he had never used before. One that had been left on his answering machine a while back, maybe as much as six or seven months ago.

It was the number of a man who believed he owed Grey Sellers something. A man who always paid his debts. As he listened to the distant ringing Grey thought briefly about the time difference between his location and the one he was calling. He knew it would still be early in the East, but he also knew it wouldn't matter how early he called. Not to Lucas Hawkins.

Apparently he was right. When Hawk answered, his voice held none of the sleepy irritation that had been in Joe Wallace's. His tone was alert, and the single word he said when he picked up was crisply articulated. "Hawkins."

Grey's heart faltered at the familiar inflection, and the years fell away in a rush. It felt like only yesterday when they had worked together.

"You left this number on my machine," Grey said.

He wasn't sure he could control his voice if he ventured anything more personal. There was a small silence, lasting less than three or four heartbeats.

"I'm glad you finally decided to use it," Hawk said.

"It's not what you think," Grey said. He didn't want there to be any misconceptions about why he'd called. "I need some information. On a couple of things, actually."

"Let me get something to write on."

Grey had known making his request would be this easy. No questions about where he was or why he needed the information he was asking for. No questions at all.

"Okay." Hawk's voice came back on the line. "Go ahead."

"If you wanted to make a horse go loco, what drug would you use and how would you administer it?"

"Okay."

Grey waited, knowing Hawk was writing everything down.

"And the second?" Hawk asked after a few seconds.

"Everything you can find on a company called Av-Tech. Missile and satellite technology. I'm not sure what else."

"Got it," Hawk said. "Anything specific?"

Grey tried to think of anything that might be relevant to someone targeting Val. "Corporate structure. Exactly what they do and for whom. Rumor. Anything that looks suspicious. Anything that sends up any kind of red flags to you."

Again there was silence on the other end, and through it came the sound of a baby crying. Grey pressed the phone closer to his ear, wondering if he were picking up another signal. This technology was not the most secure form of communication, of course, but it was all that was available to him right now.

"Sorry about the noise," Hawk said, sounding amused.

"That sounds like a baby."

"It is. Mine, as a matter of fact."

"Did you say...your baby?" Grey asked.

''Greyson Cabot Hawkins. Age two months. I think he's hungry, but I'm not too good at interpreting the signals yet.''

Greyson Cabot Hawkins. Grey's throat tightened, and he waited a moment before he said, ''You didn't have to do that.''

Hawk laughed. At least, Grey thought that's what the sound was. He couldn't ever remember hearing Hawk laugh before.

''If it hadn't been for you, I wouldn't be around to be worrying about picking out names for my son. I thought it was the least I could do.''

There was, quite literally, nothing he could say to that, Grey thought. Nothing he could get out past the knot that seemed to be blocking his throat. And he wondered why it had taken him so long to make this call. Even as he did, however, he admitted that if Val hadn't been involved, possibly in danger, he would never have punched in Hawk's number.

''You still working with Griff?'' he asked instead of commenting on Hawk's unwanted expression of gratitude. Instead of saying any of the things he was feeling.

''Griff and Jordan. And there are still openings on the staff,'' Hawk said, his voice lightened, almost amused again.

''Anybody else I know sign on?''

''A couple of people. We're being selective.''

''Not very,'' Grey said. After all, they had asked him.

That had been the purpose of Hawk's original phone call, the one where he had left this number. Hawk had called to tell him about the Phoenix Brotherhood, the protective agency three of Grey's fellow ex-CIA agents had formed. And to invite Grey to join them, in spite of what had happened on the last mission he and Hawk had undertaken for the now-defunct External Security Team.

Grey had never responded to that message because he had known he would no longer fit in. Other members of the team could go back to work for Griff, but he didn't belong with those men anymore. And what had happened last night only reinforced that knowledge.

After today's realization that he had destroyed any chance he had to keep his own agency solvent, it should have been comforting to have a repeated offer of employment. It wasn't. At least, not this one.

He suspected that Griff, and probably the others, knew everything there was to know about what he'd been doing since he had left the team. *Everything*. Even the things he wouldn't want any of them to know. That was the kind of person Cabot was, however. He would have been keeping tabs on Grey and on all the former members of his team as well. They were his people, men he had trained, and Griff would still feel a sense of responsibility for each one of them.

And in his case, Grey knew, the offer of a job with the new agency would be nothing more than charity. Despite everything, he hadn't quite reached the point of being willing to accept that, not even from Griff.

"If you change your mind…" Hawk said.

"I won't, but thanks."

Although neither of them could ever have been classified as garrulous, never before had a lull in their conversation been uncomfortable. This one was.

"Where can I reach you when I have something on these?" Hawk asked finally.

Grey had no idea where he'd be during the next few days. Here on this ridge, he supposed, unless Wallace got his act together and got someone else out here. He gave Hawk the cell phone number as well as the number at his office.

"I know it's asking a lot, but the sooner you can get back to me on those, the better," Grey said.

"You got it," Hawk agreed.

"And Hawk... Thanks."

"Thank me if I find out what you need."

"I didn't mean about this. I meant...about him."

There was another long pause, and surprisingly, despite the obvious and unaccustomed emotion that had been in Grey's voice, this one wasn't strained.

"I figure a kid needs a good start in life. I couldn't think of a better one to give him," Hawk said. "And don't worry. I'm not expecting a return of the favor. I wouldn't stick anybody with the name Lucas."

Grey laughed.

"Haven't heard that in a while," Hawk said.

There was another small silence. "So what's she like?" Grey asked, although he hadn't intended to.

The real conversation was over, the purpose for the call, and he and Hawk had never engaged in social chitchat. Of course, he had never been forced to picture Lucas Hawkins in the midst of domestic bliss before. With a *baby,* for God's sake.

"She's got guts," Hawk said softly.

"First thing you noticed?" Grey asked, grinning.

"Not exactly." There was an answering amusement in Hawk's voice. "But...in the end, it was what was important. More important than the other stuff, I guess."

"I'd like to meet the woman who's willing to put up with you," Grey said, and then knew saying that was a mistake. It was too personal and sounded as if he were eager to reconnect.

"That could be arranged," Hawk said.

"Probably not in this lifetime," Grey said abruptly. "Call me when you have something. Or even if you turn up nothing. I guess I need to know that as well."

"You got it. You mind if I tell Griff I talked to you?"

Grey thought about that. Hell, since he was asking for information, maybe Griff would think he was still doing something valuable, which ought to be a comfort.

"Tell him I'm glad he made it back," he said.

When the CIA had destroyed the elite External Security Team, they had also "destroyed" the man who had created it. Like the mythical phoenix, however, Griff Cabot had risen from the ashes of that conflagration and had begun to pull together the agents he had trained to form a new organization with a new mission—to protect those who had need of the skills they had perfected with the CIA. And Grey wished he could be a part of it, but those days were behind him. If he'd had any doubt about that, last night would have taken care of it.

"I'll tell him," Hawk said softly.

"Thanks," Grey said, his throat closing over the single word. Almost savagely he pushed the off button on the phone and put it down on the ground beside him.

He lifted the binoculars to his eyes again, scanning the area below. As he did, Valerie came down the steps of the front porch, holding on to the railing. He kept the glasses focused on her as she crossed the yard, heading toward the barn.

She didn't even glance over to where his truck had been parked, apparently assuming that when she gave an order, it would be carried out. It had been, but on his terms, of course. And now all he had to do was wait for whoever Joe Wallace hired to take his place. Then he'd be out of Valerie Beaufort's life. Which would, without a doubt, be the best thing for both of them.

HE HAD SUGGESTED getting the security guard at the grocery store, but he hadn't really thought Joe would take him seriously. The guy was wearing a uniform, for God's sake, he thought unbelievingly. One of those brown rent-a-cop things.

Grey watched as the new bodyguard shook hands with Val. He was short and stocky, with a belly that hung over the front of his belt. Gray-haired and grandfatherly. At least he was wearing a gun. Grey focused the binoculars on the weapon and, although he couldn't tell much about it from this distance, the size of the holster it rested in was reassuring.

When he raised the glasses again, bringing the two of them into view, Val was pointing toward the barn, probably directing her new bodyguard to the bunkhouse behind it. He wondered briefly what she was thinking. If she had any doubts or regrets about kicking him out last night. *And why should she? You proved you weren't capable of professional behavior.*

As a result, he had gotten fired. So he couldn't quite figure out why he was still out here, baking in the noon heat. He'd done everything he could do in this situation to make things right. Valerie Beaufort now had a new bodyguard. He was officially unemployed. And it was past time to move on.

He focused the glasses on her face one last time, freeze-framing the image in his mind before she turned and began to lead the way toward the bunkhouse. Her limp was far more pronounced than it had been the first day he'd met her.

And as he watched her walk away, a frisson of emotion again moved inside him. This time he knew what it was, however, and that it had absolutely nothing to do with pity.

IT WAS ALMOST MIDNIGHT. Everything he owned had already been packed into the two suitcases and the suit bag that were now in the back of the pickup. He had almost finished cleaning out his office, not that there was all that much there to begin with. Especially when he considered that he had been here for several months. More than a year, he realized in surprise.

He set the file on the last of the cases he'd handled for Joe on top of the stack on the corner of his desk. He planned to drop them off at Wallace's office as he left town in the morning.

Emptying the drawers of his filing cabinets was the last of the tasks he had set for himself after he'd gotten back into town. He'd played with the books before he'd done that, trying to see what, if anything, was left of the retainer he'd been given. He figured Beneficial Life had a right to ask for a partial refund, since he'd lasted on the job less than a week.

He took a last look around the room before he sat down and opened the folder where he'd jotted down the original notes on the Beaufort case. He had done that as soon as Joe left the office that day. There wasn't much information there, of course.

He picked up the pen and started to write out the resolution of the case, something he always did before he closed a file. Then his hand hesitated, hovering above the few sentences he'd written that first day. He had no idea what to write on this one. Thrown off the case because of inappropriate and unprofessional conduct? He couldn't argue with the accuracy of that statement. No one would.

For some reason, however, he didn't write it. He laid the pen back on the desk instead and closed the file without making any notation. Joe could do whatever he wanted with it, he thought, stacking the folder again on top of the others.

When the phone rang, he did a quick mental rundown of who it might be. Wallace maybe, who might have seen the lights on in his office on his way home? Hawk? Or...

Except she didn't have this number, of course. And even

if she did, he knew she wouldn't be calling him. That was nothing but wishful thinking. He picked up on the second ring, expecting to hear Joe's voice, maybe still angry about this morning. It was Hawk instead.

"I've got part of what you wanted," he said.

Av-Tech, Grey thought. It wouldn't have taken Hawk's contacts in the agency long to zero in on the few things he'd asked about Beaufort's company. He probably could have found them out himself, and he should have, he knew, even before he'd gone out there. He would have if he'd been doing the job right. If he hadn't been so damn eager to believe Joe's reassurances that there was nothing to this one.

"Okay," he said, picking up the pen he'd just put down. One-handed, he opened the Beaufort folder.

"Actually there are several drugs that might do what you described. Most of them would work faster if they were injected. A couple could be mixed into a horse's food, but it would be impossible to predict how long it would take for them to get into his system and make him react. All kinds of things factor into that—climate, condition, how much he'd ingested."

"So the surest route, especially if you wanted to make certain the horse reacted in that way at a particular time, would be to inject one of the others into a vein."

"That's about the size of it. You want the names?"

"I'm more interested in effect."

"Is this in reference to something that's already occurred?"

"I just needed to know if there was something that could have been given to a horse to make him spook. Anything on Av-Tech?"

"Griff's working on that. The name triggered something with him, some association, but he couldn't remember what. He wanted to check it out. He's still got contacts in the agency. I'm pretty much persona non grata there. Actually, I think that should be just non persona," Hawk said, sounding amused again.

Grey wished Hawk hadn't gotten Griff involved, but he knew that if anybody could uncover anything that wasn't open and aboveboard about Val's company, it would be his former boss.

"I know the feeling," he said aloud. "Whoever wiped my records apparently did it with a heavy hand."

"That seems to be the only kind they employ these days. Especially where we're concerned. I'll let you know when I hear from Griff."

"Thanks," Grey said, and heard the connection broken.

He put the phone back in its cradle, looking at the information he'd jotted down as he'd talked. Now he knew there were at least a couple of substances that could spook a horse. Something that would have to have been administered directly if they wanted to time the drug to take effect just when Val was coming out of the house that morning. Which meant that whoever had done this would have to be familiar with the routine on the ranch—at least to have been watching long enough to know what time Val usually started work. Maybe watching from a vantage spot like the one he had chosen this morning? There were plenty of those on the ridges that looked down on that isolated valley.

If someone had even given the horse something in the first place. Which was a pretty big if. That meant that whoever had done it would have to have been on the ranch that night, with no way to explain their presence if they'd been caught. And there was still the problem of figuring out what someone might have to gain by doing something to the stallion to make him go loco. Grey put the pen down, looking across the room at the darkened windows.

He was beginning to feel like one of those conspiracy nuts, looking for bad guys in everything.

Any threat the stallion's behavior represented had been pretty indirect. And his antics might just as easily be attributed to the nature of the animal as to deliberate tampering. Which left Grey right back where he had started.

Without anything to go on but an uneasy feeling in the pit of his stomach. A feeling that things he should be aware of were happening while he had been packing, shuffling folders and doing the math on his nearly nonexistent bank account.

While Val…

He took a breath, feeling the anxiety build at the thought. While Val was sleeping out at that lonely, isolated ranch, being watched over by the grocery store's security guard.

The guy had been wearing a gun, Grey told himself. Even so, he had looked as if he might be a little past using it. Using it against what? he wondered, irritated with himself. Shadows? Horses? Conspiracy theories? Because that was all he had here.

That and an incredibly strong intuition that while he was sitting at this desk, something was happening out there. Something important. Something dangerous. And whatever it was, in his gut he knew that Joe's rent-a-cop would not be prepared for it. Or capable of dealing with it when it came.

Grey was the one who was supposed to be protecting Val. And he wasn't. Instead, he had left her virtually alone out there, right in the middle of whatever the hell his gut was telling him was going on. And if he didn't do something about it, he was going to have another ghost to live with. And he knew this failure would be one he wouldn't be able to survive.

Chapter Eight

Despite the twisting roads, in less than two hours Grey was again standing in the darkness on the ledge overlooking the Beaufort ranch. In the strange green light provided by the starlight scope he held to his eye, the scene below seemed as peaceful as it had at dawn yesterday morning.

In spite of that serenity, his gut was still telling him something was wrong. Something he should have figured out by now. And if there was anything Grey had learned in his years with the CIA, it was to listen to that nagging instinct.

He had fought the urge to drive his pickup down to the bottom of the ridge and walk the rest of the way onto the Beaufort ranch. Not a smart move, he had told himself, not considering that it was the middle of the night and that he knew both the security guard and Val were armed. And there was no quicker way to get shot than to be caught sneaking onto someone else's property in the dead of night. Especially when you no longer had any right to be there.

He had stopped up here instead, hoping that simply by looking the situation over, he could ease the apprehension that had been strong enough to make him lock up his office and start on this nightmare journey. He had driven at speeds very much in excess of those demanded by the treacherous mountain roads, steering the battered truck through the hairpin turns and loops almost by memory. Or instinct.

And apparently it had been a wild-goose chase, he thought, sweeping the scope again across the tranquil scene below. He supposed he should be glad of that, despite the strength of the premonition that had brought him back to the ranch. He would spend the night up here, and then—

The movement of the glass across that eerily lit landscape below hesitated. Holding his breath, Grey brought the scope back to focus on whatever he had seen in the shadows between the barn and the bunkhouse.

Damn it, he thought, slowly scanning the area again. *Damn it.* Whatever he had seen wasn't there now. And that was the only part of the ranch so heavily in shadow that there wasn't illumination enough, not even with the night vision device he was using, to identify what he had seen.

He wasn't even sure now what had attracted his attention. A lighter shape among the shadows? Movement? If it had been, out here it could be almost anything. Coyote. A mountain lion. Or some other, far more dangerous two-legged predator.

He carefully swept the yard with the scope again, but there was nothing moving. There was only one way to find out what, if anything, was going on. Not by standing up here, of course. The only way to know for sure would be to go down and do some prowling of his own.

Not real smart, he thought again, but the knowledge that what he was about to do would be dangerous wasn't enough to stop him from climbing up off the ledge that had been his vantage point and getting back into the pickup. Val was down there. And something was moving around in the darkness.

What he was about to do was probably *worse* than stupid, he admitted. Even as his mind acknowledged that, however, his hand released the parking brake. The truck, its engine off, began to glide down the road to the ranch below.

SILENT AS A TOMB, Grey thought, making his way from shadow to shadow, avoiding the patches of moonlight. Despite what he thought he had seen from the ledge, nothing was moving out here now. Nothing that he could see.

He could occasionally hear his own footsteps crunching over the small rocks that dotted the yard, but that was the only sound. Even the air itself was still as death, a sharp contrast to the turbulence of last night's storm.

He had left the starlight scope in the truck, wanting his hands unencumbered with anything other than his weapon. He couldn't remember the last time he'd held the reassuringly heavy weight of the Glock. It fit into his palm, however, with the familiarity of a friend's handshake. Holding it again was as comfortable as listening to Hawk's deep voice on the phone.

He was moving now around the side of the house, the side away from the barn. He would check out the back of the house itself, and then head toward the shadowed area between the bunkhouse and the barn, where he had seen whatever it was.

Not that he expected to find anything. With the climb back up the ridge, clambering awkwardly over the rocks in the darkness, then the silent descent, and the walk to the ranch from the main road where he had left the pickup, it had taken him at least fifteen minutes to reach this point. Whatever he had seen from the ledge above was almost certain to be gone.

Despite the stillness, however, despite not seeing anything that could possibly be construed as being out of the ordinary, his uneasiness was stronger than it had ever been, his instincts all screaming a warning. As a result, he was moving as if he were crossing a field he knew had been mined or as if walking some dense jungle trail, surrounded by an unseen enemy.

He had rounded the corner of the house and was carefully skirting along the back porch where the chest-type freezer sat. He glanced toward the house and knew immediately something wasn't right. It took a couple of seconds, however, for him to realize what it was. The screen door, which Valerie always kept latched, was wide open, pushed against the wall.

The back door itself, however, gleaming palely in the moonlight, appeared to be closed. And locked? he wondered. Maybe the screen standing open wasn't much, but given what he had been feeling, it was enough to set off alarms.

He stepped on the first of the three low steps, intending to try the door and make sure it was secured. A warped board creaked softly under his foot. Grimacing, he lifted his boot off the bottom step, putting it on the second one instead.

As he shifted his weight from that leg to step up on the porch, out of the corner of his eye he caught a movement at the other side of the house. He had the impression that someone had been there, briefly visible before they disappeared. It had been nothing more than a fleeting image, the kind whose reality you questioned, especially in the darkness. A shape. Substance. Maybe even a color. The sensation of one, anyway.

He analyzed all that in a split second. The same second it took for him to dive into the shadows beside the freezer, putting its bulk between him and the far side of the porch where he had seen the figure.

Dark clothes. Brown. The rent-a-cop. The chain of ideas

had followed one another like waves to shore, luckily preventing him from squeezing off a shot. As soon as he'd made that very tentative identification, he had opted instead to get himself out of the line of fire. He'd be just as dead if he got shot by one of the good guys. Every bit as dead, he told himself, getting as much of his body out of sight behind the freezer as he could.

He resisted the urge to ease up and take another look, despite his anxiety about the woman who was asleep inside the house. He admitted, however, that that anxiety had just gotten a big dose of adrenaline.

Apparently, though, he hadn't been giving Joe's rent-a-cop enough credit. The guy seemed to be out here making rounds, checking things out. Grey had done that himself a few times when this had been his job. He, too, had checked out the still and silent yard in the moonlight. Not because he'd heard anything suspicious or had had any reason to think there was something going on out here. Simply because he hadn't been able to sleep. And the reason he hadn't didn't have much to do with security.

He wondered where the rent-a-cop had gone. Maybe nowhere. Maybe he was just waiting out of sight on the other side of the house. Waiting for Grey to make himself visible so he could get off a shot. Or maybe he had gone back to the bunkhouse to place a call to the sheriff's department. He probably had a cell phone out there. Everybody did these days. Grey thought about calling out to him. Identifying himself. What did he have to lose, now that he'd been spotted?

And then he answered his own question. Sneaking back onto the Beaufort ranch in the middle of the night would make everyone suspicious. And he'd play hell coming up with a valid excuse for being out here. He couldn't see himself admitting to the real reason he had come. *My gut told me Val was in trouble.*

He also couldn't see himself crouching behind the freezer until morning. Standoff, he thought, a little amused at his predicament. Two good guys playing cops and robbers in the moonlight with a couple of very real guns. Grey couldn't shoot the rent-a-cop, not even to protect himself. The guard, however, wouldn't be operating under any such restrictions.

To him, Grey was simply an intruder. Someone who shouldn't be here. The guy had either gone to call for help or was waiting on the other side of the house, hoping Grey would move so he could put a bullet into him. And now that Grey knew the security guard was doing his job and that his movement was probably what Grey had seen from the top of the ridge, the best bet seemed to be to get the hell out of here before he got himself shot.

He wondered what Val would think about finding his body sprawled on her porch come daylight. What Joe Wallace would think. Both would probably imagine he'd been up to no good, especially when Val told everyone what her friend at Av-Tech had discovered about Grey's past. His lack of any past, he amended.

He eased noiselessly to the front edge of the freezer. The metal felt cold as his shoulder brushed against it. He closed his eyes for a few seconds, preparing mentally for what he was about to do. When he opened them, he looked out once more on the tranquillity of the sleeping ranch. Then he leaned forward just enough to peek around the freezer, looking over to where he had seen the dark figure.

There was certainly nothing there now. No noise. And no reaction to the part of his body that he had exposed in order to take a look. He turned slightly, allowing his right shoulder and then his arm and finally the hand that held his weapon to edge past the freezer. Still nothing. No sound. No movement.

In a crouch, he duckwalked one step, putting his whole

body in line with the front of the appliance. Nothing. He took another step, forward this time. And then another, bent almost double and trying to move noiselessly on the balls of his feet.

A board creaked under his weight and he froze, waiting breathlessly through seemingly endless seconds for some response. There was no reaction.

It was not until he reached the other side of the freezer that he acknowledged why he was here. The smart thing to do would have been to back off the porch and disappear in the direction of his truck. Grey hadn't done that. And he knew why.

It was because of that damn screen. Maybe he had interrupted the guard in the middle of checking the back door. Or maybe the guy had seen the screen and been bothered by it being out of position, just as Grey had.

In any case, Grey knew why he wasn't hightailing it right now through the darkness toward his truck. He wanted to turn the knob of Valerie Beaufort's back door and feel the lock hold as he tried to push it open. He needed to know that the house was secure, rent-a-guard on patrol or not.

He listened again, trying to sense if anyone was on the other side of the porch. Using intuition. Listening to his instincts. There was only silence. No breathing. No reaction to the subtle sounds of his own movement. *Because there was nobody there,* he told himself.

Without allowing himself time to stop and think about what he was about to do, he stood up, taking one giant step to get around the corner of the freezer and then pressing his body against the wall of the house in relief. Then, thankful to be hidden again by the shadows, he waited. A minute. Maybe two. Slowly he reached out to the side, his fingers closing around the knob of the door. It turned under them, the door opening inward.

Grey shut his eyes again, dealing with the frightening knowledge that whatever was going on, the house where Val slept had been vulnerable. And, therefore, so was she.

There was no longer any question in his mind about leaving. Instead, he inched sideways, nearer the door, and then slipped inside the house. It was darker in the kitchen than it had been on the porch. He was out of the moonlight in here. And, for the moment at least, out of the line of fire.

He caught the edge of the door and eased it closed behind him, trying not to make any noise. He didn't relish being shot by Val's Smith & Wesson any more than he did by whatever the security guard was carrying. With the hand that wasn't holding his own weapon, he reached up to turn the night latch.

As he did, he noticed there was a dark smear on the door, almost at eye level. Exactly where he had grasped the edge to push it shut. Something left on its white paint by his hand? He held his palm out before him in the darkness, as if he could see it. He rubbed his thumb over the tips of his fingers and found moisture. Something sticky. And dark.

It took half a heartbeat before he recognized what it was. There was blood on his fingers, and the only thing he could remember touching with that hand was the doorknob outside.

The surge of fear was so powerful it almost made him light-headed. Nauseated. The only thing he could think of was Val. The fact that he had left her here unprotected. Despite what every one of his well-honed instincts had been screaming for the past twenty-four hours.

Maybe the shape he had seen on the other side of the porch didn't have anything to do with security. After all, there were no lights anywhere. Wouldn't the guard have left a light burning in the bunkhouse if he were out doing a security check? Especially if he were doing it without a flashlight.

He rubbed his bloody fingers on the leg of his jeans. Even as he did, he was turning, beginning to hurry across the kitchen, no longer bothering with stealth. No longer worrying about the sound his boots made on the tile floor.

Before he made it halfway across the room, the window over the sink exploded inward, sending shards of glass flying toward him. Some of them hit, stinging his exposed skin. He was aware of those, it seemed, even before he heard the sound of the shot. By the time he had, he was down, crawling across the splinters of glass on his hands and knees, headed for the hallway that led to the bedrooms.

He had no idea how close the bullet had come. No idea if it had been fired into the room at random or if his moving shape, perhaps blacker than the others in the dark kitchen, could have been visible through the window. And at this point, he didn't much care. He made it across the kitchen and into the hall before the lamp in Valerie Beaufort's bedroom came on.

"Get down!"

He yelled the warning as soon as he saw the light. He scrambled up off all fours, boots sliding on the worn wooden floors as he tried to get traction to run. The second shot struck another pane of glass, in Val's room from the sound. Grey was there before the echo had died away.

At least she had obeyed him, whether she'd recognized his voice or simply the wisdom of the advice. She was huddled on the floor beside the bed. The Smith & Wesson she had told him about was held out in both hands, pointed toward the doorway he was coming through. He had time to see that her eyes were wide in the pale oval of her face.

"Don't move," he warned, not even thinking about the threat represented by the gun she held. "And close your eyes."

He raised his own weapon and blew the delicate china bedside lamp to smithereens. A shot answered his, coming from outside and shattering another a pane of glass in the mullioned windows. Temporarily blinded by the sudden plunge back into darkness, Grey trained his weapon toward the sound.

As his eyes adjusted, the windows floated back into view, thin sheer curtains billowing toward him in the breeze coming in through their shattered panes. He could see nothing beyond them. No shape looking in. No gun barrel sticking through.

He pulled his gaze away from them long enough to find Val. She had one arm up, elbow bent, forming a shield between her and the windows. In the moonlight he could see broken glass sprinkled in the darkness of her hair. It sparkled like diamonds in some macabre tiara.

Not her blood on the door, he told himself, saying a silent prayer of thanks and finally remembering to draw breath into his aching lungs. He tore his gaze away from Val and back to the windows. In the silence, he listened to his own heart pounding through the veins in his temple. It was beginning to slow, however, now that he knew she was alive and unhurt.

Not Val's blood, he told himself again, savoring the realization. Putting an end to the horror he had been living with since his fingers had come away from the door frame covered with blood. And if it wasn't Val's...

"Mr. Davis," she said softly. "That's Mr. Davis out there."

"The guard?" Grey questioned. "That's his name?"

"Davis. Harold Davis," she said.

Grey nodded, although he knew she probably couldn't see him because he was much farther from the moonlight that was filtering in through the windows than she was. He began to ease toward them, keeping as low as he could.

He was aware that when he moved, Valerie put both hands around the grip of her gun again. The dark eye of its muzzle trailed him, following his progress across the room. He couldn't blame her, he supposed, although it should be clear by now that the real threat was outside.

Because he also knew that she had to be wrong about who was out there. If it were Davis, why would he shoot into her bedroom? He had to know that when he shot out the window in the kitchen, the noise would wake Valerie. She would be the one who had turned on a light. Not an invader. So it didn't make sense for her own bodyguard to shoot into her room.

Grey might buy this was Davis if the guy were trying to shoot his way in through the back door. But not for him to fire in here. Not for him to shoot blindly into Val's bedroom, the way those two shots had been fired.

"What are you going to do?" she whispered.

"See if I can see anything," Grey said.

He pulled up, hand on the sill of the window, his body aligned to the side of it. Without exposing his head, he peered through the slit between the curtains and the frame.

His view was extremely limited. Side yard, looking toward the barn. There was nothing moving in the moonlight. Grey crawled to the other side of the windows, careful to keep below them, out of sight of whoever was out there. Then he employed the same care to look across the yard in the other direction.

"Let me call him," Val said. "Tell him that you're a friend."

She was beside him now, holding her gun in one hand. Just as he made that realization, she moved, raising her head as if she intended to look out the window.

With a sweep of his arm at chest level, Grey knocked her backward and threw himself on top of her just as another pane exploded. He held her, his body over hers, as the glass showered down around them. And he continued to hold her as silence settled over them and the ranch.

Finally she lifted her head until her face was almost aligned with his. He could smell the subtle fragrance of her hair. Could feel it brush against his cheek, the tangled strands like silk.

"That's not Davis," he whispered.

"How can you know that?"

"Because *he* wouldn't be firing into your room."

After a second or two, he glanced over his shoulder at the windows. There was still nothing visible there. Reassured, he turned back and met her eyes.

"Then where is he?" Val asked. "If he heard the shots…"

Her voice faded. Even in the darkness she could probably read enough from his expression to know what he thought, although he hadn't put it into words. There had been blood on the doorknob. Not Val's, but somebody's.

"What do we do?" she asked.

"Where's your phone?"

"Bedside table."

He pushed himself up carefully. The hand that held the Glock rested on the floor, propping him up. With the other he reached behind him, feeling among the shards of glass and broken porcelain that littered the tabletop. He brought the telephone receiver down to where he was lying on top of her, putting it up to his ear to be sure. Just as he had suspected, the phone was dead.

"Cell phone?" he asked.

"In my purse. In the den, maybe. I'm not sure."

He nodded, trying to think. They had two guns between them. And they were safe here. For now, at least. He just didn't like not knowing what was going on out there. Didn't like not knowing where—or who—the enemy was.

And he especially didn't like not knowing what the guy was doing now, out there in the darkness.

"Why did you come back?" Val asked.

He eased away from her, sitting up and thinking about how to answer that question. "I felt like something was wrong."

"You *felt like?*" She sat up, leaning back against the bed.

Everything up until that first shot tonight had been nothing but feelings. Instinct. Now, however...

"I felt like someone was trying to hurt you," he said.

"Why would anyone want to hurt me?" she asked.

"Maybe...even more than that."

He looked over his shoulder at the windows. She touched his chin, turning his face toward hers.

"Someone's trying to kill me? Is that what you think? You think whoever is out there is trying to kill me?" she demanded.

He nodded and could see her eyes widen as the implication sank in.

"But...why?"

"Somehow, I'd be willing to bet it has something to do with the company you just inherited," he said, the sarcasm clear.

Slowly she shook her head. "The people who would benefit from...my death are people I *know* wouldn't be doing this," she said, looking up at the broken windows before she met his eyes again. "They're...like my family."

He laughed, the sound low and caustic. "You don't think family members kill each other for that much money? Nobody's that innocent. You know better than that."

She did, of course. At least, she didn't deny it. "Then why didn't they try to kill my father?"

He had already been thinking about that one. And after all, her father *was* dead.

"No," she said forcefully, rejecting what apparently she could read in his face. "My father died of a stroke."

"You had an autopsy?" he asked.

Her mouth moved, tightening. "No," she said, "but...I know that's what killed him. He'd been in poor health for a while. There was nothing suspicious about the circumstances of his death. They expected he might recover and then..."

Her voice faded again, and her eyes focused briefly on the windows behind him. He turned, following her gaze, but there was nothing there.

"What do we do now?" she asked again.

"Wait until dawn."

He made that decision even as he said the words. There didn't seem to be any point in going out there in the darkness. He'd have to either take Val with him or leave her alone here, neither of which he liked worth a damn.

At least this way they'd have to come through him to get to her. And there weren't but two ways into this room. They could be in a lot worse situations.

"What about Mr. Davis?" she asked. "I mean, shouldn't we—"

"Davis is a professional," Grey said. "And he's armed."

Despite the truth of those statements, he was fighting his own guilt. He was the one who had told Joe to get himself a security guard or a rent-a-cop. He hadn't thought the agent would take him seriously, but he felt responsible for that man being out here in the first place. He was someone who obviously hadn't been up to dealing with whatever was going on.

This had been Grey's job. Valerie Beaufort had been his

responsibility. He had blown it. And both he and Val knew why.

"You think he's dead," Val said flatly.

"Probably," Grey acknowledged.

"But you don't know for sure?"

He shook his head.

"Then we should try to find out. If he's hurt…"

Her eyes held his, almost pleading, and Hawk's words about his wife echoed. *She's got guts.* Val did, too. He had known that from the first morning. Watching her struggle to control the stallion. And then watching her come home on crutches and try to care for the black.

Now she was concerned about the security guard. He would be, too, except he felt certain Harold Davis was already dead. And he wasn't about to risk Val's life to find out for sure.

"We stay right here. At least until daylight. Chances are whoever is out there will be gone by then."

"And if they aren't?"

He didn't have an answer for that, and into the silence, quite clearly, a sound came from outside. Grey crawled back over to the side of the window, again looking out on the limited portion of the yard he could see. There was nothing there, but as he examined it, he heard the same noise again.

Something being dragged, maybe? It had sounded like wood moving against wood? He waited, holding his breath, but it wasn't repeated. There were a couple of thumps, but strangely enough, none of the activity, whatever it was, seemed to be taking place outside this room. It was more muffled. Distant.

"Grey," Val whispered from behind him.

He didn't turn, didn't speak. Instead, he held up his left hand, palm toward her, demanding silence.

And she obeyed for maybe ten seconds. "Grey," she

said again, and finally he turned his head, breaking his concentration, to look at her.

Her eyes were fastened on the lowest of the broken windows. He was nearer to them, but he couldn't see whatever it was she obviously saw.

"What is it?" he asked.

She took a breath, and whispered one word.

"Smoke."

Chapter Nine

"The back door," Grey said.

"Why not—" she began, before he cut her off.

"Too slow climbing out the window. We'd be more of a target. Besides, he'll expect that or the front door. So we go out the way I came in. Maybe we'll surprise him."

Knowing the rich, old Ponderosa pine from which the house had been constructed, Val had been sickened by the whiff of smoke drifting in through the broken windows of the bedroom. Far more afraid of the fire than she was of whoever was out there.

Everybody has something that terrifies them. Fire was her phobia. Her fear produced the occasional nightmare, usually not about the house being on fire, but the barn. Her horses. Kronus was the only one there now, thank God. The others were out in the pasture.

At least they would be safe, she thought, following Grey as closely as she could. However, keeping her body low was playing hell with her knee. Better than a bullet in the head, she told herself, gritting her teeth against the pain.

Grey stopped in the doorway that led into the kitchen, easing upright. When her eyes followed his rise, she realized he was holding out his hand to her. And by now, with the agony in her leg, she knew she would need his help to get to her feet. She transferred her father's gun to her left hand and took his, allowing him to pull her up. She gasped when she straightened the knee, and his fingers tightened reassuringly.

"Okay?" he asked. He freed his hand from hers and pushed her behind him, shielded by his body, her back to the wall.

"Scared spitless," she said. "Does that count as okay?"

"I hope so," he said. "Or we're both in a lot of trouble."

Surprisingly, the thread of amusement was back in his voice. And he exuded an I-know-exactly-what-I'm-doing kind of confidence, despite what he had just said about being scared.

She needed to hear both. She wanted his acknowledgment that he was scared and his assurance that it was all right for her to be. She also needed to know, however, that he felt capable of dealing with the situation, despite that fear. It eased her own terror to sense his calmness.

"Stay behind me," he whispered. The comforting amusement was gone, his voice totally businesslike now. "And be careful. There's broken glass on the floor."

She had already felt it under her bare feet, but what it was hadn't registered. She should have remembered to put on shoes. It didn't seem she was very good in an emergency, but then, she hadn't faced many of this nature in her life.

They inched around the kitchen, hugging the wall. She realized belatedly that the glass he had mentioned was on the floor because there was a broken window in here as well. That shot must have been what had awakened her.

"I'm going to unlock the door and step out on the porch. You stay right behind me. We'll skirt around the freezer, jump off the end of the porch and run toward the road. Got it?"

All except the jumping and the running part. She wondered how he thought she was going to manage that. He had apparently forgotten about her leg. And in normal circumstances, of course, she would have celebrated the idea that he had. But now...

"If anything happens to me," he added, his voice even softer, "you just keep going. Stay in the shadows. My truck's parked at the foot of the ridge where the road turns onto your property. The keys are in it."

"But will it start?" she asked, aiming for the same note of calm amusement she had heard in his.

She was trying to hold on to the remaining shreds of her courage. The smell of smoke was stronger, and she recognized that neither of their choices was good: go outside to face the gun of an unseen enemy or stay in here and burn to death.

"I sure as hell hope it does," Grey said, and then he laughed, hardly more than a breath, but unmistakably laughter.

For some reason, her body responded. A sexual response, deep and powerful. The fact that this man could laugh in the face of death reinforced what she had almost admitted to herself and had then rejected. She had fallen in love with Grey Sellers.

"I'll slow you down," she warned, feeling tears burn behind her eyes. "You'll have to go without me. I can't keep up."

She didn't want him to get shot trying to save her life. She wouldn't allow him to do that. If he were right about Mr. Davis, then whoever was outside wouldn't hesitate to add to the body count. Without her slowing him down, Grey could get away. With her struggling along behind him, however...

"You go," she said, her voice little more than a whisper.

He turned his head, looking over his shoulder. In the moonlight, his eyes were silver. Luminous and yet somehow warm.

"You probably liked those John Wayne movies when you were a kid," he said, the subtle movement she had seen that first afternoon tugging at the corner of his mouth. "The ones with the self-sacrificing heroes. Dead heroes are a dime a dozen. It's the guys who manage to stay alive that are valuable. I promise you that I'm not going to let anything happen to you, Val. Or to me," he added softly, his eyes holding hers. "You and I have some unfinished business."

Despite the smell of smoke, despite the knowledge that someone was waiting outside for them in the darkness, whatever had been in his voice echoed through her heart, eliciting an answering emotion as deep as that she had read in his tone.

Not the time or place, she acknowledged, but she also knew he was right. They had a lot of unfinished business. Not trusting her voice, she simply nodded, her eyes holding his.

"You ready to do this?" he asked.

She nodded again, and he turned back to face the door. As soon as his eyes left her face, the sense of loss was overwhelming, all the fears of the moment before crashing in.

"Now," he said.

His hand reached to turn the dead bolt and then the knob. The door opened. He stepped through it, and she followed, made forcibly aware again of the grinding pain in her knee.

It cleared her head, bringing everything that had happened sharply into focus. Back to the here and now. She felt panic push into her chest, despite what Grey had promised. *I'm not going to let anything happen to you. Or to me*. But she couldn't run. Not fast enough. Or she would fall on that uneven ground. He would try to come back for her. And then—

Envisioning her worst nightmare, she lagged behind. His hand caught her upper arm, fingers biting into the flesh. He pulled her roughly behind him, pressing her between the hard strength of his body and something cold. The freezer, she identified, recognizing it from the coolness of the metal. Which meant they were out on the porch.

After that, Grey kept his arm around her, pulling her along as he slowly eased around the bulk of the appliance. Looking over his shoulder, she thought that the yard, silvered by moonlight, seemed deceptively peaceful. She couldn't find any telltale glow of fire, although the smoke, acrid and unpleasant, burned her nostrils.

Her gaze found the dark outline of the barn. There seemed to be nothing going on out there, either. She couldn't see the bunkhouse behind it. Not from here. Maybe that's where the smoke was coming from, she thought. If whoever was responsible *had* killed Mr. Davis, then by starting a fire maybe they were trying to cover up any evidence they might have left.

They had almost reached the far edge of the porch, she realized. The high end. The end they would jump off, according to Grey's plan, and then make a run for the truck. She looked toward the road and, realizing how far they would have to travel to reach it, all her earlier terror came surging back. They would be totally vulnerable, totally exposed to whoever was out there, hiding in the darkness.

There was too much open territory to cross. And not nearly enough cover. *You probably liked those John Wayne movies when you were a kid*, Grey had said, and she wanted to tell him he was wrong. Not like this. Not this movie.

''Ready?'' he whispered, just as he had in the kitchen.

She looked at the edge of the porch, maybe three feet off the ground, and then beyond it to rough ground, dotted sparingly with low-growing desert vegetation.

"I can't," she said, fighting panic. "I can't."

"The hell you can't," Grey said, his tone savage.

"What's burning?" she asked, trying to stall, trying to distract him. "Kronus is in the barn."

"It's not the barn," he said.

His fingers encircled her wrist in preparation for urging her to take that last step, which would put her at the very edge. With nowhere else to go.

"Grey," she pleaded softly.

He released her hand and jumped, landing flat-footed on the ground below, hands held out at his side for balance, knees bent to cushion his landing. She waited for a shot from the darkness that surrounded them, but there was nothing. He straightened his knees and turned to face her, all in one fluid motion.

"Jump," he ordered, the single word only a breath.

He was looking up at her, his eyes cold, demanding. When he held up his hands, she realized he had shoved his gun into the waistband of his jeans. He was out there unarmed, waiting for her to join him. And she couldn't do it. She couldn't move.

"Jump," he said again, his voice louder this time.

Her eyes filled. Trying to clear them, she broke contact with his, looking toward the distant road where he had left his truck. And she suddenly became aware of something she should have been aware of before now. Something important.

"Listen," she said, her eyes searching the darkness.

There was a car climbing the grade that led up the ridge. She could hear the whine of its engine as it pulled the steep slope. Climbing. Going up the ridge. Not coming down here into the valley where the ranch was, but leaving it.

Her eyes fell to Grey, but he was no longer looking at her. He had turned again, facing the road.

"Is that your truck?" she asked.

"No," he said succinctly. And then he added, almost under his breath, "Son of a bitch."

"He's leaving." All she could feel was elation.

"Get in the corner. Shoot anything that moves out here. Before I come around the side of the house, I'll say your name. Anything else that moves, you shoot it." He looked back at her over his shoulder, obviously waiting for her agreement. "*Anything* else. You understand me, Val? Anyone who doesn't say your name before you see them, you shoot. Shoot to kill. No matter *who* it is," he demanded, and then he was gone, disappearing, not toward the road as she had expected, but toward the front of the house.

She pushed back into the corner formed by the freezer and the wall, holding the gun out before her in both hands, just as her father had taught her years ago. *Point and shoot,* he had said. *Don't worry about aiming.* All the long-ago lessons came back. She had been a good shot. He had taught her that.

The moment of panic had passed. She couldn't have run across that broken ground, no matter what Grey said, but she could do this. And she could pull the trigger. There was no doubt in her mind that she could shoot whoever had been out here terrorizing them.

Even as that thought formed, however, she acknowledged that the attacker was gone. That had to be the car she had heard. Grey knew it, too, which was why he had left her alone. If he had thought there was any danger—

"Val," he said. "I'm coming around the corner."

"Okay," she called, the gun still ready. She knew his voice, of course, but she wasn't taking any chances.

He stepped out of the shadows and laid his gun on the edge of the porch. Then, putting his hands flat on the floor, he scrambled back up beside her.

"I put the fire out," he said. "I don't think there was any structural damage to the house."

"Why did he—"

"I want you to go inside and call the sheriff," he interrupted. "Get them out here. I'm going to the bunkhouse."

To check on Davis. "Don't touch anything," she warned.

She heard him laugh softly in the darkness. He leaned over the gun she was still holding in both hands and kissed her on the mouth. It was nothing like the kiss in the bathroom. This one was quick and hard, like those her dad had sometimes given her mother. In greeting. Or thanks. Or congratulations.

"Don't worry," he said.

"Your prints aren't on file," she guessed.

"Not on any they're likely to have access to," he said.

He started across the porch, apparently to descend more conventionally, using the steps. She reached out and caught his sleeve. He stopped, meeting her eyes again. Then he put his hand over hers where it rested on his arm. His fingers were warm and slightly rough, comforting against the icy coldness of hers.

"We'll figure it out," he promised.

"I know," she whispered.

"Go call the cops," he ordered again. He released her hand, quickly moving beyond the reach of her fingers. She would have stopped him again if she could. To keep him with her.

He had a job to do, however, and so did she. One he had given her. It wasn't until she was dialing the number, realizing it was over and they were both safe, that her hands began to shake. She was infinitely glad he wasn't there to see them.

THE SHERIFF'S DEPARTMENT had come, filling the yard with a variety of vehicles, bar lights flashing. With people who stood together in small groups, out in the smoke-tinged night air, talking in tones so low she couldn't hear what they were saying.

They had asked her to recount for them what had happened. And she had seen them talking to Grey. They had also walked over every inch of the yard, searching the rough, broken ground. They had gone over the bunkhouse with a fine-tooth comb. And examined the front porch, where most of what was left of the winter's supply of firewood, still damp from the thunderstorm of the previous night, had been stacked haphazardly against the outside wall of the house and set ablaze.

Eventually, she had watched them carry Harold Davis' body out of the bunkhouse. She knew he had been stabbed to death, but she couldn't remember who had told her. Maybe the sheriff. Grey had gone out to the bunkhouse with them, but she and Grey hadn't had a chance to talk together after the sheriff's arrival.

Occasionally during those hours, she would look up and find him watching her. Over the heads of the deputies who stood between them. While she was describing to the one with the tape recorder what had happened. Even while he himself was conferring with the sheriff.

And for some reason, it was harder for her to meet Grey's eyes in the light that now surrounded them, glaring and so officially artificial. It had been far easier to reveal what she felt in the darkness. She wondered if he felt that way, too.

So much had taken place during those few minutes of stark terror. Not just what had happened to them, but what had happened *between* them as well. Really important things. Which, for the life of her, she couldn't seem to sort through right now. Not with all these people here.

And it had been well after daylight before they had finally left. Grey had stood out in the yard talking to the sheriff after everyone else, including the ambulance carrying Mr. Davis' body, had gone.

Standing at the sink, Val had watched the two men through the broken kitchen window, wondering what they were talking about. And remembering all the things Autry had told her. Still trying to figure out, especially after the events of the night that had just passed, exactly who, and what, Grey Sellers might be.

Someone who had saved her life. Someone who had come back to the ranch, despite the accusations she had made. Despite the fact that she had ordered him off her property. Had she done that because of what Autry had told her? she wondered. Or because of the way Grey had kissed her? Or because of the way she had responded?

In any case, she knew she had made him leave because she was afraid. Afraid of trusting again. Afraid of being hurt. Afraid that she could never know if he were really interested in her or in the unwanted money her father had again hung around her neck like an albatross.

The slam of a car door brought her back to the present. The sheriff was sitting in his patrol car. Touching the top of it lightly in farewell, Grey stepped back, allowing him room to turn in the small yard. Then he watched until the car had driven down the drive and started up the road that climbed the ridge.

Even from inside the house she could hear its straining motor. A sound she had heard for more than a decade whenever anyone left the ranch. A sound whose significance she had almost not recognized last night.

Grey turned and started up the back steps. Through the

window, his eyes met hers. Something moved inside her body, but she wasn't sure what it was. Anxiety at the coming meeting, perhaps, but there was anticipation there as well. He opened the back door, hesitating before he stepped inside, and she wondered if he could be feeling that same sense of trepidation.

"I made coffee," she said. "Do you want some?"

"About a gallon," he said, his eyes examining her face.

"I'm not sure the deputies left that much. There's plenty for a cup or two, though."

"Have one with me." Finally he crossed the threshold, closing the door behind him. He stood in front of it a moment, still watching her. "I think we need to talk."

"I know," she agreed.

She turned away from the intensity of his gaze, using the excuse of preparing their coffee. He drank his black, which didn't call for much preparation. The milk required for hers gave her a few seconds' reprieve from gray eyes that saw too much.

He was already seated at the table when she turned around, holding a cup of coffee in each hand. She walked across the kitchen, and he stood up politely, pulling out the chair catercorner to his. Instead, she put both mugs down on the table and sat in the chair across the width of the table from him.

She would be able to think better over here. If she got too close to him, as close as she had been last night, she would forget all the questions that needed answers.

She realized he was still standing, his hand resting on top of the chair she'd rejected. He didn't move, not even after she wrapped her own hands around her coffee, lifting it to her mouth to take a sip. Finally she looked up again. That slight rise at one corner of his lips was visible again. *Amusement.*

She looked down at the coffee in her mug, a little em-

barrassed. Maybe even annoyed. He saw through everything she did. Almost as if he could read her mind. Read
her emotions. And maybe he could. Maybe they were that
obvious. Maybe she was. She took a breath, lips flattening.

"It's not as bad as what you're imagining," he said.

She looked up in surprise, just in time to watch him sit
down again. He reached for his mug, pulling it toward him,
but he didn't drink from it. He held it instead, as if he
were warming his hands, his eyes locked on her face.

"How can it *not* be 'as bad'?" she asked. "A man is
dead. And I would have been, too, if…" She paused, fighting the small, unwanted quiver she could hear in her voice.
"I would have been dead, too, if you hadn't come back."

How did you ever express your gratitude for something
like that? She was so glad to be alive. As bad as she felt
about Harold Davis' death, she had been so glad not to be
the one being loaded into that ambulance. So grateful they
weren't picking through the remains of the burned-out
shell of this house, looking for her body. How did you
thank someone for that?

"That wasn't really what I meant," he said. "I'm talking about the other. What your friend told you."

"Autry?" she asked.

She needed to know the truth about that, too, of course,
but after watching Grey interact with the lawmen this
morning, she believed that her first instincts had been right.
Witness Protection. A former law enforcement officer being hidden for his own protection. Something like that, in
any case.

Because there had been nothing furtive in Grey's manner. If he were hiding *from* the law, then something as
high profile as reporting a murder and almost becoming a
victim himself would be very dangerous. And she hadn't
sensed any unease in his actions at all. What she *had*

sensed was competence and assurance, just as when she had so desperately needed them last night.

"He told you my past had been wiped clean," he said.

She nodded, waiting for him to explain. Wanting him to be able to. By now, she knew she was too emotionally connected to him to do what she had tried to do that night in the barn. Ordering him out of her life would be impossible now. Not without a lot more heartbreak than she had ever faced before. It was frightening to realize how insignificant the memory of that broken engagement seemed in the face of what she felt for Grey.

"He was right," Grey said. "That was done professionally, but probably not for the reasons he may have suggested to you."

"Witness Protection," she said softly, watching his face. Thinking she would be able to tell from it or from his eyes if he were telling her the truth.

He looked down into the mug he held, and then he looked toward the door that led out to the porch. Finally he looked back at her. "I'm afraid it isn't quite that simple."

Her heart stopped, an expression she had heard all her life. Until now she hadn't realized that it could really happen. Of course, it quickly resumed its familiar rhythm, echoing too loudly in her ears as she waited. She didn't say anything, simply watching him.

"I was a member of a special operations unit of the CIA. The details of what that unit did aren't really important, but I can tell you that it was primarily antiterrorist and highly clandestine. A need-to-know kind of operation. Not many people, even within the agency, ever knew about it."

He paused, his eyes rising to the broken window over the sink. She knew he didn't see it. He was seeing something else. Something from his past. That covert past, all of which had been professionally destroyed.

"I blew the last assignment I was given," he said softly, his eyes still on the window, still remembering. His lips flattened, and then he went on. "One of our agents had been taken prisoner by a drug cartel operating under the control and protection of a petty Central American dictator. Two of us were assigned to a find-and-rescue operation. I…misinterpreted some of the information we had, and we ended up in the wrong location. While we were on that wild-goose chase, the guy they had taken was slowly and very brutally tortured to death."

He swallowed against the emotion that had crept into his voice, the movement strong enough to be visible along the tanned column of his throat. "By the time we figured out where we should have been all along, it was all over. We got there too late. And it was my fault."

"And they…" She hesitated, unsure of the correct terminology. "They discharged you for that."

He looked at her then, his eyes widening, maybe in surprise. "They didn't have to," he said.

"You quit." The only possible explanation for what he'd just said. For the way he had said it.

"I screwed up, and someone died. And another person—a friend—almost died in the rescue attempt I insisted we make, although I knew in my gut we were too late. I botched everything. And a good man died as a result. Almost two good men," he added softly.

She shook her head. "Everyone makes mistakes," she said, and then knew how stupid that useless platitude sounded.

He laughed, unamused. "Maybe, but everybody *else's* mistakes don't result in people ending up dead."

"Mine did," she said.

His eyes narrowed. He didn't ask her the obvious question, so she told him. "If I hadn't made you leave, Mr. Davis wouldn't have been out here."

"You're not blaming yourself for Davis' death?"

"Tell me why I shouldn't."

"Because you didn't kill him."

"Did you kill the man who died on that mission?"

His mouth tightened before he opened it to say, "For all practical purposes. I wasn't where I should have been, not in time, and he died. It was my job to…" The words trailed off.

She waited, and after a moment, he started again. "It was my job to find him. I didn't do my job. And as a result, he ended up dead."

"I would think…" she began, and watched his expression close. He didn't want to hear what she thought. He had made up his mind that he was at fault. Long before he had met her.

"That's something I try to avoid," he said. "Thinking about it. Talking about it. I wanted *you* to know the truth. It's important that you know, because the reason your friend found no records for me had nothing to do with the two of us."

The phrase seemed out of place. She wondered how many times Grey Sellers had ever said anything about "the two of us" to a woman. Somehow, despite all the doubts she had had about him before, she knew there wouldn't have been many.

"And I'm not after your money," he continued. "That had nothing to do with what happened."

If that were true, then… Then what? she wondered. Why would she believe that for the first time in her life it might be true? Because she wanted so desperately to believe it was?

"Even if people don't mean to let it, even if they don't want to let it, money affects every relationship in my life," she said, wanting him to understand that her doubts were based on years of experience. "No one can truly look past it, even if they think they can. It's always there. Always in the background, a part of who *I* am. And it always has been."

He looked into his coffee. "So what does that mean?"

"I don't understand," she said softly.

"You thought I wanted to take you to bed because of the money. I've told you money had nothing to do with it. You can't believe that, so…I'm asking what that means for us."

He hadn't said, "I wanted to make love to you." To be fair, he had repeated the words she had used in the barn. He wasn't dressing up whatever he felt in romantic language, trying to make it more acceptable. He wasn't that kind of man. And he was making no promises.

"Why did you?" she asked.

His eyes came up, fastening on her face. Questioning.

"Want to take me to bed," she explained. "Why did you?"

His mouth moved, as if he were fighting a grin, and that same amusement was in his eyes. "The usual reasons, I guess."

"Because you're in love with me?" she asked, forcing her eyes to hold his as she said the words. He had started this, and they needed to clarify exactly what they were talking about. There could be no misunderstandings. This was too important.

"I've never said those words to a woman in my life," he said. "I always knew that if I did…"

Again she waited through the long pause, not willing this time to ask what he meant. She wasn't sure she wanted to know.

"I want you," he said finally. "I want very much to

make love to you. Don't you ever make any mistake about that.''

His eyes were clear, open and honest, she realized, a jolt of sensation curling inside at what was in them. He *did* want her, she realized. And given everything...

Angry with herself, she stopped the formation of that thought. Did she really believe it would be impossible for a man like this to physically desire her because she was...less than perfect? If she did, it made a mockery of her demand to be treated like everyone else. Like any other woman.

In fact, that seemed to be exactly how he was treating her. And trying to be honest about what he felt at the same time. Honest enough not to promise undying love. Except from this man, she admitted, that was what she wanted to hear.

''Val?'' he said.

''And then what?'' she asked, her voice very low.

There was another silence. His this time. And when he answered her, she knew that this, too, was the truth.

''I guess that would be up to you,'' he said. ''Whatever happens is up to you. Your decision.''

No promises. And no lies. Not unless everything was a lie, just as it had been with Bart.

''But you have to do something about the other,'' he said.

''About the other?'' she repeated, bewildered.

''About what's going on. About last night.''

Apparently, he had said all he intended to say about the two of them, she realized. He meant she had to do something about whoever had killed Mr. Davis and set fire to the house.

''Maybe if I *knew* what's going on...''

''Someone is trying to kill you. Or at least, they're trying to make you think they are.''

"Trying to make me think they are?" she repeated carefully.

"Either that, or this is the most inept murderer I've ever come across."

Which made her wonder how many he had come across. And exactly what he had done for the CIA.

"They didn't seem *inept* when they killed Davis," she said.

"Him, they meant to kill."

"But…they didn't mean to kill me?" she asked. "That doesn't make much sense."

"I know," he agreed. He lifted the cup and drank some coffee. As he lowered it, he looked at her over the rim. "Who would benefit from your death?"

She had already thought about that, of course. And she had told him truthfully that no one who would benefit from her death could possibly be trying to harm her.

"Whatever you're thinking, this isn't about the company."

"How can you be sure of that?" he challenged.

"Because I know the people who would inherit my shares too well to believe they'd want to harm me. It has to be something else," she said stubbornly.

"You inherit shares worth…several million dollars?" His inflection questioned the amount, and although it was ridiculously low, she didn't correct him. "And then you insist that doesn't have any bearing on the fact that someone is now trying to kill you? When nothing else in your life has changed?"

"None of those men—"

"Who profits by your death?" he asked again, breaking into her denial, his voice hard.

She knew he was right, but to admit that any one of those four old men could have done what had been done last night destroyed the comfortable world of her childhood, a safe, cocooned world of trust and love.

"The shares would be divided among the other partners," she said stiffly.

"Why didn't that happen when your father died?"

"Because he named an heir. Each partner is allowed to will his interests to his heirs. Otherwise, they are divided among the surviving partners in proportion to what they already own."

"It was set up that way at the beginning?" he asked.

She nodded. "They each contributed what they could afford to the start-up costs and received a share of the company in proportion to the money they'd put up. The partnership agreement about what would become of the shares if one of them died was devised then. As I understand it, it's pretty standard except there isn't any buy-out option. Each partner determines what happens to his interest in the company at his death, and the others have no say-so about it."

"So who holds the largest interest, next to yours?"

She hated to say the name. She knew it would immediately make him suspect. And despite the logic of Grey's thinking, she didn't believe the man was guilty of any of the things that had happened. Certainly not guilty of murder.

"Billy Clemens," she said.

"Then we start with him."

"Billy had nothing to do with killing that man," she said.

"It doesn't take much these days to get someone to do your killing for you. Probably a lot easier on the conscience, too. I'm sure Clemens has plenty of money to hire himself a hit man."

"But he wouldn't. And he wouldn't..."

She couldn't bring herself to say the other words aloud.

He wouldn't try to kill me, either. They were ridiculous. But she wasn't buying the other theory he had proposed. That was even more ridiculous, it seemed to her.

Whoever had killed Harold Davis had certainly been trying to kill the two of them. She knew Billy Clemens would have no part in that, no matter how much he might stand to gain by her death. She was glad Grey didn't really know how much that was.

His lips pursed, and he looked down into his empty cup. When he looked up again, his eyes were cold. "Then who do *you* think is behind this?"

She didn't have a suggestion. So it probably seemed stupid to argue with the one he had made. She knew that, but still...

"Billy's a rich man in his own right."

The movement at the corner of his mouth happened again and was then controlled. "As rich as he'd be if you were dead?"

"No," she said.

"Then he has motive."

"*All* of them have motive. Maybe they're all in it together," she said sarcastically. "Maybe coming up with a plan to kill me was on the agenda at the last board meeting."

"Which was when?" Grey asked.

"They didn't *plan* this. That was supposed to be a joke."

"Then I'll ask you an easier question. When's the next board meeting?"

"Whenever I call it, I suppose."

"Call one."

"And do what?"

"Tell them you're naming an heir."

"But..." She paused, shaking her head. "I don't have anyone to name as an heir."

"Name a charity. Create one. People do it all the time."

"So none of the partners would profit by my death." It made sense. *If* that was what this was really all about. And even if it weren't... "I ought to just give the damn shares away," she said softly.

"Give them to the others?"

She hadn't meant that. She had meant to a charity, as he'd suggested. She could do the other, except her dad hadn't.

"I don't think my father wanted Billy to have control."

"Why not?"

"I'm not sure, but...if he had, he would have left the partners his shares. I asked him to. I never wanted them."

"Then get rid of them," he said. "And then call a board meeting and make your decision public."

The company was a legacy from her father, however, so she felt she had an obligation to see that it was well run.

"It isn't that simple," she said.

"It's exactly that simple. Name an heir and put an end to the possibility that any of those people would benefit from your death. Or just give them the shares and wash your hands of the whole business. It is just *exactly* that simple," Grey said again. "And if you don't..." he added, the warning implicit.

If she didn't, then whatever was going on would just continue. She could tell by his eyes that Grey really believed that. And what he proposed was a simple enough solution: give up the money she had always hated.

She had no problem with that. At the same time, however, she would be giving up the protection of the man she loved. And that was an entirely different kind of sacrifice.

Chapter Ten

Twenty-four hours, the lawyers had told her when she phoned them. According to the bylaws, that was all the notice Val had to give in order to call a board meeting.

So she had set one up for tomorrow afternoon and asked them to notify the other partners. Having the attorneys make those calls, she reasoned, would put some distance between the little Valerie Beaufort the partners had all bounced on their knees and the Valerie Beaufort who was now the CEO of Av-Tech.

CEO only until she could find a way to dispose of the shares she'd inherited, she reassured herself. According to the lawyers, it would take time to set up the kind of charitable foundation she had envisioned and to transfer her shares into a trust. In the meantime, they'd advised, she should definitely make a will.

Having her intentions in black and white would make it difficult for anyone, like her stepmother, for example, to challenge the disposition of her shares if something happened to her. The safest way was to name an interim heir, of course, until the foundation was a reality.

Except she had no heir. And no family. Not unless she counted Connie, and she somehow couldn't bring herself to do that. Which had brought her back to her father's partners, all of whom had seemed like family.

She didn't want to believe what Grey had suggested about the partners, but it was difficult to argue with the reality that someone had stabbed Harold Davis to death and appeared to have been trying to kill her as well.

And as Grey said, the only thing in her life that had changed, the only thing she could think of that might have triggered this, was inheriting those shares in Av-Tech. In her life, money, particularly that generated by her father's company, had truly been the root of all evil, she thought again.

In addition to calling the lawyers, Val had also phoned Autry Carmichael. She was afraid he would see some press coverage about what had happened here last night and be worried. She also needed to tell him as much of what Grey had told her about his past as she felt she could share.

Autry was still trying to get a handle on what Grey had been doing before he'd shown up in Colorado. Knowing about Grey's involvement with the CIA would save him all that work.

She also knew it would make Autry feel better about her situation to have the mystery of Grey Sellers solved. Ever since she had talked to him the first time, she had been half expecting Carmichael to show up at the ranch, prepared to cross-examine her bodyguard. And she could imagine how that would have gone over.

When she had talked to Autry this morning, he had seemed just as relieved about the lack of criminal activity in Grey's background as she was. Not for the same reason, of course. Hers was far more personal.

"Did you make the arrangements for a board meeting?"

She looked up to find Grey standing in the kitchen doorway. After their conversation he had gone out to nail some boards over the broken windows, discreetly leaving her alone to make her phone call. Which had, of course, turned into two calls.

"The lawyers agreed to do that and to notify everyone," she said. "I thought that might be more professional."

"Are you expecting fallout?"

"I don't think so. Not just from the notification. The partners have probably been expecting a called meeting. They all know we've been looking for a management consultant."

"Does that mean you haven't found anybody?"

"Not yet," she admitted. "I wanted the lawyers to make that decision. However, they seem determined for me to meet with the applicants. I can't imagine why," she said.

"Maybe because you're the CEO," he suggested.

"I've tried to make it clear that's nothing more than an honorary title. I certainly don't intend to run the company."

"You've never been interested in Av-Tech?"

At one time, Val admitted, she had been very interested. After all, she had grown up with the aviation part, watching the tests of the experimental planes, some of them top secret, throughout her childhood. Later she had even tried to keep up with the technologies that had eventually transformed the small aeronautics company into the giant it was today.

That was before she had turned her back on her father's wealth and, as a result, on the company that supplied it. Now Av-Tech had moved far beyond the rudimentary understanding she had once had. The newer projects, those concerning satellite and missile delivery systems, were a foreign language to her.

"At one time," she said, her voice slightly defensive. "My father wanted me to be involved, and I tried. But since I walked away from all that…" She let the words trail off.

"Because of the money?"

Maybe it was time for her own confession, she thought.

Maybe Grey needed to know the whys and wherefores of who she was as much as she had needed to understand him. He had given her an explanation of what made him tick. Maybe she owed him the same honesty. She didn't allow herself to examine too carefully exactly why she felt that understanding might be important.

"Because I found out on the eve of my wedding that my father's money was the only thing my fiancé was interested in," she said. "It wasn't a pleasant experience, and rightly or wrongly, it became connected in my mind with Av-Tech."

She expected some reaction. An expression of sympathy, if nothing else. Grey said nothing. After a moment he walked over to the coffeemaker and poured the last of the coffee into the mug he had used before, which was still sitting on the counter.

"That must have been rough," he said. He wasn't facing her, and his voice seemed noncommittal.

"Rough" didn't begin to describe what she had felt when it had happened. Now, however, looking back on the incident from a distance of more than ten years, she thought she should be able to talk about it with some degree of dispassion.

"Someone asked my fiancé why we weren't dancing."

For some reason, despite her resolution, her voice faltered. She honestly believed she had forgotten the exact words Bart had uttered that night, but suddenly they were in her head, as clear as when he had said them. Every bit as hurtful. Maybe ten years wasn't as great a distance as she had thought. Not great enough, apparently, for dispassionate discourse about this.

Rationally, she realized how stupid that was. Stupid and juvenile. They were only words, and Bart Carruthers had been a jerk. Besides, that broken engagement was the best thing that had ever happened to her, and she knew it. Why, then, was this memory still so excruciating?

They had attended a dance at the country club, one of the many prenuptial affairs her father's friends had planned for them, and Val had been coming back from the powder room. She had almost reached the group around her fiancé, whose back was to her, when someone asked Bart why the two of them hadn't danced together that evening. She could even remember the exact tone of that question. Smug. Slightly jeering.

"He said all he was *required* to do was sleep with me," she said out loud, looking down at her hands, their fingers entwined, rather than at Grey. Looking anywhere except into those knowing eyes. "And for that much money, he said, he could probably sleep with the bride of Frankenstein. As long as it was dark enough."

And then, into the silence that had fallen after she'd finished, she heard Grey laugh. She couldn't have been more shocked if he had slapped her. It felt as if he had. She looked up to find him leaning back against the kitchen counter.

"Nice guy," he said, still smiling.

Then he began to lift his coffee to his mouth. He was watching her over the rim of the mug, and at whatever was reflected in her face, his hand hesitated in midair.

"You didn't think that comment had anything to do with *you,* did you?" he asked.

She swallowed against the aching thickness in her throat, but she couldn't think of anything to say in response to his question. She didn't even understand it. Of *course* it had had something to do with her. It was about her. About their relationship.

"He was probably sick to death of hearing about your father's money," Grey said. "He didn't have the backbone to stand up to questions about his motives, so he took the easy way out.''

''Making fun of me?''

''It must have gotten old trying to deny he was marrying you for the money.''

''Except that conversation wasn't *about* money,'' she said. ''It was about me. Personally.''

''You took it that way.''

''I'm not sure what other way I *could* have taken it.''

She had told him because she wanted him to understand her insecurities about men, her lack of trust. Grey seemed to be implying those weren't the result of the money at all. And that hurt almost as much as Bart's comment had.

''Maybe you should have taken it as a not-very-clever comeback from a jackass who was trying to make a preemptive strike at some envious friend,'' Grey said, smiling at her again. ''But it wasn't about you. It couldn't have been.''

It couldn't have been. She replayed Bart's words in her mind, the scene as vivid as the night it had happened, the pain almost as sharp. *All I'm required to do is sleep with her. I think I can probably manage that. Hell, for that much money, I could probably sleep with the bride of Frankenstein. As long as it's dark enough.*

''Of course they were about me,'' she said.

''They were about *him.* And *his* shortcomings. Not yours. There *is* a difference,'' Grey said.

Slowly she shook her head.

''You thought he didn't find you physically attractive?''

She took a breath, because that was the crux of this, of course. It always had been. And she knew why Bart wasn't attracted. She had known then.

''He didn't,'' she said.

''He never made love to you?''

She had thought at the time that the lack of intimacy in

their relationship was her choice. Until that evening, she had believed Bart was chivalrous, romantic even, to respect her wishes. And instead... *God, I was such a fool.* A wave of shame for having been so naive swept over her. The same shame she had lived with all these years.

"Obviously he didn't want to," she said stiffly. "Once I was signed, sealed and delivered—or should I say once my father's money was delivered—only then would he be willing to make that sacrifice."

"And all these years you've—" He stopped, the words cut off, but in his eyes was some emotion she had seen there before.

Pity? she wondered. *Oh, dear God, don't let it be pity.* She would hate it if he pitied her. Especially about this.

"All these years I've what?" she demanded as the silence lengthened.

Instead of finishing that thought, however, he asked, "How many men have you been involved with since that night?"

She didn't answer. No matter how she felt about Grey, that was none of his business. She wasn't asking about his love life.

"My God," he said, his eyes holding on her face. "How long ago did that happen?"

"Long enough that it's ancient history. I don't know why we're even talking about it."

She had thought he should know why she didn't want to have anything to do with her father's money and why she had made those accusations that night in the barn. She had thought he might be interested in what had created that mistrust, and instead...

"It was a mistake," she said. "Something that should never have happened."

"It's hard to know who to trust," he said. "But I guess you know that already."

"I do," she agreed, her tone bitter.

Again that movement at the corner of his mouth flickered and disappeared. He set the coffee down on the counter beside him and closed the distance between them.

He stood beside the table a few seconds, looking down into her face before he leaned forward, putting his palms flat on its surface. His face was level with hers, almost eye-to-eye.

"I don't want your money, Ms. Beaufort, but I *do* want you. I want you very much. I want to dance with you *and* make love to you. And when I do, you can be damn sure it isn't going to happen in the dark. So don't come expecting that. Or you're going to be very disappointed."

He held her eyes for a long time. She could feel the blood rising into her throat and her cheeks. And she couldn't think of one single thing to say. He had taken the essence of every hurtful word that had been festering in her soul for ten long years and thrown it back in her face.

Finally, after an eternity, he straightened, pushing his body up and away from the table. He walked across the kitchen and opened the door, disappearing through it.

Onto the back porch, she realized. Where last night he had used his body as a shield, putting it between hers and whoever had been hiding out there, waiting to kill her.

He was her bodyguard, of course, and that was his job. This, however... This was something completely different. And she needed to be very sure that she had understood what he meant. Given her track record with men, there was no margin for error. And considering all that was going on in her life right now, this was no time for a mistake of that magnitude.

For several minutes after the door closed behind Grey, Val didn't move, didn't seem to breathe, his words echoing over and over in her head. *I want you very much. I want to dance with you and make love to you. And when I do,*

*you can be damn sure it isn't going to happen in the dark.
So don't come expecting that. Or you're going to be very
disappointed.*

In her heart, however, she was sure of one thing. If she
ever did find the courage to go to him, in the dark or in
the light, she would *not* be disappointed.

SHE HAD BEEN RESTLESS since she went to bed. And she
knew why. There was no question about the reasons. All
of them. Her unease had started with the conversation this
morning about the possibility that one of her father's partners was trying to kill her. And that disturbing idea had
spilled over into dread about the meeting tomorrow afternoon. Between those troubling issues lay her relationship
with Grey. And the challenge he had issued.

*And when I do, you can be damn sure it isn't going to
happen in the dark. So don't come expecting that. Or
you're going to be very disappointed.*

Don't come… Reverse psychology? If so, it was working. Because she wanted to go to him. She had fought the
urge all day. And all night, she admitted. Especially since
Grey had told her he would be staying in the house rather
than going out to the bunkhouse. Keeping watch. Keeping
watch over her.

Which was his job, she told herself again, turning on
her side and pushing the feather pillow into a more comfortable wad under her cheek. He was just doing his job.

So don't come expecting that. Don't come… Which had
nothing to do with his job. And everything to do with her.
With her desires. And her needs. And his. *Don't come…*
Which was, of course, tantamount to an invitation.

She rolled over onto her back again, her eyes focused
unseeingly on the ceiling. All the images of the few days
this man had been in her life ran through her head. Along

with all the memories of the nights she had spent out here alone. Ten long years of nights spent alone.

Don't come... She couldn't get the words out of her head. They drifted through her consciousness, interfering with any other line of thinking. Destroying any possibility of sleep.

Maybe a couple of the over-the-counter pain pills would help her doze off. If not, they would at least deaden the ache in her knee a little. Maybe that and not the other was what was keeping her awake. *Yeah, right,* she thought, acknowledging the silliness of that blatant attempt at self-deception.

She pushed the sheet off her legs, however, and sat up on the side of the bed. She opened the drawer of the bed-side table where she always kept the bottle of pills. Without turning on the light, she searched for them, fumbling through the familiar contents before she remembered.

In her mind's eye she could see the bottle, sitting on the table beside the chair in the den. Right where she had left it, close at hand during the days she had been confined there.

Nothing to do but to go get them, she decided. She needed to be rested for the meeting tomorrow, and considering that it was after 2:00 a.m. and that she hadn't gotten very much sleep the night before, she couldn't afford to toss and turn any longer. She could slip into the den, get the pills and take them on the way back with some water from her glass in the bathroom. Grey would never even have to know she had gotten up.

When she had come to bed, he had been drinking coffee at the scarred wooden table where her mother had taught her to make piecrust. One of the proudest accomplishments of her childhood, she thought, smiling at the memory. She could still see herself, holding that first apple pie out for her father's inspection. And she hadn't made a pie in years, she realized. Maybe because there had never been anyone...

She closed the drawer forcefully, destroying the thought, shaking her head at the treachery of memory. In those days, she had wanted nothing more than to be like her mother. To have the same life she had had. Marriage. Companionship. And a little girl to teach things to, their heads close together in the fresh-baked fragrance of a summer kitchen.

What had happened to those dreams? Had she really let Bart Carruthers kill them? Or had she herself destroyed them? Out of fear? Or self-pity? Out of cowardice?

Don't come expecting that. Don't come... Except she wanted to. She wanted to go to Grey and let him create for her all the memories those long, empty years should have held. In the darkness or in the light. She didn't care how it happened.

Or why, she admitted, acknowledging the last of her fears. The final barrier. Bringing that, too, into the open and examining it. She truly didn't care *why* Grey wanted to make love to her. Not even if it was about the money. Not even if that was the only reason he wanted her.

She couldn't decide if that admission was a victory or a defeat. All she knew was that she had made it.

"GREY?" SHE CALLED SOFTLY as she stood at the bedroom end of the hallway that separated them. She could see that the light was still on in the kitchen, which was at the opposite end.

As she had entered the hall, she had remembered what he'd told her last night. She didn't want to be shot by her own bodyguard. That was not exactly the ending for this that she had been envisioning. Suddenly he appeared in the kitchen doorway, the light behind him. His shoulders filled the frame, but she could see almost nothing of his features.

"What's wrong?" he asked.

Confronted with the physical reality of him, it seemed impossible to put into words why she was here. She had hoped he would know. *Don't come...* Maybe that hadn't been the invitation she had been imagining it to be. But considering the rest of what he had said—

"Val?"

"Nothing's wrong," she said.

He waited, and when she made no further explanation, he reached over and flicked the switch that controlled the hall light. She winced against its sudden blaze, putting her hand up to shield her eyes. After a few seconds, she lowered her arm, to find his eyes intent on her face. And in them was the same heat they had held before. Again, deliberately exposed. So intense that she was almost frightened by what it represented.

This was why she was here. This heat. And besides, she knew there was nothing to fear. Not this. Certainly not him. She had never feared him, not even when she hadn't known who he was. Perhaps her instincts were as good as his.

"This isn't a good idea," he said softly.

A lot of different interpretations might be put on that remark. She took a breath, trying not to make the wrong one. Trying not to let the old ghosts or the old insecurities destroy what she felt. What she believed *he* felt, too.

Her feelings of physical inadequacy didn't fit with what was in his eyes. Or with what had been in his voice when he had said, *I want to dance with you and make love to you.* She had believed him. So she had come.

"Why not?" she asked, pleased at how steady her voice sounded despite her racing heart.

"Because somebody tried to kill you last night," he said. "And because my job is protecting you. Not…this."

The brief hesitation was provocative. She wanted him to say the words. Any of them. Even the crude, unacceptable ones. There was a surge of excitement inside at the thought of hearing any of them on his tongue and knowing they were meant for her.

"I thought you wanted to make love to me," she said. "In the light or in the dark. Either way…" She saw the depth of the breath he took then, lifting the broad shoulders. Perhaps her hesitation was as provocative as his. As deliberate. "Either way can be arranged," she finished softly.

"You aren't afraid that someone might—"

"No," she said without waiting for him to name whatever she should fear. Because for the first time in ten years she *wasn't* afraid. Not of anything. Not of whoever had been out here last night. Not of Grey. And more important, not afraid of either ridicule or rejection. Not even afraid that she might be less than what he expected.

She had only one thing that was completely and totally her own. One thing she controlled. Tonight she intended to offer that to him, and so she had spoken his name in the darkness, knowing full well what it would mean.

"Getting distracted could be dangerous," he said.

Her lips tilted in amusement. *Too sudden. Too soon. And way too dangerous.*

"Is that your intuition?" she asked. "Do you 'feel' someone's out here tonight?"

"Common sense, maybe. Not intuition. My gut's not telling me anything. At least…not anything about that." His voice had softened, becoming smoldering as his eyes could sometimes be.

"Your gut was right about what was happening last night, so maybe there really is no danger tonight. Besides, even if there were, you'll be closer than you would be sitting alone in the kitchen.'' Her tone was slightly teasing, flirtatious even, and she found she was enjoying that role, so foreign to her nature.

''The essence of good bodyguarding is proximity,'' he said, the words accompanied by that movement at the corner of his lips.

Proximity. Never before had that word had sexual connotations. Of course, never before had she been placed in this kind of relationship. It required intimacy. Required it by virtue of the threat that surrounded them. Maybe that had something to do with why, after all these years, this man had breached the barricades she had created around her emotions.

''Then…'' The word was an obvious invitation, one she couldn't believe she had been bold enough to issue. She held her breath, willing him to accept it.

''Tell me,'' he said softly. ''Tell me what you want.''

Even in the face of that demand, there was still no fear. Only need. And love. And she knew that was the answer to what he had asked. Not the mocking words she had used that night in the barn, but these. These special words.

''I want you to love me.''

''In the light,'' he said.

And slowly she nodded.

Chapter Eleven

On that first evening, when she had watched Grey's long, tanned fingers rub Harvard's nose, she had known he was a man who understood horses, a man who knew all about them. Tonight she had learned that he was also a man who knew all about women.

It had taken less than five minutes for her to understand exactly how skillful he was. How patient. Unhurried. And considering her own shivering response to his every touch, how totally in control.

He had said "in the light," but despite that, when they had entered the bedroom, he hadn't touched the convenient switch that would make the phrase a reality. He had simply led her to the bed in the moonlit darkness. Then he had released her hand and had begun to disrobe with a practiced economy of motion. He had unbuttoned his shirt first, just far enough to pull it off over his head. Every movement seemed totally unselfconscious, infinitely powerful, and yet somehow graceful at the same time.

When he sat down on the edge of her bed to remove his boots and socks, Val realized she was about to allow a man she hardly knew to make love to her, and she had no qualms about her decision. Not even one. This was right. Grey belonged in her house. In her bed.

Lost in the wonder of that realization, she was a little

startled when he stood up. Holding her eyes, he began unfastening the metal buttons down the fly of his jeans, using the fingers of one hand. He pushed them off his hips, letting them fall over his feet, and then he stepped out of them.

He had been wearing nothing under the jeans. Standing before her, completely nude, he was as elemental as the forces of the thunderstorm two nights ago. Just as primitive. Just as powerful. "Your turn," he said softly.

She took a breath, deep and unsteady. She was wearing only her nightgown, long sleeved and high necked. Hardly seductive. But then, she was a little out of practice at seduction. She raised trembling fingers to the small row of pearl buttons that ran down the front of the gown. Before she could undo more than a couple, however, his hands were there, pushing hers aside.

"I didn't mean for *you* to do it," he said.

She might have been embarrassed by her lack of understanding, but he was smiling. So she nodded, holding his eyes, her throat again too full to speak.

"My job," he said. "Not yours. There's nothing you need to do tonight."

He didn't touch the buttons, however. Not immediately. Instead, he put his hands on her shoulders, as his mouth lowered to brush against the side of her neck. Automatically, her head tilted, allowing him access to the soft, sensitive skin that lay between the lobe of her ear and the angle of her jaw.

He nuzzled gently, his lips caressing, undemanding. Some of her tension, which she had not even been aware of, melted out of her bones, turning them liquid. Pliable. Willing.

His mouth opened, sliding slowly down the ringed column of her throat, leaving a trail of moisture behind. As his lips explored the hollow formed by her collarbone, she became aware that his fingers were finally working at the buttons of the gown.

When enough of them had been unfastened, he eased the gown off her shoulders, his mouth following, tracing across the newly exposed skin above the swell of her breasts. The coolness of the air kissed the dampness it left, and she shivered again.

Just as she had gradually become aware of the draining away of that unacknowledged tension, she realized that something was happening within her lower body. A heaviness. An ache. Need. Primitive, also. And elemental.

He released the gown, and the brush of cotton over the peaks of her breasts as it fell was almost as erotic as the movement of his mouth. But it was only a precursor for what would follow, she discovered, as that tantalizing graze of fabric was replaced almost immediately by the hot, wet passage of his tongue over her breasts. It circled her nipples, one after the other, and the sensitive skin responded by tightening, engorging with a rush of blood. They lifted, reaching toward the warmth of his mouth. She heard a low, moaning intake of breath and realized belatedly it had come from her throat. Her knees were suddenly weak.

Then his mouth closed around the tip of one breast, and the hard suction, after the lightness of his tongue's caress, caught her off guard. The sound that emerged from her throat this time was louder and more uncontrolled. Uncontrollable.

It seemed she had no will. She was mindless with the wealth of sensation that grew as his mouth continued to move—licking, suckling, caressing. His fingers traveled over her skin, acting in harmony with the unceasing motion of his lips. His fingertips touched the sides or cupped the softness of her breasts, lifting them to meet his teeth and his tongue. Tormenting her until she thought she could truly bear no more.

Enough, her mind cried. Enough. But even as she thought it, she knew this wasn't nearly enough. Not for either of them. This was only the prelude. The overture. There was so much more that he would teach her. So much more she wanted to learn.

After a long time, so long she wondered that her trembling legs hadn't given way, he bent, going down before her on one knee. As he did, his lips drifted along the narrow channel of her breastbone. His fingers were still cupped around the sides of her breasts as his mouth trailed downward. Touching her navel now. Rimming it with heat. The tip of his tongue found the center of its small indention and delved inside. Circling there, just as it had over the hard, aching peaks of her breasts. Exploring every inch of her body. Learning it.

His thumbs were now on her hipbones, his fingers splayed so that the tips of them rested over her buttocks. They pulled upward, urging her body toward the glide of his mouth, which was still open. Still wet. Caressing.

And moving again, she realized. Downward. All the muscles in her stomach tensed, reacting to the realization of his destination. A slow, roiling expectation began to stir inside.

She closed her eyes, her head falling back, lips opening. One part of her wanted to protest this most intimate of invasions, and yet she knew it was what she had wanted as she lay restlessly in her lonely bed tonight.

At the first stroke of his tongue, she cried out. And the reaction wasn't completely pleasure. Neither was it fear. She wasn't sure what she was feeling, but her hands closed convulsively in the thick darkness of his hair.

He ignored the involuntary sound she'd made. Ignored her hands. Ignored everything but the tinder of the fire he had ignited. That he nurtured, encouraging the flames that were just beginning to flicker into life, sending heat rushing along nerve endings she had not even been aware her body possessed.

She had never felt anything like this before. Uncharted territory. Her body, a land unexplored until his tongue had touched her, teaching her about her own sexuality.

Prelude, she reminded herself. Only the overture. She was still unfulfilled. They both were. She couldn't imagine, however, how anything could be more than this. Or how she would bear the intensity of feeling if it were.

''Sit down,'' he said.

A command, and hearing the tone of it, she didn't hesitate to obey. She bent her knees and put her hand behind her, feeling blindly for the mattress. Her shaking fingers found it as he continued to touch her, his tongue and lips and teeth as skilled as his hands had been at the beginning.

She remembered watching him blowing gently into Harvard's nostrils that first day. And she could feel that same breath on her body, hot and so sweet. A man who knew women.

She eased down on the bed, her knees too weak now to support her. He moved at the same time somehow, so that he was kneeling between her legs, which had opened to make room, as if she had been expecting him there. She was totally exposed. Highly vulnerable. And completely unafraid.

''Lie back,'' he said.

His voice was little more than a whisper, dark and seductive. And she was powerless to resist, even if she had wanted to. Whatever semblance of control she believed she had had at the beginning of this had gone spiraling away in the darkness at the first touch of his tongue.

She lay back on the bed, half reclining, her elbows supporting her upper body. He put his hands around her ankles, lifting and positioning her legs so that her feet were flat on the bed, her knees raised. And then his mouth descended again.

She had believed she was prepared. At first, just the thought of his lips moving over her body had been exciting. Then he had proven her anticipation had been nothing to the reality. Now he taught her that what had happened before could not be compared to the exquisite torture he began to inflict.

He touched her lightly at first, the tip of his tongue flicking delicately over the most sensitive part of her body. Sheets of heat lightning, like those that had rent the sky the night she had found him in the barn, surged through every nerve pathway that led from that place into the rest of her body.

Her fingers again found the thickness of his hair, clenching and unclenching as sensations built. She writhed against the increasing pressure of his mouth, arching upward, her body unconsciously seeking something her mind could not articulate.

All she knew was that she needed to be closer to him. To become one with him. One with the pressure of his mouth, the subtle, tormenting ecstasy of its movements. She wanted to tell him what she needed, and she had no words. None that she could gather to form a coherent thought. None that would make sense.

She arched again, her breathing labored. Striving for something she couldn't identify. Something she had never experienced before. Something that was hovering just beyond her reach. A hairbreadth away...

And when it began, she didn't fully understand what was happening. Wave upon wave spread upward from where his mouth continued to move against her. A tremor started in the core of her body and shivered out into every atom of her being. She was drowning in sensation, its pleasure so intense it frightened her.

And as soon as it began, his mouth deserted her. She cried out with the loss, but even before the sound had faded to echo in the dark room, he was lifting his body over hers, entering the molten center of the firestorm his mouth had ignited.

There was a tearing pain, hot and raw. She must have reacted to it, because Grey hesitated, a check of less than a heartbeat in the downward motion he had begun. And when he moved again, there was no more pain. There was a fullness instead, a heaviness, as his body pushed completely into hers. Which had been created to accept it, a design older than time.

She waited, not daring to breathe, her mind learning what her body had only begun to know. And then Grey began to move, his hips retreating and then slowly pushing downward again. His palms shaped the sides of her face, and she opened her eyes, looking up into his, smoke gray, softened as she had never seen them before.

This is how he would look at someone he loved. And with that incredible thought, she finally remembered to breathe. It was ragged, slightly gasping, as if she had been deprived of air too long. In response to that sound, his hips moved again, his eyes locked on hers.

His thumbs found the tears that formed at the corners of her eyes and brushed them away. He bent his head and kissed her lashes, licking the moisture from them.

When she opened her eyes again, he was smiling at her, his body still moving within hers. There was no pain now. No friction. The moisture he had created inside her body eased the slow, unhurried slide of his erection, in and then almost out. Infinite patience. Infinite control.

And again the waves of sensation were building. She could feel them, stronger than they had been before. And that had been almost unbearable. A pleasure so concentrated, so intense, it verged on pain.

When it came this time, nothing had prepared her for what happened. Nothing she had read or heard. Not even the foretaste of this intensity he had already given her. Those faded into the blackness of the mindless void into which she fell.

Her body arched upward again and again, compelled to meet the downward thrusts of his hips, compelled to try to draw him into closer contact with the center of her soul. She put her hands on his buttocks, nails biting into his flesh. Under her palms she could feel the play of the powerful muscles that drove his motion. And then suddenly he shuddered, convulsing again and again as his seed jetted into her body.

After a moment, he stilled, his full weight sagging against her. His breath sawed harshly in and out, right beside her ear, the abrasiveness of his whiskers moving against her cheek. Moisture from his body, slick and wet and hot, mingled with that on her own skin. Almost too intimate. Almost.

Slowly she raised trembling hands, moving them caressingly across his still-heaving back. Now they were one. This was the need she had not been able to articulate. To be one with him. And no matter what happened after tonight, she could not regret that they had shared this.

She had given herself to him freely, without any conditions. And she had held nothing back, she thought, still running her palms soothingly over the corded, trembling muscles. After a moment, he pushed up, lifting himself onto his elbows to look down into her face.

"Why didn't you tell me?" he asked softly.

She fought off the old feelings of inadequacy. There was no accusation in his question. And there had certainly been nothing in his actions that indicated he had found what she had offered to be lacking in any way, despite her inexperience.

"I was afraid," she said truthfully.

"Afraid of me?"

"Afraid that if you knew, you wouldn't want me."

That same slow smile touched his lips, which she now knew weren't hard. Or thin. Or any of the things she had thought.

"That's not exactly how it works," he said.

She shook her head, eyes questioning.

"Inexperience is not...undesirable."

"I thought it would better for you if I had some knowledge. *Some* degree of expertise." She took a breath, still hesitant, despite what he'd said, to make this confession. "I didn't have the slightest idea what I was supposed to do."

He smiled again, real amusement this time, and something moved, deep in her stomach, almost like an aftershock of the eruption he had just caused.

"*You* weren't supposed to do anything," he said. "Nothing beyond what you did."

"*I* didn't do anything," she said, feeling her own lips tilt in relief at what was in his eyes and his voice.

Suddenly, however, the amusement that had been there was gone. His eyes had darkened; his face, serious.

"Why did you come?" he asked.

She wasn't sure what he meant. But then, she had never been sure of anything with him. So she told him the simple truth. As much of it as she could bear to confess.

"Because I wanted this. I wanted you."

"Nothing else?"

No promises, she thought. There hadn't been. Not from the beginning. And no conditions.

"Only what you want to give," she said carefully.

"What do *you* want to give?"

For a second the old anxieties surfaced. She had already given him everything that was of value. What else could he want? she wondered, a trickle of fear running cold in her veins.

"What if…" he began.

"What if what?" she asked when he hesitated. The tension he had destroyed was seeping back into her bones, and she hated it.

"You know I'm no prize," he said. "I've already told you some of it. But…there's more I didn't tell you."

His lips flattened, compressed as if to keep the words inside. She didn't hurry him. She knew part of what he wanted to say concerned the failed mission he had told her about and the sense of guilt he still carried for that man's death.

"I found out that if I got drunk enough, I didn't have to think about…what I'd done," he said after a long time.

The words hung between them in the darkness, and she waited, knowing that he needed to get all of this out. Just as she had needed to tell him about Burt.

"That night in the barn," he continued finally. "I got drunk because I knew I should never have touched you. I was here to keep you safe, and instead—"

"You kept me safe," she comforted, hearing the pain and responding to it. Wanting to ease that suffering.

He laughed, the sound short and bitter. "Only because I have very good instincts. And I got lucky. We were lucky."

"My dad used to say that, given a choice between being good and being lucky, he'd take lucky any day."

He laughed again, the sound less caustic.

"You would have liked my dad," she whispered, her throat tight again. "He would have liked you."

Suddenly she knew that was true. Maybe her judgment had been faulty before, but this time there was no mistake.

This was a good man. A man who would always put himself between her and danger, as he had done last night. And he would do that even if it weren't his job.

"Considering everything you know about me..." he began, and this time she filled in the hesitation before it could grow into discomfort.

"Would he have welcomed you with open arms?" she asked, her voice deliberately lightened. "I don't think he would have welcomed anyone that way. Not at first. Fathers are naturally pretty suspicious. That's *their* job. But...I think he would have welcomed you eventually. However, if you're looking for his approval, you're just a few days too late."

He ran the pad of his thumb across the unexpected quiver of her bottom lip. The emotion had caught her by surprise.

"I'm sorry I didn't know him," he said.

"Me, too," she said truthfully.

This silence wasn't strained. And after a moment, she lifted her hand and touched his face, running the tips of her fingers down the stubbled cheek that had moved in such exquisite torment against her body only minutes before.

The feel of his whiskers was different now. He was unshaven because it had been a very long day. He'd had less sleep than even she had managed in the past twenty-four hours. She had noticed the tiredness in his eyes earlier this evening.

He seemed vulnerable for the first time since she'd met him. Maybe because he had told her about his inadequacies. His fears. *You know I'm no prize,* he had said, skirting the real issue as skillfully as she had.

And if they continued to skirt it, neither of them willing to take that first step beyond the physical intimacy they had shared, then she knew he would disappear from her life as soon as the danger had ended, and she again would be left with nothing.

He had asked her what she wanted, and she had been afraid to tell him. A truth that was the most difficult of all to confess.

"I want everything," she said, the emergence of those words as unexpected as the urge to cry about her father's death. They had certainly been unplanned. She realized, however, that they were true, so she didn't try to soften them or take them back.

She still wanted it all. All of those dreams. The smell of piecrust. The heat-filled summer kitchen. The little girl. And at the center of that world, holding it all together, a man who was both strong and good. As this one was.

"I want you," she whispered. "I want us."

The silence stretched until it filled the moonlit darkness. And then he nodded, the movement barely discernible before his head began to lower. And when his mouth fastened over hers, she closed her eyes, knowing that after all these long years of living here in her parents' house, only now, finally, had she really come home.

Chapter Twelve

"I wanted all of you to be aware of what's been going on," Valerie said, her gaze moving around the table, "so you can understand why I'm doing this."

The shock was still in their eyes. She couldn't blame them. The story, as she had told it aloud for the first time, sounded like one of those thrillers where everyone has a motive. The kind where it seems there are no good guys, just some who are not quite as bad as everyone else. Everything in shades of gray.

That phrase triggered an association she didn't need right now. She glanced across the room to where Grey was standing under one of the security cameras, being as unobtrusive as someone who looked like a coiled steel spring could be.

She had never seen him like this, and it was not just the suit, a charcoal-gray silk blend that was obviously expensive. As were the shirt and tie he wore with it. He looked as if he belonged in this boardroom. Far more than she did, she acknowledged. Which just might be the ultimate irony.

"Let me get this straight," Billy Clemens said belligerently. "You're telling us that you're signing over your interest in this company to some damn charitable foundation. Is that what you're saying, Valerie?"

"The operative word is 'my' interest, Billy," she reminded him, feeling more sure of what she was doing right now than at any time since her father's death, despite the tone of Clemens' question. "Dad left the shares to me with no strings attached. I don't want to run the company. I don't want that responsibility. And I certainly don't want the money, considering what's been going on since I inherited. The foundation will hold my shares in trust. The profits generated by them will be used for benevolent purposes. And the day-to-day operations of the company will be overseen by a management team."

"You don't want to be involved, my dear," Harp Springfield said, rubbing the bridge of his narrow, aristocratic nose as if the glasses he had just removed pained it, "and I think we all can understand your feelings, given the events you've described. But why sign over control to some outside entity that will then have more say-so over what happens in the company than any of its founders? Why not simply divide those shares among the rest of us as the original agreement specifies?"

She knew the explanation of why she wasn't doing that could be hurtful, and which was truly the last thing she had intended.

"If that was what my father had wanted, he would have done it, Harp. He didn't. He left those shares to me, despite my repeated requests that he not."

"But it's just as obvious he didn't want his shares given away, or he would have done that himself," Porter Johnson argued. "I don't see any difference in going against his wishes in dividing the shares and going against them by giving them away."

"I'm not giving anything away," she explained patiently. "I'm putting my interests into someone else's control during my lifetime. Technically, I still own the shares.

Only if something happens to me will the foundation, as my heir, become the owner.''

"This is against the principles of the original partnership, Valerie," Emory Hunter said.

"So is murder."

The cold brutality of the word silenced them for a moment. A man was already dead, and an attempt had been made on her life. If they expected to talk her out of this by trying to make her feel guilty, they were going to be disappointed.

"Is this…foundation already in place?" Billy asked.

"Not yet," she admitted, her eyes rising quickly to find Grey, maybe for reassurance. "It is, however, in the process of being created. And until the legal work is finished, I've named an interim heir. A sort of insurance policy, I suppose. If anything happens to me before the foundation becomes a reality, my shares go to that person and not back into the partnership."

"Just who is this *heir?*" Harp asked. For the first time, there was anger in his voice.

"Not any of you," she said, "and not my father's wife, in case you're wondering about that. That's really all I'm prepared to tell you. I certainly don't want to put anyone else's life at risk the way mine has been."

"You actually believe this…nonsense?" Emory asked, shaking his head in disbelief. "You think someone is trying to kill you to gain control of your shares of Av-Tech?"

"I can't come up with any other reason," she said. She didn't attempt to tell them how hard she had tried or explain that this had been the last thing she wanted to believe.

"You're wrong," Emory said, holding her eyes before his gaze moved around the table, settling on each partner's face in turn. "I've known these men most of my life. More than forty years of friendship. I know them just as I knew your father—inside and out, flaws and all. And I'm telling you that you're barking up the wrong tree thinking any of us could have had *anything* to do with that man's death. Or with trying to arrange yours."

She could see the sincerity in his eyes, and she knew Hunter was convinced that what he was saying was true. The problem was that she wasn't. Not anymore. Simply because she hadn't been able to come up with any other explanation that made any sense.

"Which means," Emory went on, "if someone *is* trying to kill you, you're looking in the wrong place. And at the wrong motive. You be careful, honey. You be *real* careful about who you trust."

As they watched, Hunter rose and inclined his body toward Valerie in a courtly half bow. Then he turned and walked across the room toward the door. Before he opened it, he stood for a long moment, his hand on the knob, looking at the tall stranger who continued to lean at ease against the wall.

Grey met Hunter's eyes, one dark brow raised. Finally Emory broke that contact by looking back at Valerie. He shook his head again in disbelief before he disappeared into the hall, the heavy door closing behind him with a softly pneumatic thud.

Val turned back to the men still sitting around the conference table, her eyes moving over each familiar face. With the exception of Billy Clemens, who was tapping his pen against the notepad on the table before him, they met her gaze openly.

"Anyone else have anything to say?" she asked.

"This isn't right, Valerie," Harp Springfield said, "and you know it. This is *our* company. Our blood and sweat and tears went into making it, just as much as your father's did. And for you to hand it over into someone else's control—"

"Harp—" she began before he cut her off.

"Charlie wouldn't have wanted this. No matter how you try to dress it up. We were his partners and his friends. And partnership is about trust, Valerie. Nobody here is trying to kill you. I think this is something someone has dreamed up to frighten you. You used to be smarter than this."

The words battered her conscience. No matter what she said, she probably couldn't convince them that the threat she was reacting to was real. It had been hard for her to believe someone wanted her dead, and she had been there that night. With her own eyes, she had seen Harold Davis's body loaded into an ambulance. She had seen the broken windows and the charred wood where someone had tried to burn her house down with her inside.

She *had* to do this, simply as a matter of self-protection. Unconsciously, she raised her eyes and met Grey's across the room. They were almost as shuttered as they had been that first evening when she had found him sitting on her front porch, the black Stetson pulled down over his face.

"Then I suppose that's all," she said. "I'll keep you informed. As soon as the lawyers have found a management team—"

Harp stood up. "Don't bother to inform me," he said coldly. "I'll give them my law firm's number. We can communicate through our attorneys. I never thought I'd live to see this day."

Val didn't allow herself to flinch before his fury. She had done nothing wrong. She wasn't taking anything away from the four of them. Their anger was probably more about the implied accusation than the creation of the foundation that would hold her shares in trust. She was sorry about that, of course, but doing what she was doing still made eminent sense to her.

Harp walked out of the room, followed by Porter and

Billy. None of them said another word. When the room was empty, except for the man still standing against the back wall, she raised her eyes from the papers on the table before her. She had to blink a couple of times to clear them of the tears that threatened.

"For some reason, I hadn't expected it to be that bad," she said softly. "I should have been better prepared."

"Gut reaction?" Grey asked.

She shook her head, trying to think about what had been said. About their expressions. Tone of voice. "I don't know that I have one. Other than regret. But…not Emory. I think that hurt the most. The fact that he was so disappointed in me."

"One of them's involved," Grey said, pushing away from the wall and walking over to stand behind the chair Clemens had been sitting in. "They have to be. Nothing else makes sense."

He moved around the table, looking at the notepads that had been placed before each partner. There didn't appear to be anything written on any of them, not even on Billy's, but Val would never have thought to check.

That's why he's the CIA agent, and I'm not, she thought. *Ex-CIA agent,* she amended as his eyes came up to meet hers.

They hadn't talked about last night. Or about anything. And although Grey could never have been called loquacious, he had said less this morning than at any time since she'd known him.

"You ready?" he asked. "The quicker we get out of here, the better I'll like it."

"I don't know why," she said, gathering up her papers and putting them in her briefcase. "No one has anything to gain anymore by getting me out of the way. I thought that was the whole point of this. To destroy any possible motivation to murder. I did that, I suppose. But in the process, I alienated almost everyone left on earth who has ever cared about me.''

''Not quite everyone,'' Grey said. He walked around the table and put his hand against the small of her back to direct her across the room and through the door. ''Did you really name an heir, or was that just cover until the foundation becomes fact?''

She had known when she told the partners what she'd done that Grey would ask this question. She had had a lot of time to prepare an answer—at least since she had written up her ''will.''

While Grey had been out checking the horses this morning, she had sat down at her computer and, going by the copy of her father's will the lawyers had given her, she had typed in the exact wording of the section in which he had designated her as his sole heir. Exact wording except the name of the heir. Then she had printed out two copies and signed them both, sticking them in her briefcase. They were still there.

And she had already decided who she would ask to witness them. The one person who had nothing to gain by her death. A person she trusted to understand the necessity of what she had done with her shares, as paranoid as it might seem to her father's partners. A person who would understand her demand for secrecy.

I certainly don't want to put anyone else's life at risk, she had said. How true that was, she acknowledged, glancing up at the face of the man walking beside her.

''It wasn't a cover,'' she admitted, feeling a sense of dread over this confrontation, too.

Grey had been scanning the deserted hallway ahead of them. By this time on a Friday afternoon most of the employees had already left the building. Maybe because of her tone or maybe because his instincts were as good as he claimed, he stopped walking, his hand still at the small of her back. He turned and looked down into her eyes, his questioning.

"I put your name in my will," she said.

She had believed she understood all the ramifications of what she was doing because she had thought about it so long, during all those dark hours last night as he lay sleeping beside her. But watching Grey's eyes change as the import of her words impacted, she knew she hadn't been prepared for this, either.

"*My* name?" he repeated incredulously.

"I couldn't think of anyone else I could trust."

"That's insane."

"I think it's probably the sanest thing I've ever done."

"You can't make me your heir."

"Actually, according to the lawyers, I can make anyone I want my heir. As long as I'm of sound mind."

"I'm beginning to wonder about that. Did you tell the lawyers this…crap? If you did, you can damn well get on the phone and tell them something else. *Somebody* else."

"I don't *have* somebody else," she said.

No one but you, she added silently. That was even more true after the meeting today. And she didn't understand why Grey was so opposed to this. She thought he wanted the same things she did. She thought that's what his nod had meant last night, so putting him into her will had seemed to make sense. A natural progression of their relationship. But maybe she'd been wrong about what Grey wanted. She had been wrong once before.

"Is this some kind of test, Val?" he asked softly.

"Test?" she echoed in bewilderment.

"You've let that money warp you so much that it affects every emotion you ever have. If you're not careful, it's going to destroy the part of you that makes it possible to trust."

"This *is* trust. This *proves* how much I trust you. If I—"

"I'm not your fiancé," he broke in, speaking over her words. "And I don't give a damn about your money."

"I know that," she said. "That's the reason—"

"If I let something happen to you, then I'm a multimillionaire. Is that what you're telling me?"

His eyes were like stone, slate-gray and cold. She didn't understand why he was twisting this all around. She had never even thought about *that*. It had never crossed her mind.

"Nothing's going to happen to me," she said. "You wouldn't let anything happen to me. And besides—"

"And if I don't, then you can be completely sure I care more about you than about your money. Is that the deal?"

Is that the deal? Was it? Was that what she had done? Was it possible she *had* done this to set up the ultimate test—a test of him and his love? But that made no sense. By naming an heir, she had destroyed whatever motivation anyone might have to harm her, so nothing was going to happen to her. No one would benefit now but Grey, and he was the one person she knew she could trust.

"How could this be a test?" she argued. "There's no reason for anyone to want to harm me. No one has anything to gain now."

"No one but me," he said bitterly.

"I did what you told me to do. I don't know what you're so angry about," she said, feeling her own temper beginning to rise.

"I never told you to put *my* name down. I damn well never suggested that."

"There was no one else I could be sure of. No one but you."

Into the sudden silence that fell after those words came the sound of a phone ringing. Not the one at the reception desk, which lay at the end of the hallway where they were standing. The tone of this was different. Muted.

"Damn it," Grey said angrily, reaching into the inside pocket of his suit coat. He pulled out a small, flat cell phone, and snapped it open with an impatient flick of his wrist.

"Sellers," he said into the mouthpiece. And then he listened, holding her eyes.

Val fought the urge to walk away. She had anticipated that Grey would be reluctant to be her heir, of course. She knew him well enough by now to expect that, but she had never dreamed he would suspect her motives.

"As soon as I can," Grey said into the mouthpiece. He closed the phone, shoving it back into his pocket, and then he took her arm, his fingers closing around it tightly enough to be painful. "Come on," he ordered.

Still angry, she tried to pull away, but he wouldn't release her. "You're hurting me."

"Good," he said succinctly.

"You don't mean that."

"Right now, I just might."

"Grey—"

"We'll talk about this later. I have to find a pay phone."

"Why?" she asked, finally reading the urgency of his tone.

"Because they're more secure."

She glanced up at his face, but he wasn't looking at her. His eyes were searching the hall, obviously more concerned about what he'd been told during that brief phone conversation than about what they'd been talking about.

"Through the lobby. There's a bank of phones in a hallway off to the left," she said. "What's this all about?" she asked as he began to pull her down the corridor toward the lobby.

"I'm not sure," he said. "They weren't willing to tell me over a cell phone. The signals are too easily picked up."

"They?"

He glanced down at her. "A couple of old friends," he said. "People I used to work with. I asked them to do some checking on Av-Tech. They've found out something they think I should know."

People I used to work with. CIA.

"But they didn't give you any hint—" she began.

"They don't hint," he said brusquely.

By that time, they had reached the telephones she had directed him to on the far side of the marble foyer. Grey put her behind him, her back against the wall, his body between hers and the glass entrance doors. He seemed to be watching them and the lobby as he dropped a quarter into the slot and punched in a number. Old habits die hard, she supposed.

She waited, imagining a ringing she couldn't hear. Grey said only one word, "Okay." And then he listened again, his eyes occasionally scanning the lobby and the front doors. After a couple of minutes, she put the heavy briefcase down on the floor.

The longer he listened, the stronger grew her sense of anxiety. Finally she turned her head, determined to look at anything other than the back of Grey's head.

Autry Carmichael was standing at the other end of the short hallway that housed the phones, watching them. Which shouldn't be surprising, she realized. This wing also housed the security offices. Autry must have come out of his and noticed her standing here. He would have figured out very quickly who was with her.

And since Carmichael had never met Grey, Val knew he would be sizing her bodyguard up, just as her dad would have done. After the animosity of the board meeting, the thought of Autry assuming that kind of fatherly role was touching.

Suddenly she remembered that she had planned to ask

Autry to witness her will. Val smiled at him, motioning him forward. She watched as he began to walk toward them, crepe-soled shoes making no noise on the carpet. She turned to see if Grey had finished his conversation. His back was still toward her, however, his head lowered as he listened, the phone to his ear.

And then everything seemed to happen at once. Autry rushed by her, the butt of the big semiautomatic he always carried raised high. He brought it down against the side of Grey's head, striking a blow so vicious Grey was thrown into the bank of phones. He slid bonelessly off them, collapsing onto the floor.

Too stunned to scream, her mind trying to find some logical explanation for what Autry had just done, Val looked up from Grey's body to find that Carmichael had reversed the weapon. The muzzle was pointed at Grey's head now, Autry's eyes on hers as he used his free hand to place the dangling receiver back on the hook.

"Don't say anything, don't make any noise, and you won't get hurt. I promise you that, sweetie," he said softly. "You do what I say, and he won't get hurt, either. Now walk."

He gestured with his head toward the end of the hallway where she had first seen him. Her eyes followed that movement before they came back questioningly to his face. Then, because she couldn't help herself, despite the threat of the gun, she looked down at the motionless figure sprawled on the floor.

Blood was beginning to pool under Grey's head, staining the cream carpet. Val looked across the lobby toward the reception area, hoping that there was someone there who would help. She could see only the edge of the mahogany desk, which sat back in a small recess. And that meant they couldn't see her, either.

"Now, Valerie," Carmichael ordered, his voice still soft

but menacing. "You make any noise, and I'll have to kill you both. I've got nothing to lose if you attract attention to this. You do what I say, however, and we get out of here without anybody seeing us, then nobody will get hurt."

Going with an assailant was the last thing you should do. She knew that. She should start screaming right now and not stop until Autry stopped her. That's what her logic was telling her. What everybody told you to do in this kind of situation. But maybe "everybody" hadn't been in this situation.

Autry Carmichael had already killed one man. Killing the two of them couldn't make what would happen to him if he were caught any worse. *Nothing to lose* echoed again and again through her brain as the slow seconds ticked by.

She could tell from Autry's eyes that he really believed that. He was prepared to pull the trigger if she opened her mouth, because he thought it would then be all over for him.

And if she went with Autry, at least he wouldn't hurt Grey anymore. Someone would find him and help him. He was too close to the heart of the building for that not to happen. Or Grey would regain consciousness on his own and call out for help.

That realization produced a new terror. If Grey woke up while Autry was standing here, he would do everything in his power to prevent Carmichael from taking her. And Grey was in no condition right now to do anything. She couldn't count on him to realize that, however.

And even if he did, she knew he would still try. Finally, holding Autry's eyes, wanting desperately to believe his promise that if she did this, no one would be hurt, she nodded. He gestured again, using the gun this time.

Knees trembling as much as they had last night, but for

a very different reason, Val started down the hallway, leaving Grey unconscious behind her, far too much of his blood seeping out onto Av-Tech's pale, expensive carpeting.

Chapter Thirteen

Now Grey knew what had really been going on at Av-Tech, but with the "Anvil Chorus" in his head, he was barely capable of thinking about the "who" behind the "why" Griff had discovered. His brain couldn't seem to get past the fact that Valerie was missing. And that keeping her safe had been his responsibility.

Of course, protecting Val had been more than a responsibility. More than an assignment. And if he failed to find her in time, as he had failed once before, he knew it would also be more than he could live with.

No one had witnessed Val's abduction, however. He didn't have any idea who had taken her. And not even a clear idea of what they believed they had to gain. All he knew was that whoever was behind all this had already tried to kill Val at least once. And that they had brutally murdered Harold Davis in cold blood.

Grey closed his eyes, refusing to let the flood of despair about what he *didn't* know overwhelm him. Just because he had gotten there too late before didn't mean—

"That should do it," the paramedic said, pulling him out of that fog of fear and self-recrimination. "You ought to have a scan. With an injury like this, all kinds of stuff could be going on that we aren't aware of."

All kinds of stuff could be going on.... The guy was right about that, Grey thought. He stood up too quickly and was forced to put his hand on the door of the mobile unit to steady himself. If he wasn't careful, they would shove him into an ambulance and take him to the hospital, no matter how much he protested.

And he had a job to do. His job. His responsibility. He had already done everything he could think of that might help him get a handle on where Valerie had been taken *before* he had let the paramedics take care of the gash on his head.

The cops were searching the building and the grounds, not that he had much hope they'd find anything. And Grey had sent for Val's partners and for Autry Carmichael, who was head of security. If anybody could answer the questions Griff had raised, those five men could. And if they couldn't...

Again Grey pushed that possibility out of his head. All he had to do was figure out who was behind what had been happening at Av-Tech and then figure out why they had taken Val. And where. Then he would have to get to her before...

As he realized the enormity of the task, he took a deep breath, fighting a growing despair he knew would paralyze him. He couldn't afford that. He couldn't afford anything that might get in the way of his ability to think clearly and logically.

He needed to apply to this investigation everything he had learned from his years with the agency. He also needed every particle of those vaunted instincts he'd bragged to Val about. And on top of those, he needed a hell of a lot of luck.

I'd rather be lucky than good, Val's father had said. Grey knew he had to be both—both very good and very, very lucky.

"WHEN THE LEAKS WERE first discovered last year," Grey said, "there were a number of possible sources. Several companies dealt in the technologies involved. But the latest one came straight from Av-Tech. There's no other possibility, because no one else has this particular technology."

"From Av-Tech?" Harp Springfield repeated. "That's impossible."

"Not according to the CIA," Grey said. "And they don't make mistakes about something like this. Someone within this company, someone who has access to the most sensitive defense contracts you handle, is selling technology to this country's enemies."

It took some of the starch out of the old man. Grey could still see disbelief in Harper Springfield's eyes. According to Cabot, however, there was no doubt about what had been going on.

"You need to talk to Autry about this," Harp said. "Autry Carmichael is in charge of security. Has been for years."

"But this is *your* company," Grey said, remembering the bitter words Springfield had thrown at Val this afternoon. "Your 'blood, sweat and tears' was the phrase that was used, I think. So you *all* had an obligation to make sure this technology never ended up in the wrong hands. An obligation to the American people, who, through those defense contracts, have paid Av-Tech a hell of a lot of money during the last forty years."

"You've got no right to come in here and make these kinds of accusations," Billy Clemens said. "When Carmichael comes, he'll tell you about our security. It's the best in the business. The government's never had any complaints."

"According to the agency," Grey said, "Av-Tech was

warned more than two months ago about what was going on.''

"Who'd they talk to?" Clemens asked, still belligerent.

"It's customary to go through the CEO. Given Mr. Beaufort's service record and the company's long involvement with military contracts, that's what was done in this case."

"Charlie never said a word about any warning," Clemens said.

"Because Charlie would have turned anything like that over to Autry," Harp Springfield offered. "He wouldn't have handled something like that himself. Security was Carmichael's job."

"And he's always done it well," Clemens argued. "I don't believe for one minute that our security has been breached."

"Hell, Billy, the government can't even secure their own nuclear labs," Porter Johnson reminded him. "You can't know for sure that what this man is saying *hasn't* been going on. You ever look at what Carmichael was doing? You ever ask him whether he'd beefed up security, given those stories of other kinds of technology being leaked to our enemies? I sure as hell didn't."

"And just because Charlie trusted him all these years," Harp added, "doesn't mean Autry was capable of dealing with the kind of espionage that goes on today. And we sure aren't. None of us knows the first thing about the computer systems we use. How do we know we aren't vulnerable to some high-powered hacking?"

"And he's right about the other, too," Porter said, lifting his chin to indicate Grey. "This company is *our* responsibility. As much ours as it was Charlie's. Or Carmichael's. Val tried to tell us something dangerous was going on. We didn't want to listen because we were so afraid things were gonna change around here. Afraid somebody was gonna come in and tell us we were taking too much money out of the company or something. Afraid somebody was gonna rock our nice, profitable little boat.''

''Well, if this is true, the boat's rocked now.'' Harp shook his head, lips tight. ''And where the hell *is* Autry?''

''The police are trying to find him,'' Grey said. ''His car's not in its parking spot here, but there's no answer at his home.''

''Of course not. It's the weekend,'' Emory Hunter said.

''What does that mean?'' Grey asked.

''Carmichael's got a place up in the mountains,'' Hunter explained. ''Good weather, he heads up there on the weekend, just to get away from it all. You could talk to his assistant.''

''I already have,'' Grey said. ''He didn't mention a cabin.''

''Carmichael doesn't talk much about what he does. He and Charlie were close. The rest of us…'' Porter Johnson hesitated, apparently reluctant to finish the thought.

''Autry wasn't one of us,'' Harp said. ''Charlie hired him because he'd served in his command in Korea, but Autry didn't contribute anything to the start-up costs of the company. What Porter's trying so hard to avoid saying is that we didn't make any effort to be friends. To us, Carmichael was just another employee. We had different social circles. Different lives. Different…circumstances, I guess you could say.''

Grey nodded. He understood more about the relationship between Carmichael and these men than had been openly expressed. Autry had been the outsider. Apparently he hadn't shared in the phenomenal success of the company Charlie Beaufort had founded with the money provided by these four men.

So to them, Carmichael had been only the hired help. Hired help who was in charge of protecting some highly sensitive technology. Information that would be extremely profitable on the international black market. So what if, after all these years on the outside looking in, Carmichael had decided to cut himself in for a piece of the very rich pie the others had been enjoying for so long?

It made sense, Grey thought, with the first stirrings of excitement since he'd regained consciousness and found Valerie was missing. Carmichael had the opportunity. And the oldest motive in the world—sheer old-fashioned greed.

It wasn't much to go on, but Grey's gut was telling him that it was enough. Especially when combined with the fact that Autry Carmichael was the one person who wasn't here. The one person involved in Av-Tech who wasn't present and accounted for.

"Anybody know where this weekend place is?" Grey asked. And then he watched as, one by one, they shook their heads.

"WE CAN STRAIGHTEN all this out together," Val said, knowing she had to be very careful in framing her arguments.

She had to convince Autry he couldn't get away with this abduction, that someone would figure out where he had taken her. At the same time, however, she couldn't afford to destroy the possibility of his achieving whatever it was he had been hoping to accomplish when he brought her up here.

"I'll do everything I can to help you," she offered. "I know Dad would have wanted me to do that."

"Charlie's the only one of those bastards who ever treated me decent. Like I was part of Av-Tech. Like I was valuable. The rest of them," he said, taking her elbow as she struggled, without the use of her hands, up the rugged path that climbed toward the cabin above them, "they always acted like they were better than me. I put just as many years of my life into that company as they did. And a lot more hard work.''

"I know," Val said soothingly.

Her wrists were tied together, the thin nylon rope so tight her flesh had swollen over it. Autry had done that as soon as they got into his office. Then he had taken her down to the deserted underground parking garage and made her get into the trunk of his car. He hadn't let her out until they arrived here.

At least she was in the open, she thought, savoring that after the near claustrophobia of those hours in the trunk. She could no longer feel the ends of her fingers, however, which looked bloodless and discolored. Of course, worrying about the condition of her hands in this situation was a little like worrying about the *Titanic* having a few mice.

"Your dad could have made it right if he'd wanted to," Autry said. He took a firmer grip on her arm to steady her as they mounted the low wooden steps that led to the front door. "All those years, I really thought he would. But he had his stroke and married Connie, and I knew then he wasn't going to do right by me. She wouldn't have let him. I thought she'd get his shares, and I'd be left high and dry. Instead, he left everything to you."

"If you tell me what you think is right, Autry, I'll do it."

If he would let her go, he could have the money. All of it. *The root of all evil,* she thought again.

While her mind repeated that familiar refrain, her eyes examined the interior of the cabin. She had known Autry had a mountain place, but she'd never been here. She also knew Carmichael had built it with his own hands, working on weekends, just as her father had once built the ranch. In emulation?

"It's too late for that," Autry said. "You know what I've done. I killed that man. I thought *he* was the one from the CIA. I thought they'd sent him here to figure it all out.''

"Figure what out?'' Val asked in bewilderment.

"They never meant for me to have my share. Those old bastards were just going to milk the company until they died and then leave it to their kids. Not even your dad saw that was wrong. But there's more than one way to skin a cat, sweetie. I learned a few things during the last forty years.''

"Like how to get your share?'' Val asked, her mind less engaged by Carmichael's harangue than by the problem of extricating herself from this situation. Because there would be no rescue, she thought, remembering how still Grey had been.

Just unconscious, she told herself fiercely, fighting the memory of that spreading stain under his head. But Grey would be in no shape to come after her, even if he were able to figure out what was going on. And she didn't see how he could, since she was right in the middle of it and still didn't know.

"There's plenty of money to be made if you know what I know,'' Carmichael said, bringing her attention back to him.

"And what is that, Autry?'' she asked, acting as if she were really interested in his ravings. "What exactly do you know?''

"That there are a lot of people out there prepared to pay plenty for what Av-Tech's got. And we got a lot of it.''

It took Val a few seconds to make the connection, but when she did, what he had said earlier about the CIA sending someone out finally made sense. It also explained why he had come to the ranch that night. He had intended to kill Grey Sellers and had ended up killing poor Harold Davis instead.

"You've been selling the technology,'' she said.

For just an instant she wondered if Grey *had* been sent to her ranch to uncover a traitor. Wondered until she remembered how far off base their thinking had been about the reason for the attacks on her. What had been going on was not about her shares. This was about another kind of greed, the kind that betrayed not only friends, but country.

She was glad her father hadn't lived to see this. His patriotism was real and deep, and the idea that technology his company had developed might one day be used against the United States would have sickened him. Especially since this had been done by a friend. By someone he trusted completely.

"I deserved *something* after all these years," Autry said.

He pushed her down into a chair he had pulled out from the kitchen table. Of course, there wasn't really a kitchen. The entire structure was only this one room with an enormous chimney in the center and a sleeping loft above one end.

"I still don't understand why you brought me here," Val said. Maybe if she understood what he wanted—

"You're going to tell me where that will is," Autry said.

"The lawyers have it," she lied, meeting his eyes.

"Could be," Autry said, his mouth pursing a little as he considered her face. "But somehow, sweetie, I don't think so. For one thing, you didn't have time to do that. You talked to them, but you didn't go to their offices. And you didn't tell them anything over the phone about naming an heir."

"How could you know that?" Val asked.

"Security's my job, remember," he said, almost smirking.

"You've been listening in," Val said.

"Only when I had to," Autry said, as if that made it right. "After I found out they'd sent somebody out here to spy on us."

Spy on *us?* Val thought. As if everyone at Av-Tech was in on this. "Grey Sellers isn't even with the CIA anymore."

Carmichael laughed. It was obvious he didn't believe her. "You should have left well enough alone, Val. You didn't want the money. You should have just given the others those shares and walked away. Instead " He shook his head, lips pursing again as he considered her. "You were going to get someone in there to start looking at things. Somebody who was going to be asking a whole lot of questions about what we were doing."

That's what this had all been about, Val realized finally. This was what Autry had been so afraid of. He didn't want anyone new nosing around Av-Tech.

"You were afraid the management team I wanted to bring in might discover what you've been doing."

"When the CIA contacted your dad, he came straight to me. I told him I was handling it, and he believed me. Maybe because he wanted to. Charlie was already bad sick, and when he died…"

"No one else knew what the CIA had discovered," Val said, slowly putting the pieces together. "And you didn't intend for anyone else to find out. How long did you think you could get away with what you were doing, Autry?"

"Long enough to get what's my due. Then you got involved."

"So you tried to frighten me off," she said. If anyone had tampered with her stud, it had been Autry. And then the next time he had come out to the ranch in the middle of the night, Grey had been his target because of what Carmichael had found when she had asked him to check into Grey's background.

"You didn't want the responsibility of running the company. We both knew that. I figured if things got too unpleasant, you'd bail out. I figured you'd hand over your dad's shares to the others and run away like you did before."

He meant when she had run from what had happened with Bart, she realized. *When she had run away from life.* And Autry was right. That was exactly what she had done ten years ago.

"But I never meant to hurt you, sweetie," he said softly.

Maybe that was even the truth. His attacks on her had, as Grey had said, seemed pretty inept. The shots that had come through the windows of her house had been high; the wood he'd piled against the front wall too wet to do much more than smoke.

Autry *had* meant to kill Grey that night, however. He had just found the wrong man in the bunkhouse. And she was the one who had told him her bodyguard was sleeping out there, Val realized, nausea thick in her throat. She had mentioned that when he'd called to tell her what he'd found out about Grey.

And Autry must have found out far more than he'd told her when he started looking into Grey's past. At least enough to make him suspicious. Enough to make him think the CIA had sent Grey to get to the bottom of the technology leaks.

"If you don't want to hurt me…" Val said hesitantly. "I want that will."

Maybe she was slow, but she still couldn't see… *Oh, dear God,* she thought, the realization of what he intended sending an icy stream of dread through her veins. Autry wanted to find the will that named her heir so he could destroy it. Then he would kill her, and with the trust not yet a legal entity, her shares in Av-Tech would revert to the other partners. And things would go right back to the way they had been before.

As the new majority owner, Billy would become CEO. And as always, he would spend more time on the golf course than at Av-Tech. The partners resisted change, so Autry was probably right in what he was thinking. Clemens would leave him in charge of security, which was exactly what Autry was counting on.

"If you don't want to hurt me, Autry," Val said, trying to think of anything that might make him reconsider, "then why don't you take what you have and leave? Go to Mexico or somewhere."

"Because of a little thing called extradition. And if that doesn't work, the CIA would track me down. They'd send somebody like your friend to find me. Besides, I want *everything* I've got coming to me. I want every cent that's owed me for the last forty years. I've already killed a man to get that, so I'm just not walking away and leaving what's mine to those jackasses."

"And if I tell you where the will is?" Val asked, her voice very soft because she already knew the answer. "What then?"

"I never meant for you to get hurt, sweetie. I wanted you to stay out of it. Why couldn't you have just stayed out of it?"

The question was plaintive. As if he were the one who had been betrayed. But of course, he believed he had been. There was enough revealed in his eyes to let her know how far gone he was into that delusion. He felt he was the injured party here.

"I can do it now," she said. "Give them Dad's shares."

He smiled, and the trickle of ice slid along her veins again. "It's too late for that, baby. I know you. Hell, I ought to. I helped raise you. You're just like Charlie. You wouldn't let me get away with what I've done, no matter what you say now. But I'll promise you this. You tell me where that will is, and I'll make it quick and painless. I want that as much as you do, baby, believe me. Because otherwise, you know what I'm going to have to do. And it will be awfully hard on both of us.''

His eyes rested on her face, as if he expected her to just tell him. One part of her really wanted to, because she knew a lot about pain. More than most people, she supposed. But she also knew what would happen as soon as he had the information.

First he would kill her. And then he would kill Grey. He wouldn't be able to take the chance on leaving him alive. Not with what he believed about Grey's purposes in coming here. But the longer she could keep him occupied...

Hope is a remarkable thing, she thought, feeling it stir in her heart, giving her a rush of courage like the injection of a drug. As long as she was alive, there was hope. That Grey would find her. That someone, maybe Grey's friends in the CIA, would realize what was going on and track Autry down.

Hope... And so, looking into the eyes of a man she had known all of her life, and now knew she had never really known at all, Valerie Beaufort slowly shook her head.

IT HAD TAKEN GRIFF CABOT less than two hours to track down the records for the property Carmichael had purchased in these mountains almost forty years ago. Grey could have done that himself, maybe even faster, if it hadn't been the weekend. The records office was closed, so Griff had used the agency's computers and satellite data to give him a map to this location.

And he would never have found this place without it, Grey acknowledged as he scanned the cabin and the surrounding area through his starlight scope. The curtains were drawn over the windows, but there appeared to be no lights inside. No movement. And no sound, other than the subtle noises night creatures made, which had resumed with Grey's continued stillness.

Grey fought off the terror that he was wrong. That while he was out here, spying on an empty cabin, Carmichael was somewhere else, doing to Val the things that had been done to Paul Simmons, the agent who had died on that botched mission.

But that was only the residue of the old nightmare, he told himself. There was no reason for Carmichael to torture Valerie. Deliberately, Grey cleared that memory from his consciousness. There was no room in this for that fear. He had a job to do. Another chance. A chance to do it right this time.

And according to Griff, Hawk was already on his way. As soon as Hawk landed at the airport Cabot would fax to him the same map he'd sent Grey. And when Hawk got here...

By the time Hawk gets here, it will be too late. Grey wasn't sure where that certainty had come from. It was suddenly there in his head, a conviction so strong there was no need to try to fight against it. *Do it now,* his heart demanded, despite what his brain told him. *Do it now, or it will be too late.*

Even as he began to move, his training screamed it would be better to wait for backup. The anxiety that was driving him to do this now was only a product of his failure two years ago. Trying this rescue by himself increased the odds that Val could get hurt, as well as the odds that Carmichael might take him out of commission and then move Val to another location where they might never find her. The entire time his intellect posed those arguments, he was moving, instinct-driven compulsion overriding training and reason. Val was in trouble, and if he didn't want what had happened two years ago to happen to her—

The piercing sound arrested his careful movement, paralyzing his muscles, as that internal debate had been unable to do. He had never heard Val scream, but there was no doubt in his mind that was what he was hearing. And the sound tore through whatever restraints evolution, civilization and more than fifteen years in intelligence work had imposed.

Grey had never bought into the action movie sequence where the hero bursts into a room by kicking down a door. He'd been trained in the technique, and he knew that it usually didn't work. However, without knowing exactly where Val was in that room, he couldn't afford to try to shoot off the lock. Not unless he had no other choice, he amended.

The thoughts ran through his head faster than his straining legs could move over the broken terrain leading up to the cabin. He hit the wooden porch at a dead run, gathering his body for the attempt. Then, left leg raised, he slammed the flat of its booted foot into the wooden door, striking just above the knob.

Surprisingly, it flew open. It had probably not even been locked. He landed inside the room, knees deeply bent to maintain his balance, his body low. The semiautomatic was out in front of him, gripped in both hands, classic shooter's stance.

The scene before him was the same one he had seen played out endlessly in his nightmares. Everything was exactly the same as those night terrors. The pounding of his heart, the inability to draw air into his lungs and the absolute horror of what he was seeing. Except Valerie was the one in this dream, not Paul.

The only light was from a low, flickering fire in the fireplace. Its oppressive heat had made the cabin a dark little corner of hell. And what was going on here…

The man standing beside the kitchen chair where Valerie was tied was holding a knife, its tip heated to a yellow-white glow. He had turned to face the door when it had come crashing into the room. Sweat gleamed in greasy-looking rivulets on his face, and his eyes had widened in shock. Grey had never seen Autry Carmichael, but the age-lined face and the gray hair were right. Somehow they made what was going on even more obscene.

Unable to resist, Grey's eyes flicked to the woman tied to the chair. Her head sagged against her chest so that he couldn't see her face. The adrenaline that had flooded his body at the sound of her scream was suddenly sucked out of his blood, leaving his knees so weak they trembled, his guts like water.

Val, he thought, in despair. *Please God, don't let me have been too late. Not again. Not Val.*

The man began to move, bringing Grey's attention back to where it should have been. Everything seemed to be happening in slow motion. Time enough for Grey to recognize what Carmichael was doing. Plenty of time to react to it. His brain, however, seemed numbed by his terror over Val, muscles still paralyzed.

Carmichael's fingers had closed over the gun that lay on the table, fumbling to pick it up. He was trying to get his hand wrapped around it, to get the muzzle pointed toward Grey. As he did, Val lifted her head, eyes widening just as her captor's had.

Alive. There was only time for that one thought. Then Grey's finger closed over the trigger, squeezing off the shot as if he were on the firing range. No tremor. And no mistake.

The single bullet Carmichael got off exploded through a window on the other side of the room. Grey would always believe he had felt its passage, a scant millimeter from his head. The sounds of the two shots seemed to ring out at the same time. Carmichael's was wide by a hair-breadth, Grey's as true as any he had ever fired. The security chief's hands flew up, his gun sailing across the room behind him as he was thrown backward.

Grey never could remember hearing the sound Carmichael's body made as it hit. By then he was kneeling on the floor by Val's chair. She hadn't taken her eyes off his face since she had raised her head and looked into his eyes. She didn't now.

"It's over," he said, searching her features.

They were completely drained of color. The faint freckles, even in the dimness, were stark against the chalk of her skin. Her pupils were dilated. He couldn't be sure if that was because of what she had seen him do, the lack of light, or her fear. Or maybe because of the pain.

"He's dead?" she asked.

She tried to turn, attempting to see Autry's body, which lay behind her, and Grey realized that she was still tied to the chair. He found the knife Carmichael had dropped as he went for his gun, and used it to cut the cords.

"He's dead," Grey assured her. Considering that he'd hit him exactly where he'd been aiming, right in the middle of Carmichael's forehead, he had no doubt about that.

As soon as Val was free, she was in his arms. They knelt together on the rough boards of Autry Carmichael's isolated weekend cabin and held each other too tightly. Val wasn't crying, but maybe that wasn't a good sign, he thought.

"It's all over," he whispered again, his lips brushing against the small line of stitches on her temple. It seemed that had happened a lifetime ago, and yet it had been only a few days. Too little time to explain the depth of what he was feeling.

"I prayed you'd come," she said. "I knew if you were still alive, you'd find me."

He closed his eyes, fighting the horror of what he had

seen when he opened that door. And if he hadn't found her...

"Let's get out of here," he said. "Can you walk?"

"About as well as I ever could," she said, a hint of laughter in her voice.

Hysteria? he wondered in concern. She'd been through enough to be hysterical, but it worried him. It wasn't like Val.

"Did you mean it?" she asked as he helped her to stand up.

"Mean what?"

"I said I wanted it all, and you nodded. I do, Grey. I know that now. I kept thinking about it, making myself think about it, instead of thinking about...what Autry was doing. I thought about my mother's kitchen. About making pies. And little girls."

"About making little girls?" he repeated carefully, trying to make sense out of this and still wondering about hysteria.

And then she laughed, and the sound of her laughter, her ability to laugh after what she had just gone through, touched all the dark places the past two years had burned into his soul. Soothing them. Healing.

"That wasn't what I meant, but..." She drew a shaky breath. "Actually, maybe it *was* what I meant. Because it sounds like a good idea to me. I know you need time to think about it. But I guess I should warn you. I'm not running. Not from life. Or from you. I'm never running away again from anything I really want."

"I don't have any idea what you're talking about," he said truthfully, bending to put his lips over hers.

"Let's get married," Val said as soon as the kiss ended.

"Married?" he repeated.

It wasn't that he hadn't considered the idea. He had. A lot. He just hadn't been able to figure out why Val would want to marry him. After all, when he thought about who she was… He destroyed that doubt because he *knew* who she was. And it had nothing to do with Av-Tech and nothing to do with the money.

"Unless you don't want to," she said. She pushed away from him a little, so she could look up into his eyes.

She was waiting for his answer, he realized.

She's got guts, Hawk had said. *In the end, it was what was important. More important than the other stuff.* Far more important than anything else, Grey acknowledged. Except love, of course.

"I want to," he said.

"And do you want to make little girls?" she asked, beginning to smile, the freckles less stark.

"One for you," he said, bending to kiss her forehead. "And one for me." His lips touched the tip of her nose, brushing over the freckles.

"And a little boy," she said, leaning back again. A single tear had escaped, but she was still smiling. And her eyes were soft and dark in the firelight, searching his.

This is the way she would look at someone she loved, he thought, still surprised that the someone she loved could really be him. "I think that could probably be arranged."

"Soon," she said. "I've got a lot to catch up on."

Grey nodded, fighting an unfamiliar burn at the back of his own eyes. "Me, too," he said softly.

Because, he acknowledged, like Val he was through running. No longer running from his failures. And there were some people he needed to say that to. And to say thanks to, as well.

"Let's go home," Val said.

And wherever she was, Grey knew it always would be.

Epilogue

"This is my dance, I think," Grey said.

Surprised, Valerie turned from her conversation with Claire Cabot to look at him. As it had in the conference room that day, her heart turned over at the sight. Even in the elegant evening attire, Grey was so obviously, so completely and utterly masculine. Beautifully male. And now he belonged to her. Her husband.

Although the wedding had been very small and private, almost everyone she knew was in attendance, including all her father's partners. Emory Hunter had stood in for her dad, walking her slowly down the aisle, his pace carefully adjusted for her limp. Beaming, he had placed her hand in Grey's as they stood before the altar.

She had realized at the reception that all of Grey's friends were here, as well. The tall, quiet man they called Hawk, who for some reason reminded her of Grey, had served as best man. Griff Cabot, who had been Grey's boss when he had been with the CIA, was here. And a handsome man named Jordan Cross, whose deep voice held traces of an unmistakable Southern accent.

And they had each brought their wives, who seemed to be the perfect mates for these strong men. *Perfect,* she thought again. *All of them so damn perfect.*

The thought formed without her volition. And it was

unwanted, especially today. It was too much a bitter echo from the past, which she wanted to be nothing more than a distant and faded memory. As she reminded herself of that, her gaze fell to Grey's hand, still held out in invitation.

"I told you before," Grey said, and questioning, she raised her eyes to his face. He was smiling, that small, almost secret smile she had seen during the most intimate moments they had shared. "You really can't say I didn't warn you."

And suddenly in her head were the words he'd said that day, leaning over her kitchen table, holding her eyes, just as he was now. *I want to dance with you and make love to you. And when I do, you can be damn sure it isn't going to happen in the dark. So don't come expecting that.*

She had, however. She had never believed he would ask this of her. She couldn't dance. Maybe if it were just the two of them. If they were safely alone and in private. But she could never do this in front of all these people. In front of his friends and their wives...

Perfect reverberated in her heart. Painfully.

And then, as if it were a lesson, she remembered what Autry had said. He had believed she would run away at the first sign of trouble. That she would give up her shares and retreat to the same safe isolation she had sought before. She had sworn then she would never do that again.

If Grey could find the courage to go to work for Griff Cabot in the Phoenix Brotherhood, despite what had happened two years ago, then surely she could manage to stumble around a dance floor if he wanted her to.

Let them watch, she thought, retreating behind the familiar protective shield of pretending she didn't care. *It doesn't matter what they think. Nothing matters but this,* she told herself, putting her fingers into Grey's, which felt incredibly steady under the trembling of hers. So strong.

Strong enough to keep her safe, she thought, looking up into his eyes again. And she realized with a deep sense of wonder that they were filled with pride. Pride in *her?*

When Grey swept her into the dance, however, she was conscious of nothing but what was in the smoke-gray softness of his eyes, looking down into hers. Conscious only of the feel of his arms, holding her securely, as he guided her carefully around the floor. As if she were fragile. Or infinitely precious.

And by the time the quiet applause started, echoing around the circle of all those friends who were watching them, Valerie, too, was smiling with them.

*   *   *   *   *

Please watch for Gayle Wilson's next release,

MY LADY'S DARE,

Harlequin Historical #516,
which will be out on bookshelves in early June.